THE WITCHES TRILOGY: BLUE/BLACK

Cathleen Dunn

The Witches Trilogy: Blue/Black / Cathleen Dunn -- 1st ed.
ISBN 978-0-9899310-3-8

My sincere thanks to The Circle: David, Ann, Tami, Lee, Stephen, and Karla... and to Julie for making the F1 drivers real...

The quartet of witches gossiped over their expensive drinks at *La Tremoille's* hotel bar in the *Le Triangle d'Or* district of Paris as they watched Olivia, Alejo, and Taylor having lunch in the furthest corner of the room.

"That's her–I heard she killed Dantin. Took out a sword and cut his head clean off, or some such thing." Thane gestured with his drink toward Olivia. He was really enjoying this moment. There'd only been rumors since Dantin had disappeared, and he relished that he had a morsel of actual information, and knew *who* was responsible at that. It was so delicious to be the first.

"I don't believe you." One of the women stared at Olivia as if she could divine the truth just by looking at her. She turned back to Thane. "Details."

Thane set down his martini on the low table between them and leaned toward the others. He was annoyed at being questioned; now he'd have to admit his shortcoming.

"Well, I don't know exactly how it happened. Somehow she got ahold of a charmed weapon that Dantin used to own. Only her close friends know for sure what went down, but the bottom line is she took matters into her own hands and just did it. Unbelievable."

"But she's a Silver-Tint, isn't she?" The woman was still doubtful. "They're all about not using magic to kill or it comes back on you sevenfold or some similar nonsense." That concept was foreign to her. Blue/Black witches reveled in their power and weren't afraid to use it for anything. She couldn't imagine restricting herself or paying back the use of magic by being kind to everyone else. She looked down at the eight thousand dollar Valentino leather dress she was wearing. What–just because she paid for it with magic she should feed filthy little starving urchins on the other side of the planet? Disgusting. They were witches and the magic and power were theirs for the taking.

The other man was analyzing the news. "How could she have gotten to him? We're stronger than they are." He reached for his bourbon. "Besides, don't they think they'll turn Blue/Black if they harm something intentionally? I can't imagine one of them taking the risk."

"That doesn't mean she's one of us," the woman added. "I wouldn't know what to do with her."

"So who can you trust less? A Blue/Black who's always been Blue/Black or a Silver-Tint who turned?" Thane took a sip of his martini. "I wouldn't be friends with her if she turned. At least we all know where we stand with each other."

They all watched the trio of Silver-Tints as they stood and left the lounge, crossing the hotel lobby to the front desk.

"So they're staying here. I'm keeping that in mind." Another sip of his bourbon. "I wonder how long."

"Another two days, that's all. I spelled the concierge to tell me everything she knew about them." Thane was satisfied he'd regained his dominance as the one with the information.

The witch in the red dress leaned back on the sofa, crossing her arms. She gave a sidelong, cozen look at the other woman sitting with them.

"If I were you, Malila, I wouldn't let her get away with it."

The man drinking bourbon turned to the last witch, an exotic-looking woman with long dark hair and turquoise eyes. "That's right, Malila. You and Dantin were pretty close, weren't you? What are you going to do?"

Malila didn't answer him or even look at him. She simply watched Olivia, Taylor, and Alejo with narrowed eyes as they left *La Tremoille*. The others didn't ask her again.

Alejo cast a brotherly gaze on Taylor where she stood surrounded by three assistants in the huge private salon at Chanel. The experienced hands were tucking and pinning her choices from Chanel's Spring Collection and that evening they would be sent to the maestro's workshop to be perfectly tailored to fit her.

"Hard to believe she's the same scruffmuffin you found in Seattle a year ago." Alejo took the piece of brie Olivia was about to eat right out of her hand and ate it himself.

"Hey, you scum…" Olivia laughed and took a strawberry off his plate in retaliation, then dropped it into her flute of champagne. "Yeah, I know. I don't think she'd ever had a new coat before I met her. Those old Doc Martins and ripped Levi's of hers? Still her favorites, God help us." She shrugged. "Well, so what? She's still pretty grounded."

"It all depends on what's inside the clothes. Olivia, I've seen you covered in mud and you still manage to look good somehow." He extended his long legs and stretched back in the cushioned chair. "This is perfect. Beautiful women in beautiful clothes and I'm in the dressing room with them."

Olivia saw Taylor smile and nod as two of the assistants asked her a question in French. The two slid covert looks over at Alejo, and she distinctly heard "*Il est un homme sexy,*" and the other replied "*Oui–il peut aller à la maison avec moi.*"

They were barely speaking, they whispered so quietly, but Olivia could hear them. Magic could allow you almost anything when you focused hard enough on it. Olivia knew Alejo well enough to know that he also had heard the two women talking about him–although he didn't show it.

He must have heard them from the start. She decided to tease him.

"Do you ever get tired of women trying to get into your jeans?" As expected, he turned to her, looking a little scandalized.

"Why, Olivia..." He feigned shock. Then he grinned. "Of course not."

She laughed at their old game. "What is it about being an international polo player? Everyone thinks you guys must be the most exciting, the sexiest things on the planet, but I don't know; you look pretty ordinary to me."

She knew that was ridiculous: he was tall, lean but muscular, Latin, and had one of the warmest smiles she'd ever seen. Couple that with a matching temperament and she counted herself lucky that she and Alejandro Baquero were friends. And had been for the last several hundred years.

Alejo smiled and reached over to take her hand and play with her fingertips. "But this spring I'm just me, traveling with the two of you. Nothing to take us away from our vacation together." He nodded toward Taylor. "So wonderful for you to give her this experience– Chanel's *haute couture* in their private salon."

"I know a few people."

"To say the least. Paris was the fashion seat of the world when you were an aristocrat here before the Bastille was taken, Olivia. You knew them all then, too."

"I'm glad you came and rescued me when you did." Olivia took more of Alejo's hand in hers and gave it an intentional squeeze. "Thank you." She dropped his fingers just as the Head Assistant came over. "And don't let the French hear you call it Bastille Day. It's *le quatorze juillet* here."

The Head Assistant was flawlessly chic in her grey trousers and sweater, a huge sparkling pin at her shoulder the only accessory. It always amazed Olivia how so many people underestimated the drama of simplicity in their attire–but never the French.

"How are we doing, Arienne?" she asked.

"It will take two weeks for Taylor's couture to be completed and shipped to her in Monaco. Six gowns for the galas surrounding the Monte Carlo Spring Art Festival, but suitable for anywhere formal that you decide to go. Fourteen pieces in the day couture trunk for the Monte Carlo Tennis open and the Grand Prix at the end of May as well as luncheons and red carpet events."

"*Merci.* And for the bill." Olivia handed her credit card to Arienne. "I don't need to see it unless it is over ninety thousand Euro." Olivia knew exactly how much Taylor's fashion should cost, including the alterations and transport of the *couture* to Monaco. Arienne took her card with a quiet nod and slipped away to settle the paperwork.

Taylor passed Olivia and Alejo on her way to the dressing room where her clothes would be carefully removed to preserve the alterations. Olivia stopped her.

"You know, I'm surprised you like something as classic as Chanel. I would have thought Moschino or one of the edgier designers for this trip."

"Oh, but I can always punk it up with something. I like Chanel because it's classic, like my vintage wear only better. So easy to mix my more unusual pieces with it." She looked at what she was wearing. "Olivia, you know I can pay for these. I have the money."

"Yes, but I want to do this. Otherwise it's not a gift–it's just us killing time while you shop. I love showing you things and taking you to all these new places." Olivia regarded her apprentice affectionately.

"Okay, Olivia." Then suddenly Taylor broke into a huge smile. "Oh, Livy, thank you! I just love you both." Taylor tried to fold both her and Alejo into a single hug, but they threw up their hands to block her.

"Be careful–pins!"

One of the assistants came and steered Taylor away carefully and Olivia signed the receipt for the couture. Once Taylor was back in her own clothing she sat next to the tray of leftover champagne, brie, and fruit and ate like she had been on a deserted island.

"Oh, my God. I thought I was going to die of hunger. I didn't want to get anything on my new clothes, though, so I waited." She closed her eyes and savored the mouthful of flavors on her tongue, then ate steadily until the little tray was empty. When she'd finished they stood up to head downstairs, making sure to thank the assistants; it had been a very long day for all of them. Then they exited Chanel onto *Avenue Montaigne*.

"What would you like to do?" Alejo asked Taylor. "This trip is all about you; we've been here before."

"Well, I don't want to waste a minute while we're here in Paris, but I'm really tired after six hours of trying on clothes and pinning and standing still with my arms out and trying not to move."

"All right, Taylor. Then we'll just walk back to the hotel and enjoy the city along the way."

They strolled down the Avenue at Taylor's pace, past the cream-colored stone buildings that housed the most exclusive and expensive designer boutiques on the planet. They were basically storefronts, yet they sat behind clipped green hedges and gold-tipped iron railings. Taylor understood why people said this was the most beautiful city in the world. Serene manicured gardens softened every niche and gold leaf ornamented the most mundane of objects, and Paris's soaring architecture and heroic statues gave it an ethereal quality.

Since last Thanksgiving she had been in Europe with Olivia and Alejo. They'd spent December and January traveling and staying in Austria, where they'd gone to the *Kristkindlmarkt* in Salzburg and the opera in Vienna. They'd spent another month in Switzerland where she had loved watching Alejo and the other teams play snow polo in St. Moritz. That had been a beautiful mystical world in white; watching the horses run through falling snowflakes and kick up snow as they galloped down the field.

Taylor had fallen completely spellbound by polo; the beauty of the horses and riders had captured her heart and the moves on the field were powerful and thrilling. Not only that, Alejo always made sure she was part of the inner circle even though he was famous in his own right and she was not.

And just when she'd thought life couldn't be more wonderful they had come to this amazing city of Paris, just to dine, and go to the theater, and walk the beautiful streets, and shop in the most exclusive boutiques in the world, and all for her. Her life had changed so much since becoming Olivia's apprentice. Life as a witch was incredible.

Alejo, Taylor, and Olivia walked into hotel *La Tremoille* after dark had fallen. It was early April and the sun had set around seven-thirty. It was almost time for dinner in Paris; most restaurants had opened for the evening and would begin to fill around eight or eight-thirty. As they were crossing the hotel lobby Alejo turned to Olivia and Taylor.

"What next? Shall we go out to eat or are you still tired, my *sobrinita*?" He addressed Olivia's apprentice.

Taylor hesitated. They had only one more night in Paris and she didn't want to miss anything, but in Europe the night life started between eight and ten and ran into the early morning hours, unlike the city of Seattle she and Olivia called home. People there went to dinner and entertainment early and then rushed home afterward instead of going out for dessert or drinks. Something about avoiding the traffic or missing the ferry was the usual excuse. Taylor had almost gotten used to the later schedule here in Europe, but today had been especially tiring.

"I'm going to stay in tonight."

"Me too." Olivia was looking in her handbag for her room key.

Alejo was about to protest but then didn't. In the hotel lobby he had glimpsed a woman looking at him with the slightest hint of a smile. She was witch; he could tell by the familiar adrenaline rush they all felt whenever one of their kind was nearby. He'd almost ignored it as Olivia and Taylor had, but this was a witch that he knew. Intimately, in fact. It had been years since the last time they had seen each other and he was about to excuse himself from Olivia and Taylor and go over to her when she turned away and walked out of the hotel lobby. He watched her go, noticing how her hips moved under the silk dress. Damn, he thought, feeling a pleasurable heat start to grow in his loins. He turned his attention back to his two companions.

"You're both right. We have to leave for Monaco tomorrow so we need to get some rest." He took the elevator with them up to their separate suites, setting a time to meet for café and croissants in the morning before they all said their goodnights.

Sleep was the last thing Alejo wanted, however. He couldn't get his mind off the woman from the lobby. He prowled his room, looking out the window and picking up magazines only to set them down unread. He considered scrying her to get another look at her and find her location. The question of course was: did he want her to know she had captured his thoughts? Well, that was childish, he realized. He wasn't a teenager anymore to be so coy and unconfident–far from it. Of course she was hoping to be on his mind, and he wanted to be on hers as well. After all, she had appeared in the lobby to get his attention. Well, now she had it.

He darkened the lights and cupped his hands, watching as magic filled them with a shimmering fluid that he spread on the bed until it was smooth like a mirror. Looking deeply into it he concentrated on her, asking the magic to show him where she was, but the vision wouldn't focus and he found himself rebuffed. She was blocking him! Blocking his view so he couldn't see her! Well, then, obviously she'd been waiting for him to try. He chuckled and gave up; she was right to block him. It was impolite to scry without permission like a Peeping Tom, but they both had their answer; They were waiting for eachother. Confidently he waved his hand over the scrying medium, and it flowed upward into his palm where it dissipated into vapor. Then he stepped into the shower to refresh himself before dressing and going downstairs.

The hotel bar was split into two sections; the walled area in back had private tables for dining, but in front couches made for casual intimacy. Alejo walked the full length of the room to see if she was there before choosing a spot within sight of the entrance. He ordered a scotch and was still waiting, keeping an eye on the entrance, when he felt that familiar tingle on his skin. It came from behind, though, and this time it was augmented by a hotness in his thighs that spread up through his belly. Oh, it had to be her. No one else affected him this way. He loved how she'd sneaked up behind him as well. How had she simply appeared in the back section of the lounge without anyone noticing, he wondered?

Standing up, he turned to give her *faire la bise*, the cheek kissing without really touching that is the French custom. It was all he could do keep his head from swimming while she was so close to him. In the past he'd considered asking her if it was a sex spell that she wore, but he had to admit he didn't really care as long as he was the recipient.

He gestured next to him on the couch and she sat. "What would you like to drink?" he asked her.

"Perrier, thank you."

Alejo caught the waiter's eye and then looked back at his companion. "How did you find me?" he asked her.

"I saw you in the lobby the other day. I'm staying here."

"You must have just arrived."

"No, I didn't get close enough for you to tell until tonight."

Alejo smiled. "Ah, and I could never forget how you feel–and there's no way I would want to." He drew in a deep breath and let it out as he looked her over. "How long has it been?"

"Nineteen fifty-nine. You were Juan Gutierrez then, I think."

"Yes–I have your magazine articles from that year. We had a wonderful season together, didn't we? How in the world did you get your publisher to send you around the world to write about the polo teams?"

"Same way you get away with playing polo so publicly decade after decade. Magic. How do people not notice you are the same person for centuries?"

Alejo shrugged. "They see what they want to. I use a spell to make them see slight differences, and I need only do it for one or two generations before people forget and I can start over."

"You look the same to me."

"Of course I do–you're witch. And you want me to look the same."

She leaned closer to him, her breasts almost touching his arm and her voice as smooth as cream. "I'm hoping everything about you is the same."

He was looking down at her, feeling the warmth spreading into his chest now and trying to think of a polite way to suggest leaving with her when the waiter came with her Perrier. She stopped to greet him and took her drink, saying, "Please charge both drinks to my room, number 604." Then she stood with her water and faced Alejo.

"Are you coming?"

Alejo looked down at his chest where her fingernails had dug into him. The marks would stay there for days and he knew he'd be hard again just looking at them and thinking about her. He felt stirrings even now, right after their ardent lovemaking, and he wanted to be inside her again.

"*Dios*, how do you manage to do this to me?"

"I'm not doing anything. I'm just lying here enjoying the moonlight." She was stretched naked on the rug beside him, bathed in the moon's pale blue wash that made her café crème skin glow. He ran his hand over her breasts and down her belly to her inner thighs and brushed them lightly, lazily, trying not to pull her against him again so soon.

"It's a good thing we don't see each other all the time or you would truly kill me. I've never known a woman that was so *voraz ala hacer en amour*–so ravenous with sex."

"I love it when you fall back into Spanish. Your accent is like soft red wine. A full-bodied Rioja."

"Don't change the subject. No, do. Tell me what you've been doing since last time. You're not still reporting on polo matches or I would know about you."

"No, I'm not. I follow some matches but mostly go where I want. I prefer a lower profile now. A simpler life."

"Perhaps you are thinking of settling down?"

"Alejo, you're a fine one to talk. You never stay with anyone for very long."

"That's not quite right; I've had the same friends for hundreds of years. I would be open to the right woman, however..."

"Well, it's not me, and we both know it. I like to go where I want, when I want."

"Not even for the right man?"

"And let someone think they can tell me what to do? No way in hell. Not ever."

Alejo laughed and relaxed back on the carpet, lacing his fingers behind his head. "I would never presume to tell any woman what to do. I like strong women with a mind of their own. And they are going to do what they want to anyway, so why fight them?"

"You're smarter than you look."

"I've just known lots of women."

"That much is obvious to me." She turned on her side and reached over to play with the mat of dark curls on his lower belly. "Tell me about the two women you were with today. I know of Olivia–everyone knows you've been friends for centuries, but who is the other?"

"Her apprentice, Taylor. She's been training less than a year, but she's very powerful. We're trying to make sure she gets the most experience and protection we can give her."

"How old is she?" "She looks seventeen or eighteen."

"Eighteen, maybe nineteen by now. Human years. She's *nuevo*–truly brand new."

"And how about Olivia? How is she doing? Anything new on that front?"

Alejo raised his head to look at her with suspicion. "What do you mean?"

"You two have been friends so long and usually have separate lives, but now she's traveling again with you. No regular lover this long after Tristan's death?"

"No." Alejo was quiet a moment.

"I'm sorry. I know losing him like that must have been horrible for her. I can't really blame her for falling apart." She slid closer to Alejo and put her head on his chest, her long dark curls spilling down his ribs to pool on the floor. Alejo slid his hands over the curls to stroke them for a few moments.

"Alejo, you're a wonderful friend to her."

"But you were the one who let me know where she had gone when she disappeared, where to find her in that group of debauched aristocracy. I'm sure she was waiting to die, either with the other *Noblesse* at the guillotine or from too much wine and snuff and who knows what else? I won't tell you what I had to do afterward to heal her."

"I'm glad she has you."

"But you would never let me tell her about you–that it was you who told me where to find her. Why?"

"I don't know. I didn't want accolades. Maybe I don't like to be noticed."

"There's no way in hell you aren't noticed everywhere you go, Malila." Alejo let his gaze wash over her body. The globes of her breasts looked absolutely succulent in the moonlight. He turned on his side and pressed his belly against her thigh, groaning at the urgency he felt rising in him. He put his arm around her waist to flip her on her back and knelt over her. He was entranced by her eyes, the color of the Caribbean, by the way she moved, by how he wanted to plunge himself into her every second he was with her or saw her or even thought of her. He'd been intimate with hundreds of women in his lifetime and no one had ever controlled his desires like this.

"No more talking about other people right now." His voice was husky with drive, that primitive moment with men where sex took over and it was only about lust. Malila loved him this way. She drew up her knees to let him between them and Alejo spread them apart with his hands, exposing the pink tender flesh hidden between her thighs. She had a Brazilian wax and her labia were completely bare, more tender and delicate and sensitive than when covered with hair. He had an almost overpowering urge to simply shove himself into her and lose himself in her warmth, but knew he couldn't deny her–or him–the pleasure of some lengthy foreplay.

He let his hands slide down her inner thighs slowly, watching her face as he moved downward. She was most beautiful when uncontrolled, he thought, showing taut ecstasy and slack relief without self-awareness, without inhibition.

Alejo stayed between her thighs a long while, savoring the feel of her bare labia under his lips. It always astounded him how incredibly smooth and delicious they felt that way. Her reactions– the sharp intake of breath and groans of pleasure–only drove his desire harder. Finally, when neither could stand it anymore, their breath coming in thick, heated gasps, he slid himself upward, pressing himself tightly against her as he mounted her until he filled her completely. Malila gasped a long "Aahhh" with the pleasure of that first moment, and as they stroked together he could hear her soft grunting with each plunge. After a while it was all he could do not to come just from listening to her. She could tell he was close too by the change in his movements, the hesitation in his hips. She stopped moving.

"Do you need me to hold still for a moment?"

Alejo looked down at her face. Seeing her moist lips parted by panting and her eyes half-closed with sex only made it harder to control himself. He looked away, but Malila wrapped her legs around his waist and whispered in his ear.

"Don't wait. I want you to come in me, and come hard. I love it when you make me slippery and messy with it. Put it deep inside me."

He didn't need any more urging than that. Very few women he'd known spoke that way and it drove him over the edge. He nearly saw stars as the orgasm pushed through him in waves and he felt acutely her plush warmth encasing him. Oh, God, he thought, I could die right now and be fine with it...

They woke up a half hour later, spooning, Malila's back to Alejo's front with their legs still entwined.

"What time is it?" Malila murmured.

"Four o'clock. Do you need me to leave?"

"No–I just wondered how long we had before sunrise. When are you leaving Paris?"

"We're taking Olivia's jet to Monaco at noon. Do you want to have breakfast with us?"

"No." Malila was quick to answer him over her shoulder. "I have people to see here. I may find you in Monaco, though; I'll be there for Grand Prix." She was referring to the Formula 1 race held there every year.

"So will we. Let me know when you arrive," Alejo told her.

"I might not tell you right away. I want to be on my own first."

Alejo knew her comment wasn't rejection; Malila had always been a little secretive. He assumed she simply savored her freedom.

"That's fine, but at least let me introduce you to Olivia this time. And to Taylor. I won't tell Olivia it was you who told me where to find her back then."

"All right, Alejo." Malila couldn't believe her luck. This is perfect, she thought. I need to get close to Olivia and here he is placing her right in my lap. She twitched her hips side to side, rubbing her bottom against him. "I would like that very much."

"Good then. It's settled." Alejo wrapped his arms tighter around her, enjoying the feel of her skin and amazed that he still felt amorous. Once again, he was on the edge of asking her if it was a talisman or spell that made him crave her so badly, but it was hard for him to think through his haze.

"Oh, hell, who cares?" he muttered as he dove again into her ready embrace.

The next morning, Olivia, Taylor, and Alejo lingered over breakfast on Alejo's garden terrace for one last look at Paris while their stack of luggage was dispatched with efficiency by the *La Tremoille* staff into waiting town cars. With some regret, they said goodbye to the hotel staff and the city and drove south of Paris to the airport at Orly.

The day was bright and golden as their limousine pulled up to the Citation X jet where it was warming up on the tarmac. One of the best things about flying with Olivia, Taylor thought, was that you almost never flew in the same plane twice. No sense letting an expensive plane sit around seventy-five percent of the time, Olivia had always said. Therefore, she subscribed to a private jet service that could have any one of their fleet available for her at a moment's notice. Flying by jet did two things for a witch: one, it saved valuable magic that had to be paid back to the logos for using it, and two, it was a damned sight more luxurious and fun than flashing to wherever you wanted to be. After all, life was an experience to savor.

Once they boarded, Taylor settled in on the ultra-soft, cream-colored leather and ran her fingers over the polished wood trim. She still wasn't used to such luxury, but she hoped she never lost her appreciation for it no matter how many times they flew privately or where they went. It would be a shame, she thought, not to appreciate something right in front of you because you thought you were too cool, or you took it for granted. With that in mind she made sure to thank her flight attendant, a handsome young man who made sure she was buckled in properly and somehow knew everything she needed without her saying it, starting with a glass of iced tea. She thanked him again as he set it down and then looked out the window as they lifted into the sky.

Barely two hours out of Orly they touched down again at Nice's *Cote d'Azur* airstrip and then took a car to Monaco along the M6098, *Beaulieu-sur-Mer*. With the top down it felt like freedom as they drove along the winding road that embroidered the edge of the Mediterranean and took them to gorgeous, glamorous, exciting Monte Carlo.

The tiny principality was an amazement to Taylor. Its curving streets were cut into a narrow hillside along a dazzling blue harbor filled with sleek yachts, and elegant Belle Epoch buildings of cream-colored stone staircased up the slope. Monaco was tiny, just over a mile wide and two miles long, but they certainly had made the most of it; luxurious buildings were nearly on top of each other in order to take advantage of the ultra-prime real estate. Taylor loved how the lush palms lining the streets gave the city a semi-tropical feel, and beyond them were the sun-kissed hotels, fronted by opulent gardens and glimmering reflective pools.

"Oh, these buildings are so beautiful!" Taylor craned to look at an ornate edifice as they drove by.

Alejo regarded Taylor in the rearview mirror. "Well then, we will drive you through town instead of straight to the hotel so you can see more of them."

They made a loop through Monte Carlo, enjoying the sights. Livy pointed to their right as they drove up the *Avenue des Beaux-Arts*.

"Look–there's the Monte Carlo Casino."

Taylor gaped at the ornate building with its domes and finials set off by a circular drive around a sparkling fountain. Its massive triple-door entry was flanked by statues on either side.

"You must see it at night," said Alejo, "with the lights. The whole city is lit up after dark like a jewel in a museum." They took a left up the *Avenue de la Madone*, then a quick right, and they were welcomed into the cypress-lined, private drive of the *Hotele Metropole*.

It was their habit to take suites next to each other on the upper floors, but this time Alejo had insisted on securing a huge suite on the ground floor. "I like the dark wood and leather in this suite, and these old books in the bookcases. It feels like my home in Argentina." He ran his fingers over the row of volumes in their ornate bindings. "Plus, it's perfect for the Grand Prix."

"How can you say that?" Olivia stared at him, incredulous. "From our luxury box at the *Virage* next to the harbor we can watch the cars exit the tunnel, round the chicane, and see the whole harbor area up to *La Rascasse* corner and maybe the finish line as well."

"Ah, but Olivia," he said, leading her by the hand to the terrace where the race course would run below them along the *Place du Casino*, "that's all day up in the crowded restaurant with everyone else. When we get tired and want some privacy we can transport ourselves back here for a while and still see this part of the race while we relax."

"Oh! And then magically pop back to the *Virage* any time for the winner's ceremonies or whatever else we like. Handy, you are a dream." Olivia fell back into their pet name for him and he knew she was pleased.

Alejo accompanied the two women to their suites on the top floor and was concerned when he saw how small Taylor's was compared to Olivia's. He motioned to the bellman, who was setting Taylor's luggage next to the bureau, to stop for a moment and then voiced a question to Olivia's novice.

"You don't want something larger, *mi niña*? Your bed is right here, practically in your sitting room and we'll be here for over two months. We could have the bellman move you right now."

"No." Taylor looked around. "This is perfect. In Paris my suite was too big–it felt empty even when I was in it. Besides, I'm with you and Olivia most of the time and you always have huge rooms."

Alejandro looked at her intently. "You are sure?"

Taylor smiled and nodded. "Yes, Alejo. Quit trying to spoil me so much. This smaller room is exactly what I want. It's cozier and I'm happier."

Alejo eyed her a moment but then was satisfied.

"All right then. You go ahead and get settled just the way you want, and then you and Olivia come down to my suite and we'll go to dinner. Then tomorrow, we'll show you this beautiful city of Monte Carlo."

The next morning Taylor was up before either Olivia or Alejandro, excited to explore Monte Carlo and know her way around. She started with the concierge, asking for advice and brochures, and what was fun to do, and where were the best places to eat. By the time Olivia and Alejo found her in the lobby two hours later, she already had a list of ideas and places she wanted to see, and a tote full of information.

"Let's start with breakfast at *Côté Jardin*–it's not far away, I think. While we're there I can show you my plans. I really want to..." She began to rattle off her wish list while both of the other witches listened in astonishment.

"Whoa, slow down." Olivia finally put up her hands. "We just got up, you know. I may have had a shower, but I still haven't had coffee yet."

"Let me see what you have." Alejo peered into her tote and Taylor began pulling out brochures, but Olivia stopped them.

"Let's do that at *Jardin*–over coffee." She drew out the last word, making it sound like "kahhh-feeee" as she plucked the tote from Taylor's hand. Then she turned and headed out of the hotel, leaving no doubt as to their first priority. The other two followed.

For all its fabulousness, Monaco really was tiny; it was barely a block from the *Metropole* to the Casino and then the *Hotel de Paris* was next door to that. Within fifteen minutes they were having nice strong espressos on the famous *Côté Jardin* garden patio. From their outdoor table they could see the yachts in the marina and the famous *Rocher de Monaco*, the huge fortress-like cliff that jutted out into the Mediterranean.

"So," Olivia said as she looked over Taylor's brochures, "Alejo and I know Monaco well. Can we start by giving you the layout so you can find your way around?"

Alejo cut in. "I thought showing you the Grand Prix course first would be a good idea. It winds completely through town in a loop and has a little bit of everything. That should help you find your way around later. Would that be okay, *sobrinita*?"

Taylor was undecided. "There's just so much I want to see."

Olivia leaned back in the patio chair and sipped her *café au lait*. "We'll be here for over two months, Taylor. Take your time and relax. You will get to see everything." She was the very picture of continental, reclining in her white dress and Prada sunglasses with the sun kissed Mediterranean behind her.

"Why don't you start by just eating breakfast and looking at the view?" she said. "For the next ten weeks you're not a tourist. You live here in Monaco, at the *Metropole.*"

Ah, Taylor thought, when she put it like that, it was very sophisticated indeed. A whole different mindset. With that in mind she took her time, picking at her breakfast and drinking a mimosa while she looked around and enjoyed that she was actually, finally, in Monaco.

It was after twelve o'clock by the time they finished and they flashed themselves up to the *Palais du Prince* situated on the *Rocher de Monaco* and started with the panoramic view there.

"That's where we just came from," said Alejo, pointing across the *Port Hercule* harbor at the *Hotel de Paris.*

Olivia gestured toward the massive *Centre de Congrès Auditorium*. It was a bold building: a gathering hall jutting out over the sea.

"And we'll be in there for a few swanky parties while we're here in Monte Carlo," Olivia assured her. "The Grimaldi forum is beautiful."

They walked around the palace grounds along the edge of the cliff, pointing out other places they would take her and parts of the Grand Prix course.

"Right there, just opposite the marina, will be the pits and the start and finish lines." Alejo knew the most about this subject; he had friends who drove Formula 1 race cars. In fact, they would arrive next month to compete and Taylor would meet them both.

"...then see over there, Taylor? Look farther away, to the right along the water ... that's where the cars exit the tunnel at full speed, then have to brake hard to make the chicane, and then speed up again before *Tabac* turn." He was behind Taylor, his head at her shoulder so he could point more accurately for her.

"Oh! I see it now." She looked at the distance between the tunnel exit and the sharp left turn. "How fast do they come out of the tunnel?"

"I think...ahhh... maybe two hundred eighty-nine kilometers." At Taylor's confused look he said, "A little over one hundred sixty miles per hour."

Taylor looked back across Port Hercule at the tight streets, trying to envision it. Very dangerous indeed.

"Can we go down to the harbor next?" Taylor wanted to walk along the marina and get next to those sleek yachts in their slips. She'd never been close to a yacht before. They were like floating secrets, with their smooth white sides and pointy angles hiding pampered guests on board, living a luxurious life.

After visiting the yachts Olivia and Alejo walked Taylor through Monte Carlo, pointing out their favorite places and sharing memories from earlier visits. It was late afternoon when they ran out of sidewalk and stories, for the moment at least, and Alejo suggested they go to dinner first and then the Casino after.

"You will love it, *mi niña.* It's beautiful inside and we will show you how to play roulette, or Baccarat, or anything else you want to try."

Olivia added, "It's the European-type casino from those spy movies that you like. Some of them were filmed here."

Alejo regarded Taylor with a look of surprise. "Is this true? I thought you only liked classic movies from the thirties and those little romantic comedies from the fifties." He shook his head. "I think you will always surprise me."

"Why? I like the rat-pack stuff from the fifties. Besides, Ian Fleming wrote the Bond novels between nineteen fifty-one and nineteen sixty-four. That's in the fifties mostly."

"How in the world do you know that?" Alejo was astonished.

Taylor considered a moment and then was blank. "I don't know."

They both looked at Olivia and she shrugged. "Why are you looking at me? Let's go get ready for dinner." She turned and headed back to the hotel.

A couple hours later, after a short rest, refreshing showers, and a change of clothes, the three stood in the *Metropole's* lush lobby.

"Where do you want to eat?" Olivia asked the two of them.

"I don't know. Are there restaurants in the Casino?" Taylor asked.

Alejo turned to Olivia, a sudden grin on his face. She broke into a smile as well, and they both turned to Taylor at the same time.

"Buddha Bar," they said in unison.

"What?" Taylor laughed at their comic timing.

"Buddha Bar," said Olivia. "It's an Asian restaurant inside an old concert hall at the Casino complex. Come on; follow me."

Olivia led the way to a small unassuming entrance to the side of the elegant Belle Epoch building, but when they arrived inside Taylor stopped in her tracks.

"Wow."

The cavernous lobby with its domed ceiling, delicate friezes, and graceful curving stairways was obviously that of an old theater from the nineteenth century, but the décor was Asian. Everything was painted in translucent, shimmering hues of red and gold and blue and violet. Rich, embroidered fabrics and carved woods glowed in the soft light. It was an amazing mix of the lavish and eclectic. There were two levels to the restaurant; the twenty-four-foot high dome gave way to an open dining balcony upstairs which encircled the restaurant and overlooked the lounge below.

And what a lounge! A gigantic mahogany Buddha dominated the patrons there, serenely observing it all between crystal sconces on the walls and miles of cushioned banquette wrapped in satin brocade.

Livy and Handy waited with while Taylor took it all in. Finally Alejo turned to the hostess.

"Three for dinner."

"Do you have a reservation?"

"Yes." Alejo looked at her reservation ledger and immediately Taylor knew he had just put their names there by magic. They hadn't even known where they were going when they started out.

Alejo went on. "In fact, we have two reservations; one upstairs for dinner and then one downstairs at a quarter to eight for *la fée verte.*"

Taylor looked at Olivia and mouthed: "What's he talking about?" But Olivia only smiled at her inscrutably.

"Sounds like you've met The Green Fairy before." The hostess attempted to engage Alejo in conversation.

"Olivia and I have, but tonight we are introducing her to my niece, Taylor. You wouldn't want to expose our secret, would you?" Alejo turned his warm smile on the hostess and of course, she couldn't say no. Smiling back at Alejo, she went silent and made a big show of nodding her complicity before she turned away to lead them upstairs.

All during dinner Taylor tried to pry the Green Fairy Secret out of both Olivia and Alejo, but they wouldn't budge, even when they had to stretch out dinner and discussion an extra half hour to get to their seven forty-five reservations in the lounge. By the time they were re-seated downstairs Taylor was about to burst.

"Okay, you two, I've waited long enough; tell me right now. What is The Green Fairy?"

"You have to say it in French first." Olivia was really enjoying this torture.

Taylor was exasperated. "Really? Fine. *La fée verte*," she said with perfect Parisian inflection.

Alejo opened his mouth to tell her, finally, but Olivia interrupted. "Oh, look. Here it comes."

Taylor watched in fascination as their server brought an ornate tray carrying strange items. He set it down on the table, arranging three oddly-shaped glasses in front of them. Each had a reservoir at the bottom, a heart-shaped little bulb. They looked old, too, like from Edwardian times. The server then laid a perforated piece of silverware on the rim of the glass, balancing its perforated middle over the center of the cup.

"Beautiful design," Taylor said, looking at the perforations, and then when the server placed a sugar cube on them she had an epiphany.

"Oh! I know this!" She cast about for the words and then saw the bottle. "Absinthe!"

"Yes. Absinthe." Olivia smiled at her. "Watch."

Taylor had heard somewhere about this ritual with the green liquid and the sugar cube but knew nothing else. She watched as the server poured a neon green liquor through the sugar cube until it filled the bottom reservoir. Then he poured chilled water over that to fill the glass.

"Do you want the rest of the sugar in your Absinthe?" he asked Taylor. She looked at the other two witches.

"Yes," they both said together, and then they all laughed. Olivia and Alejo seemed to be sharing one brain tonight.

The server stirred the rest of the sugar into her drink, and slowly the liquid turned from sparkling emerald to cloudy pale green, almost like mint ice cream. With that taste in mind, Taylor raised the glass to her lips and drank while the other two watched. She paused, letting the flavor bloom in her mouth–and then abruptly screwed up her face in a sour expression.

"Gack! Ick–that's not what I expected at all!" She shivered involuntarily and banged her drink back on the table to reach for her water. "Whoa!"

Olivia was laughing. "Here, you need more sugar." She put another cube in Taylor's glass and stirred it. Then she and Alejo took a sip of their own concoctions. A very small sip, Taylor noticed.

"That was like black licorice only bitter."

"That's the wormwood. It has anise in it, too. More sugar will help, I swear to you." Olivia continued swirling Taylor's glass until the sugar was liquefied and then handed it back to her.

"Here. Try it again."

"Man, Olivia. I must really trust you to do this again." Taylor shook her head and barely wet her lips with the fluid. Much better. "I like black licorice, but that was way too strong."

Alejo held up his glass in salute and the other two did the same before taking another tiny sip.

Taylor put down her glass. "What's the story behind Absinthe? It's got a pretty racy reputation."

Olivia sat back and smiled. "People used to say it caused hallucinations from the wormwood, but the only thing I ever saw was everyone just plain drinking too much of it."

"I don't know how anyone could drink that much of this stuff." Taylor held up her glass and looked through the bulb at the bottom. "Why was it so popular back then?"

Alejo shrugged. "The unusual ritual. And its Bohemian mystique. Artists and models and writers drank it so it got a scandalous reputation. When you have all those artists and writers creating green fairy paintings and writing outrageous stories about it, well then..."

"That's pretty cool. I don't think I'll drink the whole thing, though." Taylor reached for her water again.

"You don't have to finish it, of course." Alejo agreed. "It's a ... *hábito adquirido.* An acquired taste. We'll stay a few more minutes and then go to the Casino. I want to teach you to play Baccarat, and Olivia has a penchant for roulette that I suspect she will want to pass along to you as well. One time..." He continued, relating a story from Olivia's past where the two of them got into quite a bit of trouble with Casino security when Olivia was using magic to win.

The three didn't notice the glazed looks on the faces of a couple sitting at the table next them. They appeared completely normal, each seemingly engrossed in their smartphones, but through their eyes, Malila was watching Olivia, Alejo, and Taylor.

It was a trick she had learned from Dantin, spying on witches through the humans around them so they couldn't feel her witch's energy or block an intrusive scry. Malila knew many of Dantin's secrets, but this one wasn't getting her what she wanted. She should have guessed they weren't going to discuss witchery out in public, but she had spied on the three in their rooms through the hotel staff, too, with no results.

Malila was irritated; she needed to know more about Olivia, this supposed weakling Silver-Tint who, if rumor were correct, had taken out one of the very strongest of the Blue/Blacks. She needed far more intimate details.

Malila would have to get very personal with Olivia.

At half-past midnight, the center door of the Casino's broad entrance swung open to release Alejo, Taylor, and Olivia from inside its rarefied world. It was a wonderful end to their first full day here and they exited the gaming house relaxed and happy. In her hand Taylor held a fistful of Casino chips.

"Pretty good–my first time playing Baccarat and I ended the night up a hundred and seven Euro."

"That's because I'm such a great instructor." Alejo was all self-admiration for his handiwork with Olivia's novice, completely forgetting that it was Taylor who had the winning streak and not him. In fact, he was down by over four hundred Euros and there was no way Olivia was going to let him get too full of himself just for teaching Taylor how to play Baccarat.

"Oh, please, Handy. You're such a guy–taking all the credit for her winning. Unless, of course, she won because you used magic to cheat on her behalf. And if you did, that just means you suck because you cheated and that's dishonest. And because even if you cheated through magic, you still couldn't keep your own money at Baccarat. Not so skilled after all. Hmmm?"

She was immensely pleased at her own circular argument. "Let's see you get out of that, Alejo."

"Easily. I didn't do either one because Taylor didn't need cheating to win, and you don't have much faith in her abilities for you to say that she did." Alejandro was pleased at how cleverly he diverted Olivia away from her original argument.

"I didn't say that."

"Yes, you did."

"Did not."

"Did so."

"Did not!"

"Did so."

Then all three started laughing because they sounded exactly like two children bickering on a playground. That was one of the things Taylor loved the most about the two of them—no pretense in their friendship. She knew they could be serious; they had certainly backed each other in some dire situations over the centuries, but they also had innocent fun like two little kids. It was delightful.

As they stepped out from under the glass portico into the balmy evening Taylor stopped short, looking around.

"Oh, Alejo—you were right. Monaco sparkles like a jewel at night."

All around them hidden uplighting illuminated the foliage and pale buildings and the halo from streetlamps danced through trees, giving the palms and branches extra depth. The contrast of night sky and glittering city was stunning, and even the two older witches took a moment to enjoy the sight. A kiss of warm breeze came in off the Mediterranean, gently ruffling the palm fronds and bringing the fragrance of freesia blossoms.

"What a perfect night." Olivia lifted her nose to inhale the perfumed air and closed her eyes.

Alejo stood beside her, watching her for several seconds before he became aware that Taylor was watching them both.

"Come on," he said suddenly, and started down the broad stairs toward the garden that encircled the fountain. "Let's go the long way home and enjoy the walk back to the *Metropole*."

The trees were a little thicker on this side of the garden and clematis vines draped through some of the branches. They strolled through the heady scent of blossoms, not in any hurry to get back to the hotel–or anywhere for that matter.

They were walking along, Olivia telling them the latest news she'd heard from Dan and Julia, friends of theirs that lived in Houston, when Taylor suddenly stopped.

"What was that?" Taylor was looking at Livy and Alejo but listening off to the side. The three stood still and quiet until the noise came again: small, quick steps through the grass somewhere nearby.

"I'm going to see what it is." Taylor walked toward where she had heard the sound and peered into the bushes. She caught the tail end of a very gangly, very matted-looking dog squeezing through a hedge to hide from them on the other side. She turned to the other two.

"It's a dog! I'm going to try and find it. I can't imagine that it's supposed to be out here alone."

They spread out to try and get another look at it but couldn't catch more than a peek. They knew it was still nearby; occasionally they could hear it rustle a branch or step on leaves and loose twigs, but it didn't run away. It seemed to be curious about the three of them as well.

"Here." Olivia conjured a small mirror. "Let's scry for it." The three looked in the reflective surface of the mirror, letting its magic work, and soon they could see where the animal was hiding. It had circled around and was now peering at them from behind a mimosa tree.

Taylor conjured some food in her hand and held it out, crouching low to the ground to make herself smaller and hopefully, less intimidating. The dog came from behind the tree but wouldn't come closer, no matter how much Taylor cajoled or offered the food.

"I'm going to flash over to it and catch it."

"No!" Olivia put a hand on her arm. "You'll scare it and then it will never trust you. I wish Eidolon were here and could possess it. He could tell it we're okay." Eidolon was Olivia's familiar. She knit her brows, thinking. "To spell it and make it obey we'd have to find something it's sure to touch, or we'd have to get close enough to touch it or breathe a spell on it..."

The three had their heads together trying to find a solution when the scruffy thing suddenly stuck its long nose into their midst. The nose poked into Taylor's hand, gulped down the chunk of meat, and then backed away, but only a few feet. The dog now stood close, watching Taylor through soft brown eyes.

Taylor looked at the dog and then back at her companions, astonished and open-mouthed. She didn't dare say a word for fear of scaring the animal. She conjured another piece of meat in her palm and lifted it in front of her. The long nose came back silently to eat, the canine face barely a foot from hers.

No one moved. Carefully, Taylor conjured more snacks for it, which it ate hurriedly. Surprisingly, it didn't leave after Taylor quit feeding it, so she stroked its neck slowly and looked it over. It was skinny and neglected-looking. It had a collar that was nice once but now scratched and worn just like the dog. Poor thing. Taylor felt her eyes grow hot with tears.

"Olivia, I'm going to keep it."

"Okay." Olivia didn't bat an eye and Taylor was a little surprised.

"Just like that?"

Now it was Olivia looking surprised. "Why not? Have you forgotten all about karma, Taylor? Taking care of it could be payback for all the magic you've used lately, or maybe something that will happen in the future. It crossed your path for a reason. It even came to you. But mostly you should keep it because it needs you. I mean, just look at it."

Taylor didn't need any coaxing. "There's no way I'd leave it out here. I couldn't live with myself."

Olivia was proud of her apprentice's affectionate nature. "It's certainly not a problem for us; we'll just pay the hotel for the extra service. Big deal."

"I'll need to take it with us everywhere." Taylor wanted to make sure she wasn't raining on Alejo or Olivia's vacation plans.

"That's fine. I miss the greyhounds anyway." Olivia had two rescued greyhounds at home who were now staying with her friend JaneAnn while they were traveling. About once a month they flashed home to visit them for a few days. Taylor looked at Alejo for agreement and was happy to see it.

"I agree, *mi niña*. You should do this. It's right to."

Taylor suddenly realized how very happy she was to have something of her very own to care for. It was hard being the novice all the time. No matter how wonderful Alejandro and Olivia were to her, she was their dependent. Not only that, she missed her sister, Karen, who was away at college and wasn't witch. Karen didn't know Taylor was witch, either, and it was difficult to keep it from her because they used to be close. Now they were drifting apart without shared experiences or anything else in common. Karen talked about college and her friends there, and Taylor couldn't tell Karen any of her real experiences or thoughts. For a very short time Taylor had known another novice named Nicole, but that hadn't worked out, either; their lives had been destined to take different paths.

It hit Taylor that she needed not just a companion but this companion. This poor neglected thing that she could fill with love and turn its life around. First though, they needed to get it home with them.

Alejo was still crouched with them, softly scratching the dog under the chin while Taylor rubbed its neck.

"Taylor, *es maliolente*–smelly." He cooed to the dog. "You need a bath, don't you?"

"He's right. *Un clébard.*" Olivia had a penchant for French the way Alejo did for Spanish, and the term was not flattering. It meant mutt or mongrel.

"Okay, that's it for the badmouthing." Taylor felt she had to come to its rescue. "My dog now. Part of the family."

"Well then, let's get it back to the hotel so you can give it a bath as quick as possible." Olivia wrinkled her nose and stood up.

Taylor conjured a leash and attached it to the collar after making sure it was sturdy enough and they headed toward the *Metropole* with the smelly pup. To everyone's surprise, it went obediently, walking perfectly by her side as soon as it heard the leash clip onto its collar as if it were used to it and knew what to do. That was a relief after how skittish it had been at first.

Alejo was inspecting the thing as they walked through the park. "What is that, anyway? It has a long nose and is shaped like Olivia's hounds, but it has more hair."

"But it's so tangled I can't tell what it's supposed to look like." Olivia was inspecting it, too. "Well, maybe after the bath and brushing..."

"A Wolfhound? Borzoi? Scottish Deerhound?" Alejo was ticking off the possibilities. They were coming up to the hotel entrance by that time. They all stopped.

"We'd better not walk into the lobby with this thing the way it is. I don't feel like dealing with any questions or even looks. Alejo, would you care to put a glamour over this thing? And don't forget to mask that smell."

"I can do that Olivia. Alejo showed me how, remember?" Taylor wanted to do everything for her new charge.

"Yes, I forgot. Sorry." She and Alejo stood back to let Taylor smooth her palms lightly over the dog. Wherever Taylor ran her hands it appeared smoother, clean, the hairs silky and unmatted. She stood back to check the effect.

"Much better," Olivia cocked her head to one side. "I still can't tell what kind of dog it's supposed to look like, though."

"Well, I didn't know what I should make it look like. I was just thinking about giving it shorter, cleaner fur. As if your greyhounds had longer hair."

Olivia burst out laughing. "That's exactly what it looks like–a fuzzy greyhound! I see you've still got to practice exactly how you want your glamours to turn out. If you don't think a clear picture you won't get it. Well, that's okay. Pick a scent to mask that thing and let's go."

She was still chuckling as they entered the glass doors to the *Metropole's* lobby.

Clicking canine toenails announced their arrival to patrons in the lobby and a few turned to look as the four of them crossed the diagonal checkerboard of floor tiles. One person, they could tell, was trying to figure out just what breed they were looking at, but otherwise no one seemed to mind them. Wealthy patrons and their dogs were a common sight in the hotels here. Even though Taylor's glamour wasn't the best, they still made it to her suite without any incident, even when they shared an elevator with some other people. It tickled Taylor to think how magic allowed them to sneak this thing in right under their unknowing noses.

Once in the privacy of her suite Taylor gave it a bath and then tried to brush the tangles out of its fur, but they were too tight and it whimpered once or twice when Taylor pulled too hard on the brush. She finally had to give up.

"Well I can't leave it like this, and I don't know what it's supposed to be under all that so I can't conjure it." Taylor was stymied. "What do you think?"

"Just remove the mats," Olivia advised, "like a short haircut. We'll find out what it is once it grows out on its own."

Taylor did just that, smoothing her hands over it and leaving only an inch of fur that was clean and smooth. Then she stood back with the other two to look it over.

"Damn, that is a goofy-looking thing." It was a pale champagne color all over and had a little bit longer fur on its ears, but that was the only thing they could tell for sure. That and it was damned skinny. Taylor fed it a few more treats.

"A Saluki? A Borzoi?" Alejandro was still trying to figure it out. He peered underneath it. "Well, it's a female. I can at least see that."

"I don't care what it is. Here–come on." Taylor sat on the bed and called it up to her. It complied immediately, jumping up onto the bed. Then it turned around twice and curled up next to Taylor, resting its nose on her leg.

"I think I'm going to name her Lexie."

"Why Lexie?" Alejo couldn't imagine.

"I can't tell you right away–you'll laugh."

"Why would I laugh?" Now Alejandro's curiosity was up.

Olivia cut in. "You two can discuss that at length if you want, but I'm going to bed. It's nearly two in the morning." Then she thought of something important.

"Taylor, don't forget you'll need to take it out to pee every five or six hours. Here's food and water for you." She pointed at the floor next to the wall and there appeared two stainless steel bowls, one filled with water and the other with kibble. She walked over to pet the dog and hug Taylor.

"Good night, you two. Lexie, you really do smell a lot better," she said to the dog, who looked intently up at her, as if trying to understand. Then it rested its head back on Taylor's leg.

Alejo said his goodnight as well and then both of them walked out the door.

Alejo accompanied Olivia to the door of her suite. "Just like being parents."

Olivia looked a little startled at the statement and Alejo added quickly, "I mean, we introduce her to everything, take her on vacation with us, she gets a dog...your other apprentices seemed more grown up, or at least less new to everything. And Celeste was more your confidante than your novice."

Olivia considered. "Well, they all grew up knowing about their powers. I also got them early and they traveled with me from the start, so even when they were little they seemed older. And you didn't meet Celeste until she'd been with me for decades. By then we were long past being teacher and student. But Taylor... well, it's been less than a year that she's known she's witch and she's nineteen. Everything is new–her powers, traveling, having anything nice at all."

"You did tell me she grew up really poor. You said she didn't even finish high school?"

"No. That goddamned stepfather of hers–he abused her so much she couldn't study. She couldn't concentrate most of the time, or she hid and didn't go to school to hide the bruises from the beatings."

"I thought you told me she and her sister only had their mother, and she died just before you found them."

"Oh, God. That's right, I never told you." Olivia looked down at the carpet, deciding something, and then back at Alejo. "You know, the more people that know a secret the more it's sure to get out." She pointed an index finger at him. "You tell no one about this. No one. Only JaneAnn knows."

Alejo nodded. "Of course."

"Taylor asked me to remove those memories from both her and her sister, Karen, and give them new ones. Her stepdad was a real bastard, I mean beating and raping Taylor since she was twelve. She would protect her sister from him, usually by diverting his attention to her. Sometimes that only pissed him off and he beat her more, but at least he stayed away from Karen. Taylor doesn't remember anything about him and doesn't want to, either."

"*Madre de Dios.*"

"Yeah. No kidding. That's how she knew about those Bond books but couldn't remember how she knew it. Don't poke that stuff too hard, Alejandro. We don't want her to remember."

"That's why she's so innocent now; everything is new to her."

"Yes, I could give her more memories, but there's a limit to the learning that goes with them when they're false. Maturity happens when you need to deal with adversity, but I couldn't bear to give her any more pain. There's another thing that only I and that bastard stepfather know. He beat their mother to death and dumped her body in the woods."

"How did you discover that?"

"I confronted him when I took the girls so he wouldn't come after them. Easy enough for me to read his mind with magic when I was invisible. What a sick bastard." She smiled. "It was great scaring the hell out of him. He'll leave them alone now, I guarantee it."

Alejo smiled; Olivia was quite a woman. He didn't know another that he loved nearly as much and he found himself on the very edge of telling her so. He'd wanted to for so long.

"Olivia, you are the most fabulous woman I've ever met."

"Thanks." She smiled up at him.

"I love how you take charge of everything and I love how wonderful you are to Taylor. And to me." And then he stopped. There it was ... he'd said everything *except* I love you.

Goddamn it. He could have punched himself for being such a nancy. Just tell her, he thought. He found himself looking at her lips, wondering what it would be like to kiss them.

"What are you smiling at?" Olivia's question brought him out of his fantasy.

"Nothing. You're just not scared of anything."

"Ha. You know better than that. I was terrified of Dantin for centuries."

"And you took care of him."

"Yeah, well, we'll see how that goes." She turned the handle of her door. "Goodnight, Handy. See you in the morning." She stood on her tiptoes to kiss his cheek and he caught her face in his hands for a moment, but then only kissed her on the forehead and watched as she turned away to enter her room and close the door.

He let his fingers rest on the door handle where she had touched it last and pressed his forehead to the doorframe. *Maldita sea dios! Aarrrgh!* He hated himself; why couldn't he just tell her?

In the hallway behind him, Taylor's voice startled him.

"Alejo, what time are we meeting in the morning?"

Alejo spun around. "How long have you been there?"

"Just a second or two. I'm surprised you didn't feel me, but you were giving Olivia a goodnight kiss." She pointed at her door behind her. "Lexie fell asleep and I didn't want to wake her by getting up or opening the door, so I flashed myself here."

Alejo was relieved. "Oh. Well, in the morning call us after nine or ten and we'll decide what to do then. You'll have to get up earlier to take Lexie out. You know, I think most of our plans will have to change because of your new pet."

As if on cue they heard some scratching at Taylor's door and a soft canine whimper.

"Oh, I shouldn't have left her alone. I don't want her to think I'd leave her." Taylor was instantly gone and the hallway was silent again.

Alejo looked back at Olivia's door.

"Fuck," he said under his breath, and disappeared back to his own suite.

For the next several weeks the three Silver-Tint witches enjoyed the warm spring weather and a surprising array of enticements offered by the tiny country. Lexie fit right in, adjusting easily to being taken so many places where she could still be with her newfound pack of humans. They explored the old *Grimaldi* palaces and museums, had lunch and drank wine in each of Monaco's four exotic gardens, and of course spent a whole day on a yacht just for Taylor, lying in the sun and looking back at all the earth-bound inhabitants on the shore. The day was hot and the azure sky spread out above them as they lounged on deck. Even Lexie lay flat on her side in a piece of shade on deck, her long tongue lolling out the side of her mouth.

Lying on her back and stretched out in the sun, Taylor languidly mused aloud, "How is it that a simple day on the water can make you feel so special?"

Olivia had her eyes closed behind her sunglasses. "I think it's the blue of the sky and the Mediterranean that's so soothing."

"But there's something different about it from out here," Alejo agreed with Taylor.

"Hmm." Olivia couldn't bring herself to exert any more effort than that.

Taylor was still musing on the question. "I think it's the flat water, and the open sky, and because there's no one around to make noise or intrude."

"I think you are right, *mi niña*. It's beautiful, and calm, and very private even though we can see the people on the shore. They're very far away, though." Alejo had his eyes half-closed as he looked back at *Port Hercule*.

"Will you two teach me how to sail?" Taylor asked.

"Sure," said Alejo.

"No," said Olivia. "Too much effort. I like yachting better than heaving sheets and canvas."

Alejo snorted. "You haven't been part of a schooner crew for two hundred years, Olivia. You could make the effort for Taylor."

"Oh, great. I have to now that you've shamed me into it." Olivia pulled up her sunglasses to squint at Alejo. "You're such a jerk."

Alejo simply laughed. Olivia would be happy to teach her apprentice anything she asked for, and he knew it.

Olivia was back under her sunglasses again, shaking her head but smiling. "Jeez, the things I have to do to keep you two happy."

Yachting was only one of their days in the sun, however. Monaco also offered land bound spectator sports, like the Monte Carlo Tennis Open, where the view of the courts opened onto the expansive Mediterranean, or watching soccer from a luxury box at Louis II Stadium. Taylor had thought Monte Carlo would be just a series of shopping and sightseeing days, but April was coursing along with a full and varied calendar.

April was also the month of the Monte Carlo Spring Arts Festival. Olivia and Alejo each contributed hundreds of thousands of dollars to different Monte Carlo charities and tonight Olivia was presenting at a fundraiser for the organizations that contributed to the Festival.

As she and Alejo sat at their table waiting for Olivia to come onstage, Taylor looked up at the thousands of blossoms cascading out of the crystal chandeliers overhead. They looked like one of those huge Chihuly hanging glass sculptures, only these were far, far better because they were real flowers. And they smelled heavenly, like vanilla and ginger and something faintly oriental. No wonder people got so dressed up to go to these things, Taylor thought, they had to compete with the décor. The Hollywood Academy Awards had nothing on these attendees tonight.

Taylor was glad she'd worn her Chanel gown of vivid cobalt blue. Alejo also looked resplendent in his tuxedo and tie–something extra dressy for this special event–and Olivia had commented on it before they had left the *Metropole* that evening.

"Handy, you look completely fabulous. If only more men would realize–when they dress up for women, they would get a lot less arguing and a lot more sex from them."

Alejo looked startled for a microsecond and then laughed and kissed her hand affectionately. Taylor smiled again thinking about how much she adored the two of them and watched the celebrities and local glitterati take their turns at philanthropy.

Backstage, Olivia was talking with another presenter while awaiting her turn. One by one, the others went onstage to present their pieces as the stage manager gave the cue. Finally Olivia was next in line and she turned her attention to the mirror for one last check on her gown. Okay, she thought, everything is zipped up and tucked in; there'll be no wardrobe malfunctions tonight. She smoothed her hands over the salmon-colored satin bodice and got ready to step out.

Suddenly she heard Dantin's dark voice dripping in her ear: "Ahhh, my beauty. I love you in this corset dress. Look how it shows off your waist and the curve of your hips. And you feel so... luscious under my hands."

Olivia jerked her palms away from her waist and spun around, not sure at all what she might see and terrified it would be Dantin. But there was no one there. Of course no one was there, she thought. Dantin was dead. Still...the voice had been so real, and hearing him while she was running her hands over her own waist and hips felt distinctly creepy, as if he had been touching her.

She shuddered. She had felt him; the more she thought about it the more she was sure of it. Her head swam. That's impossible, she told herself. She knew it was impossible and with an effort she shook it off. They were stupid thoughts. She had stabbed Dantin in the throat, and she and Alejo had burned his body. He was dead months ago and he was gone, finally. The bastard.

But even while she wanted to hate him, she was a little sorry for him. He'd been so obsessed with her—his twisted version of love. Maybe if he hadn't been a Blue/Black he wouldn't have been so mean, and maybe they could have been a couple...

She snapped her head up at that line of thought. What was she thinking!? Where in hell did that total bullshit come from? A couple indeed! He was psychotic and vicious and those were the facts. How could she think they could be together, even for a second?

She took a deep breath and let it out, telling herself, be logical, Olivia. It was that damned cursed sword she'd had made to kill him with, that was it. She'd known there would be unexpected effects for using her powers to hurt someone and for using that sword. She closed her eyes and tried to calm herself. Maybe she was just feeling sorry for him because he was dead.

She was still standing there, not realizing the stage manager had called her name twice when a stagehand tapped her to get her attention. With a start she apologized and went onstage to give her speech.

As Alejo watched Olivia walk smoothly to the podium he knew something was wrong; he'd known Olivia too long not to tell by the look on her face. It was too still, too posed, her thoughts half somewhere else. He wondered what could possibly be troubling her. As he watched her begin her piece though, she quickly warmed up to the crowd and then the look was gone and she was herself again. But Alejo was sure something serious had happened.

The limo ride back to the *Metropole* after the fundraiser would have been silent if not for Taylor chatting about tomorrow's plans. Both Olivia and Alejo were distracted and quiet; him wanting to ask what had happened and her hoping he wouldn't, although she could tell he was wondering. When they got to the hotel Olivia begged off for the evening, saying she was tired, and when Alejo tried to see Olivia to her room she wouldn't let him.

"I really just want to get to bed, Handy. Taylor and I are on a whole different floor than you are, and we're right next to each other. It makes more sense for us to drop you off down here while Taylor and I go upstairs. I'll see you in the morning."

Alejo nodded, foiled for the moment, and they left him at the entrance to his first floor suite before taking the elevator to their rooms.

After saying goodnight to Taylor, Olivia didn't pause to use her key as she went into her own suite–she simply faded and walked through the door, crossing through walls to get to her bathroom without so much as a look to either side. Her gown, once one of her favorites but now tainted by the backstage memory, faded away and was replaced by a simple terry robe tied at her waist. She sat on the edge of the tiled tub and pushed up the sleeve of her robe to peer at her wrist.

She could see the blood in her veins, semi-visible through the translucent skin. Like any human veins they appeared faint blue, the blood starved of oxygen on its way back to the lungs. But what about exposed to the air, not hidden under the skin? What tint would it have? She closed her eyes and took a deep breath to steady herself. She'd have to get a closer look, but she was afraid of what she might see.

Olivia didn't bother to conjure a blade; she needed to see her blood and right now, before she lost her nerve. She winced as she traced her finger over the vein, opening up an inch-long incision through the skin and vessel walls. The sanguine fluid welled out in a pool, flowing over her arm and dripping onto the tiles before she closed it up again. Raising her forearm closer to her face she looked at the burgundy stain, apprehension making her chest flutter. Was it different than it had been a few weeks ago? Was it turning darker?

Yes. Definitely. A few weeks ago it had only a few dark blue streaks. It had been mostly red with a silver sheen to it; the comforting Silver-Tint blood she'd known her whole life. It was her identity, who she was. One of the good guys.

Now it was darker, a claret fluid with equal amounts of blue/black and silver running through it.

Yes, definitely. Darker...Blue/Black.

Olivia realized her breath was coming out in gulps. Her chest felt crushed with the weight of what she was seeing and her head spun. There would have to be more changes than simply the tint in her blood. Blue/Blacks were vicious, suspicious, power-hungry, and Dantin had been especially so. She didn't want to be like that.

Unwanted tears welled up in her eyes. Stop it, she thought. Stop being so weak and scared. Get control of this.

She conjured up a very old and dusty-looking Lesser Key of Solomon–the most accurate of all grimoires, according to the witch community– and looked through it for maybe the fiftieth time. There has to be something in here somewhere that can help me, she thought as she bent over the parchment. Page after page after page she turned, scanning the contents to find a spell for eliminating Blue/Black blood, but of course there was nothing. Just like last week and the week before that and the month before that.

Olivia couldn't count on her familiar, either. Eidolon was a chimera, a creature of magic that lived in the logos, the dimension of magic. He hadn't been back since he and several other chimeras had captured Dantin's vile familiar in October and taken it away, allowing Dantin and Olivia to face each other alone. They were out in the logos and there was no telling where they were right now, let alone *when* they were at this point. The logos didn't have the same rules about time and space that human worlds did. Eidolon could be gone a very, very long while.

An icy thought passed through her; what if Eidolon knew she was turning and had abandoned her? Their agreement had never included her being Blue/Black. She had the sudden sense that her whole world was caving in. She gritted her teeth against the tears that were now falling hard.

She considered for the hundredth time calling Schmidt. He was one of the most gifted charmsmiths around, maybe *the* most. He had helped her and Alejo craft the weapon that had killed Dantin. They hadn't told him the entire truth about what he was creating, although he may have guessed. She didn't see how could she ask him now if he could get rid of Blue/Black blood; she was sure he would know what was happening. How could he not?

A sudden knock at her door made her jump. She wondered who in the world it could be at this time of night. I won't answer it, she thought, but the knock came again, harder this time. She'd better take care of it, whoever it was. Since it would take her longer to scry the other side of the door than to simply look through the peephole, she flashed herself to the door and saw for herself.

Alejo stood on the other side. That surprised her; she'd thought she'd been clear when she'd said she was tired but apparently not. She spoke to him through the closed door, feeling a bit stupid for doing it, but she didn't want him to see her face right now, tear-stained and scared as it was.

"What's up, Handy? It's late." She knew she didn't sound like herself, and typically she would open the door and let him in, but she didn't know what else to do.

"Are you all right, Livy? You were so quiet in the limo."

"Yes. Of course, Handy. I told you I was tired."

"Are you sure? It felt like more than that in the car, and I saw in your face that something was bothering you."

Damn it, she thought. She'd tried not to have any expression after she'd heard Dantin's voice. Maybe that had been the problem. The trouble with having close friends was that they could read you.

"I don't know what you mean."

"Livy, let me in. It's *estúpido* to be talking through the door. You know I could just transport myself in there with you."

"Don't!" Olivia pressed her eyes closed, trying to maintain her composure. "Come on, Handy, powers or not, you know that's not right. This is my room and I want some privacy." She spat out the last sentence and was a little surprised at how forceful it was. What was she doing? She never spoke to him this way, and they always shared everything. She changed her tone.

"Handy, please. I'm really, really tired and I want to be alone. Just leave. Go back to bed, or your room, or to the bar, or anywhere else. But leave me alone, please." She felt like a shit for being so unkind. He was her best friend and she loved him a lot, but...

She felt the brush of magic on the other side of the door, and he was gone. She made sure to block him from scrying her and seeing what she was doing, and then let her tears come in raging waves as she made her way to her bedroom and crawled onto the bed. Everything was falling apart and she had no idea what to do.

Olivia couldn't let anyone know about this. She may as well have had a virulent, highly contagious poison in her blood that would infect other witches, like the Bubonic Plague or Ebola virus. She was sure if they knew, her own kind would ostracize her.

She felt a bigger alarm suddenly. She couldn't count on the Blue/Blacks if she turned, either. The Silvers and Blue/Blacks had been enemies for centuries and previous overtures at friendship had quickly been squelched with Blue/Black treachery. They trusted no one; should she fear for her own life?

Even worse, if there could be such a thing in all this, she was hearing Dantin's voice. I had to have imagined it, she thought. It had been months since his death and nothing like this had happened until now. Oh, God, she thought. Will I start hallucinating?

She sat on the bed and cradled her pounding head in her hands, the dark blood staining her robe a bitter reminder of her predicament. Olivia couldn't take the chance on anyone knowing about this. Not even Alejo could know. Especially not Alejo.

She'd never felt so utterly alone.

Alejo poured himself a drink and stood on his terrace overlooking the city. The late night air was lush and balmy, but he was disturbed, in fact really concerned, about Olivia rejecting him the way she had. The only time she ever did when something was really wrong, like after Tristan had been killed and she'd disappeared completely.

Tristan had been Alejo's best friend and Olivia's lover, and after he was gone, Olivia and Alejo clung to each other for comfort; they were all that was left of him. Then she had disappeared, letting herself waste away in Paris until he had found her and rescued her. That had deepened their friendship and since then they'd become almost one. For over five hundred years they'd been tight, always there for each other no matter what was needed. Olivia had even insisted on protecting Alejo from magical blowback by dealing with Dantin herself. Now something serious had happened backstage tonight, and he couldn't imagine what. That also meant he couldn't help Olivia, and that was killing him inside.

He knew about the Blue/Black blood. He'd seen the streaks in her blood right after she'd killed Dantin, but they were faint and he had told her it was probably Dantin's blood that had mixed with hers as they fought. After all, she'd had some serious wounds. But that had been months ago and nothing had happened so far. Olivia was the same as she'd always been—until tonight.

No Silver-Tints had ever turned dark. At least not that he knew of.

He swirled his drink, listening to the ice clink comfortably in the scotch. He was probably being stupid, he told himself. Some guy backstage was probably overly friendly with her, or overly short with her and she had taken care of it but was still annoyed, that was all. He didn't need to be in on every little thing that happened with Olivia, and she certainly wouldn't appreciate him coming to her rescue over such a little thing and unasked at that. She was always insistent that she could handle herself.

He made himself sit and nurse his drink as he listened to the nighttime sounds of Monte Carlo, trying not to think of Olivia. Looking out over the city, he could make out the top of the Casino and its highlighted domes; inside the gaming would be in full flower. He could go over to the Casino for distraction, he decided. He would definitely meet the dress code; he was still in his tux. It was nice that there were places where people were still expected to dress well. In particular the women at the Casino were always spectacularly turned out, and he needed to get his mind off Olivia.

Suddenly he wondered if Malila was in Monte Carlo yet. He'd like to play a few rounds of Baccarat at the Casino with her–if he could keep his hands off her long enough. The thought of that made him smile. He thought he knew just how to get her attention...

As it turned out, at that very moment Malila was in Monte Carlo and already at the Casino playing roulette. She'd just placed her bet when a touch on her left wrist caught her attention. She looked down to see the outline of a bracelet start to appear and smiled warmly when she recognized it as one Alejandro had bought for her in Brazil when they were together so many years ago. Well, it was a copy, of course–he didn't know where the original was. She'd kept it all this time and never told him. It was nice to see that he'd thought of the same thing she had when choosing a memento from their time together.

She sighed silently; she really did like him. It was too bad about Olivia, maybe. She hoped she could keep Alejo from finding out what was going on. For a second she considered leaving him out of it completely but didn't see how she could. The two were tighter friends than anyone she'd ever seen. It was too late now, anyway.

Malila pulled out her iPhone, murmured a charm under her breath, and then spoke to a very surprised Alejandro on the other end.

"I thought you would just appear here," Alejo said. "I didn't know what to do with the phone that appeared in my hand until it rang."

"Well, I can't just disappear if I'm in public, you know. What are you doing? On your own tonight?" She hoped he was.

"Yes."

"Would you like company?"

"Yes. I was thinking of Baccarat, like the last time we were here."

"Well, I'll cash in and move over to the Baccarat table then."

"Oh, you're already at the Casino."

"Why are you surprised? We're in Monte Carlo. And anyway, why aren't you at the dessert reception following the Arts Fundraiser? You always attend those things." Be careful Malila, she thought. Alejo probably assumes you're a Silver-Tint and that you do the same. But he didn't seem to notice.

"Livy said she wasn't feeling well. She wanted to leave and go back to the hotel right away. Of course, Taylor didn't know what was wrong–I mean, she'll go wherever we go until she's developed her own life. After her powers mature, of course."

Something in his voice alerted Malila. "Wrong? What's wrong with Olivia?"

Alejo hesitated. He didn't know how to answer her. He considered that maybe there wasn't anything to worry about, or Olivia could keep something to herself if she wanted to, but it just felt wrong. There was something about the way she acted, and it felt different. Bad different. Something not good had happened with Olivia that night.

"Alejo, what's going on?" Malila decided to push. "I can tell there's a problem from your voice and the fact that you're not answering. You don't play games." She needed to know if it was true. Was Olivia turning? It could make all the difference in the world for Malila.

Alejo still didn't respond, however, so she took another tactic.

"You don't really sound like you want to go out. Give me a few minutes and I'll come to you."

"Yes, please come and visit me, Malila. That sounds really good right now." Alejo hung up and watched the magical iPhone dissolve in his hand.

Malila had already left the roulette table to find a private nook where she could think. It was a good thing the Casino was from another era. It was opulent and old-fashioned enough to still have a sitting room in the ladies' lounge and Malila picked a spot in a far corner away from curious eyes. She needed it for what she was going to do.

If Alejo was this bothered by something that had happened with Olivia, then right now was the time to spy on her. She didn't dare go there in person; Olivia would be able to feel her presence, and there wasn't a human in her room to look through. She'd have to split and send her essence. Looking around to make sure she was alone, she whispered a few magical syllables as she postured herself.

Slowly a transformation began to take place around Malila. The bronze glow that lit her entire body was too faint for a mortal to perceive, but inside it Malila's body was suspended, held alive while her essence was absent from it. Any mortal looking at her would see her reading her smartphone, but across town at *Hotel Metropole*, Malila's essence emerged in Olivia's sitting room.

The lights were off throughout the suite and the room was silent. In the sitting room a crisp satin evening gown lay draped over the sofa, shoes and accessories on the coffee table nearby. Malila navigated the room, feeling the energy to see what she could pick up. She peered through the bedroom doorway. Dark there, too, but she decided to look there last. Guardedly she made her way to the bathroom.

She could see the ghostly outline of herself in the mirror as she moved through the bathroom, gliding her hand over personal items to see what images she could pull from them. Nothing was strong enough to generate any information she was interested in.

Until she stepped on the tiles next to the tub.

A jolt went through Malila. Images of a sobbing Olivia and her feelings of absolute desolation sliced through the Blue/Black witch. There was also...terror. Olivia had been terrified by something when she was here earlier, but Malila couldn't tell what. It was definitely Olivia she was feeling, that was for sure. She could see her clearly, although the images were fleeting.

Malila closed her eyes and drew in an astral breath to let the energy in the room permeate her inside and out. Eventually the images slowed down and coalesced. Now Malila could feel it was

Olivia's horror over turning dark, but also something else. Something far more deadly and evil accompanied that horror.

Malila lifted her foot and looked carefully at the tiles there, trying to see if any visual clue was evident. Nothing but pristine ceramic glinted back at her.

She turned her focus to the bedroom and slowly moved through it. A motionless Olivia was lying on the bed in a white terry cloth robe. As she passed her Malila got the impression that she had cried herself to sleep but didn't dare go near her, even in her astral state.

One very careful step after the other Malila moved through the bedroom, passing her hands over items to see if she could glean more information from them, but she didn't want to touch anything that might alert Olivia she'd been there. Not only that, she didn't have much time. Projecting like this was a dangerous and foolhardy thing to do. There was no guarantee she could regain her body without help if she didn't match it exactly, and the longer she was separated the more out of sync her essence and body would be.

She made it to the sitting room and was taking one last look around before leaving when her eyes fell upon the satin dress. She must have been wearing it tonight, Malila thought as she reached for it. I'll take the chance on touching it. It might be able to tell me–

"Oh, my God."

The whisper escaped her before she could stop it. No, she thought. That's impossible. But there it was. *Dantin.*

The realization was so piercing that Malila was frozen. She knew she was creating magical waves in the suite that Olivia would feel, like ripples in a pond, but couldn't help herself. Malila's shock at feeling Dantin so strongly in the gown was pulsing outward in rings that absolutely would awaken Olivia when they got to her.

In the bedroom, she heard Olivia start to stir.

No time to get any more information. Malila had about one second before Olivia would know she was there. She disappeared immediately and returned to her human self, still sitting on the chaise in the ladies' lounge and ready for her to combine. Malila framed herself in line with her body and sank back to reintegrate, but she didn't blend. She fell through it and ended up still spectral, staring in shock at her suspended form.

Coming back from an astral projection was a three-dimensional puzzle. All aspects had to line up perfectly–including mentally–and Malila was still rattled, in a hurry, and now alarmed at failing to blend the first time.

She tried to relax. You're out of Olivia's room now, she told herself. You won't get caught. There was her human form, right in front of her, and again she tried to meld but couldn't. She was so frightened by what she'd discovered that she was too out of sync with the person who'd left this body and getting worse every second. Multiple times she tried to slide back into her form but without success, and now she was frantic.

"Locke!" She shouted the name into the logos.

The glow surrounding her physical form expanded, becoming brighter, and from it an arm appeared with an open hand that reached out to Malila. She took it gratefully, tucking it into her chest with her own hands and hanging on tightly. As the glowing form surrounded and encompassed her, she was able to relax and align while the glow retracted to her body, creating one cocoon that blended until both the Malilas were one again. She would never have been able to get back on her own, she realized.

She sat there, trembling and in shock as the surrounding glow faded. That was way too close, all of it: Almost getting lost forever in the astral world. The shock of suddenly feeling Dantin there in Olivia's suite. Almost getting caught by Olivia. And Olivia with the possibility of Blue/Black blood. Oh hell. I have to get Olivia's blood, she realized sharply. And as soon as possible. There is far, far more to this and it may change my plans for Olivia. At least at first.

Then Malila remembered Alejo. She was supposed to meet him in his suite. She hoped he wouldn't key in on her nerves, but thank goodness the infatuation spell would distract him. She was lucky she could handle its effects on her. She was almost as captured by it as he was; that was the problem with those things. But it would get her what she needed from him and with the scare she'd just had she could use an energetic, animal, no-holds-barred bounce with Alejo. That should take care of these butterflies in her chest. She disappeared and flashed to him, appearing in his room.

Alejandro felt Malila several seconds before he could see her and strongly this time, too. Good, because he didn't want to think about Olivia. He wanted a distraction that could push Olivia out of his head, and Malila was exactly who he had in mind.

When she appeared he didn't even say hello. He crossed the space between them to kiss her immediately, wrapping an arm around her waist and pulling her to him. His other hand went lower to grab a handful of her bottom through her dress.

God, he thought, how can she have such a tiny waist and a round voluptuous ass at the same time? She's like a Vargas pin-up from the fifties, all luscious and pointy and soft and round at the same time. He thought how athletic and sleek Olivia's body had looked in her swimsuit the other day on the yacht. He closed his eyes against that vision, and with effort he shoved her out of his mind and pulled Malila so close to him she gasped for breath.

"I'm sorry." He released her, but she grabbed him tightly and wouldn't let go.

"No. Keep doing it–I want to lose myself in sex with you tonight. I don't even want to think."

Alejo felt the heat coming up through him. God, she was like no one else; she seemed to always match his mood, his desire of the moment. He growled, low and guttural, and buried his teeth in her neck. He felt like a stag in rut tonight and it was perfect that she wanted the same from him as well because right now he couldn't be gentle if he tried.

He jerked open the neck of her dress to expose her breasts and gripped one in each hand, pushing them together while framing her nipples in the circle between his thumbs and forefingers. They were rosy pink, the tender tips erect and perfect to suck on and he did, going from one to the other and licking the rounded flesh in between.

"Ah, yes–that's exactly right." Malila gasped. "Suck harder. And I want you to leave them wet all over." She had her fingers entwined in his hair and it was hard not to pull it, she was so wound up.

Alejo was right there with her. He wanted to bite through the luscious skin, swallow her whole, devour her if it could keep this intensity of feeling going. Suddenly her breasts weren't enough and he wrapped an arm around her waist again to grasp her closer to him and grind himself against her. He wanted to feel her everywhere, all at once and his hands showed it, going from breasts to waist to thighs and back again.

"Here," Malila whispered and cupped her breasts together for him. "I'll hold these for your mouth while you do whatever you want with your hands."

It took a second for him to understand what she meant, and then he readjusted his stance and complied. She was right; he could bury his face in her cleavage and grab everything else, too, but it still wasn't enough. For either of them.

"Alejo, I want to be at the bar." Malila looked over her shoulder to the cocktail bar in his suite. Perfect, he thought. The mahogany counter behind the bar was just the right height. And the best thing about being witch? They were instantly there. No staggering across the room trying to keep hold of each other, no break in the action—now she was up on the counter with her knees up on either side of him and her dress high on her thighs. He caught his breath when he looked down; bare pink flesh, no panties, nothing to get in the way of this roaring hard-on he had for her right now. He waved a hand over his tux to get rid of it and stood naked between her thighs. A sweep of his fingers between them told him how ready she was.

He hooked a forearm under each of her thighs and pulled them wide. Oh, this dress has got to go, he thought, and willed it away so he could see her complete nakedness.

Malila was looking at him from between her wide open legs, her gaze focused on his mouth, but Alejo pulled her closer on the mahogany bar, sliding her bottom to ride against his flat belly.

"I'll do that later, I promise. Right now I just want this." He shoved himself into her hard and was not disappointed by her reaction. Her exclamation, arched back, and bare throat exposed to him as she threw her head back told him he'd matched her desire. He watched her closely as he drove himself into her, not wanting to hurt her, but she urged him on.

"Let yourself go in me. Tonight, that's what I want. Hot-panting, growling, animal sex. I'll tell you if I want less."

With that Alejo let go and closed his eyes, losing himself in the softwarmsquishy cloud of feeling inside Malila, thrusting himself into her hard with every stroke. He could hear it force a grunting breath out of her each time he drove deep and that heightened his lust more. Her soft thighs were sweeping against his hips with every stroke, too, and her soft bottom was squishing his balls against his thighs with each deep plunge. It was a vortex of pleasure that gave him vertigo.

Malila braced herself against the counter to match his force. Her adrenaline was still loaded and she needed to burn that off, and Alejo was doing a great job for her. She gripped his biceps, digging her nails into him, and used the leverage to keep her hips from sliding back on the counter as he jacked himself into her.

"Yes, perfect! More..." She urged him on.

They kept at it, half delirious with arousal until finally they had to slow down because they were just plain tired, but by that point they'd had their fill. Malila reclined back on the polished mahogany to enjoy looking at Alejo while he used slower, more thoughtful strokes. He gazed down at her, taking in the combination of the view and how it felt.

"How are you doing?" Malila asked him.

"How about you? What would you like now?" Alejo asked instead of answering her. In his experience her question, when things were slowing down, meant his partner was ready for a rest.

"I could stop here," said Malila. "Oh, that felt great."

"Sorry I didn't give you a big finish." Alejo hoped Malila wasn't disappointed; they'd never ended without climaxing that he could remember.

"Are you kidding? For me it's not about the ending; I love how it feels all along the way. That was exactly what I wanted, Alejo, thank you."

She stretched out on the bar. "Aaaaahhhh. I feel so much better."

Alejo looked down at her as she lay on the mahogany bar. "Now I won't be able to help thinking of you naked right here whenever I make a drink."

"Good. Take a nice long look then." She fanned her hair out, drew her knees up and arched her back off the counter in a centerfold pose.

"*Oh Dios, tu eres como un picara!* What a scamp you can be. Come here; I want to lie next to you." He scooped her up and carried her to the bedroom so he could lay her on the bed, then walked naked to the mini-bar to get water for both of them.

She watched him in the half-dark. His broad shoulders descended into beautifully muscled hips and legs. All those years of riding, she knew. It was a pleasure to watch him walk back to the bed where she waited for him.

"Do you want anything else?" He stood silhouetted against the light coming through the sheer curtains.

"Can we open the French doors in here? It's warm and I like listening to the nighttime sounds."

She piled up the pillows while he opened the doors so they could sit up and talk awhile. Malila intended to find out what Alejo knew about Olivia, but it was a delicate dance she was doing. She'd never pried into his affairs before or volunteered much about her own life, and it might seem odd if she did now. She started off slowly; she couldn't afford to get caught.

"So, what have you been doing in Monte Carlo?"

"Oh, Taylor's never been here before so we're showing her a little bit of everything. Actually, Taylor's hardly been anywhere her whole life."

"She's Olivia's novice but hasn't traveled?"

"Not until she met Olivia. Her family was very poor."

"How did they meet?"

"Taylor lived in Seattle, in a run-down section not far from Olivia's neighborhood. Livy ran into her in the local market one day and could tell that the girl didn't know about her powers. She knew if she didn't take her in and teach her, then something *malo*–something bad– would find Taylor and take advantage."

That startled Malila, Alejo's use of the Spanish word that sounded so close to her name. She hoped he wouldn't pick up on it. Her parents, both Blue/Blacks, had chosen it proudly because of its connotation. She quickly continued the conversation in Taylor's direction.

"Taylor is lucky, then, to have found Olivia. Oh, now I remember you saying she's been with Olivia less than a year. Yes, I suppose you'd need to introduce her to everything." But Olivia's apprentice wasn't really who Malila wanted to know about.

"Alejandro, when you said Taylor didn't know what was wrong or why Olivia wanted to go back to the hotel right away, was it some sort of witchcraft problem she hadn't learned yet? I'm sorry, but I don't understand what you meant."

Alejo knit his brows, thinking. He shouldn't be telling Olivia's business to anyone, but Malila had helped him find Olivia in Paris when she had needed him, so he could trust her, he thought to himself. But he didn't know what the problem was–Olivia wouldn't talk to him tonight. He decided to tell Malila the truth.

"I don't know what's wrong with Olivia. Something happened backstage when we were at the *Grimaldi* and I don't know what. She won't tell me."

"But what's the problem with that? You don't always tell each other everything, right?" Malila couldn't imagine that much openness.

With the Blue/Blacks you always had to watch your back.

"Usually we do, or at least almost." He paused again. "And she doesn't ever cut me off and not talk to me at all, well, except that time she disappeared in Paris."

"Oh. She didn't say anything? Not a clue?"

"No."

Alejo actually looked pained about it, Malila thought. She didn't dare ask him any more now; she would have to settle for half-information. She had another thing she could use to her advantage, though; Alejo had offered to introduce the two of them, and she reminded him now but very carefully.

"Well, I'll be here for the Grand Prix and we might run into each other. I have Paddock Club VIP passes for the race."

"That's wonderful—we're at the *Virage* but have pit passes so we might run into each other if you go there. The Paddock is pretty exclusive, though. I imagine you will have more special access than we will." He had a thought. "Two of my friends are driving in it and they have come early. Why don't we all have dinner together?"

"I'd love that Alejo. Just let me know when. You know how to get ahold of me." She thought she'd better change the subject at that point.

She pushed her breasts together again, inviting more attention on their already bright pink tips. Alejo looked at them. There were tiny purple spots where he'd given them such bruising attention earlier. "You know there'll be teeth marks tomorrow."

"That's okay. I did ask you to, after all. I was feeling primitive."

"Still, I didn't want to hurt them." He leaned over and kissed them again, very lightly this time. Little kisses meant to apologize to her breasts for being so rough earlier. Somehow even that small thing impassioned him again, but he held himself in check. The whole night had been unsettling and at this point he just wanted calm. He wanted Malila's closeness right now, not her sex, and his desire for her was getting in the way. He tried to just spoon with her and felt himself growing lustful again, but that wasn't how he wanted to treat her after being so rough earlier.

Finally he pushed himself away from her. They had only quit ten minutes ago, for heaven's sake.

"What's wrong?"

"I feel *devestar*–that I want to ravage on you again." He sometimes stumbled in his wording when he was agitated. "But I don't want that; I want to relax." Even at this moment he felt like he needed–*needed* every inch of her touching him, inside and out.

Malila knew what was happening. His agitation over Olivia was adding its strength to the spell, mixing with it. She couldn't control that, but she could try and match his need for warmth instead of aggression. Slowly, carefully, so Alejo wouldn't see, she drew in a silent breath to pull in the magical haze around them and then exhaled to dissipate some of the energy. She could feel the power become less aggressive, less in turmoil.

"Here." She lay back on the pillows, drew up her knees, and patted her chest. "Come and lie here between my legs."

Alejo looked at her suspiciously.

"No, I mean lay your head on my chest, and I'll put my arms around your back, and we'll lie still."

After a second or two of looking at her narrowly, he complied. Seems like he couldn't say no to her at all, even when it was for no sex. Still, he had to admit she was right. It was a comfortable, companionable position. Just what he wanted. He began to feel calmer and was soon in a warm, dreamy state. Why did I ever think Olivia had a problem? he found himself wondering. He was drowsy, his thinking thick and sluggish. I must be getting sleepy, he told himself, and decided to go with it.

Malila could hear his breathing become regular, softer, and she knew he was asleep. She let her thoughts relax and tipped her head back on the pillows, putting her fingers lightly in Alejo's soft hair to play with it. It was the perfect length: just an inch or two past the haircut stage which gave a tousled, friendly look to his handsome face.

Olivia really has an effect on him, she thought. But they are best friends after all. Exactly how much did he know about Olivia's involvement in Dantin's disappearance? He had told her they shared everything—well, except for tonight when Olivia had shut him out—but it might take her too long to pull that knowledge out of him.

She decided she couldn't wait any longer to be introduced to Olivia, and she needed to test her blood, which meant she had to get some of it first. And she needed to find out for sure why she felt Dantin in Olivia's room that night. Usually a dead witch's essence dissipated out into the logos and added itself to the other magic out there. A horrible thought struck her. If Dantin wasn't dead then she had bigger problems to fix than dealing with Olivia.

When Alejo woke up Malila was gone. Of course. She never stayed if they weren't already traveling together and in the same room.

He was still a little out of sorts, remembering the string of things that had happened the night before, ending with Malila helping him to relax. She was the only good thing that had happened last night, he thought. He lay there a while to wake up and then looked at his watch. Eleven o'clock. His two driver friends were arriving today to prepare for the Grand Prix, and he was meeting them for drinks at their hotel, then going to a late lunch with Olivia and Taylor to introduce them all. Until then, Olivia, Taylor, and Lexie had plans of their own today.

Finding Lexie had turned out to be ideal for Taylor. Since Taylor needed to walk her, keep her occupied, feed her, and be with her constantly, the novice had gained more independence from the two older witches. She was out much more on her own with Lexie, planning and deciding everything for the both of them and not asking Olivia for direction or companionship all the time. It was a marvelous development. Being responsible for another creature and having to care for them both was making Taylor bloom.

Thinking about that made Alejandro smile. Even his worry over Olivia moved further away as he thought of the apprentice, and as more time stretched out between last night and this morning. He got out of bed, strode to the shower, and hit the spray to get ready for his day.

Across town, Olivia had been out for hours. She needed time alone after last night's drama, and it was lucky Alejo had friends coming in so she wouldn't have to deal with him. She had purposely risen early and left the hotel before Alejo could ask her to have coffee with him. She'd gone to *Larvotto* beach, walking along Avenue Princess Grace until she was at the far end, next to the Monaco Sporting Club. Getting her spot in the sand early also meant there would be fewer people and sure enough, no one came near her for three solid hours.

The alone time didn't do her much good. After casting back and forth about whether to tell anyone her problem, she realized she needed a witch with knowledge of Blue/Black. The problem was, she didn't know anyone like that except maybe Schmidt, but did even he know more than rumors and legend?

She desperately needed Alejo's friendship but was still afraid he'd reject her if he knew. Becoming Blue/Black was very different than being victim of one, like she had been. The irony of her situation wasn't lost on her, either. She might be turning into the very thing she had finally escaped from, all because she took action to free herself from it.

By this time the beach was filling up, even her end. Tourists were flocking into Monte Carlo because of the Cannes film festival in Nice that happened in May. Nice was only an hour's drive to the west so of course everyone and their Aunt Nan and the family dog had decided to swing by Monte Carlo while they were in the area.

Olivia gathered up her things and walked up the road, intending to find a place to stop for lunch but it quickly turned into a mammoth expedition. The city was preparing for the Grand Prix and the usual pedestrian pattern was disrupted. Even worse, the crosswalks and public lifts were full of gawkers and souvenir buyers and people who zigzagged up the street without real purpose and caused bottlenecks in the moving sidewalks set up through town to expedite traffic. Olivia didn't want to go back to her hotel yet so she was trapped in this crowd for now.

It took Olivia nearly an hour of stop and go and detours to get to the Casino and its nearby shops, and she was a little surprised at how impatient she was becoming with all the bustle.

As she was crossing the *Avenue des Citronniers* a diminutive, mild-looking woman in front of her stopped abruptly and turned to the right, then changed her mind again and turned back the way she had come, cutting Olivia off as she tried to continue crossing.

For some reason this small inconvenience infuriated Olivia, and with magic she dashed the poor woman to the ground where she landed on hands and knees, her purse and shopping bag both skidding across the pavement. Olivia could hear some delicate thing in the bag implode with a sickening musical crunch.

Olivia stormed by her at first without helping, more intent on her own discomfort at having to pause in her stride and then stopped, shocked at her actions–why in the world had she done that? She was never impatient or mean. The poor woman was simply enjoying her day. Olivia was suddenly, deeply ashamed.

She went back to the woman, helping her up and gathering the purse and the shopping bag that now held shards of a treasure the woman had probably selected carefully, a memento of her trip. She'd probably had to save awhile to afford this trip, too, from the looks of her, and couldn't afford to replace what Olivia had broken.

Olivia introduced herself and asked if she was all right. The woman gave her name as Donna and looked at the pavement around her for some bump or pothole that had caused her to fall.

"I don't know how that could have happened. I'm so embarrassed."

Olivia felt like a shit. The woman was embarrassed, and it wasn't her fault at all. She brushed the street crumbs off Donna's clothes for her.

"Can I help you somehow? Where are you staying?"

Donna named the hotel where she was staying– one of the less expensive places on the outskirts of town. The more Olivia listened to this small, sweet-natured woman the sicker she felt. As Olivia had suspected, this was a scraped-together trip for her, the one in a lifetime. As she handed Donna's purse back to her, she conjured a hefty amount of cash to appear in her wallet, her traveler's checks, and then put a few extra dollars in her pocket as she held her elbow to steady her. After a moment, Olivia paid off her credit card bills, too, but it still didn't assuage her shame at being so cruel in the first place.

With a few more kind words, making sure she wasn't injured, and wishing her a happy vacation, Olivia left Donna and walked up the street. All her fears of the night before came flooding back. What was wrong with her? she wondered. She stopped at a café and ordered a coffee. She needed to think.

At least she could feel other witches around her. It wasn't unusual for them to congregate in a place like Monte Carlo with its chi-chi lifestyle and an exciting event like the Grand Prix. Something like that was always sure to attract lots of them, especially since three or four of the drivers were witch. Feeling the vibrations from the other witches was comforting because while Olivia still felt isolated by her secret, she didn't feel quite as alone. Well, she thought, at least no one else suspects my horrible situation. They're not all screaming and running away from me.

A sudden commotion and a crash startled her, and then she was astonished to find an impossibly beautiful woman in her lap and white wine running down her leg.

"Oh, my God, I am so sorry! Let me clean that up." The woman pulled herself off Olivia's lap and then dabbed Olivia's wine-covered leg with a napkin while venting her anger at a pair of very expensive looking shoes.

"These goddamn shoes. You'd think for seven hundred dollars they'd last longer than two weeks! Man, that really pisses me off!" She pulled at her shoe while she held the napkin against Olivia's leg until she was able to jerk the stiletto off her foot. She looked at the slim ankle strap with its dangling broken buckle. "Son of a bitch!"

Then she stopped, looking at Olivia. "Oh, I'm so sorry–again. Gods, you must think I'm insane, getting so mad over a pair of shoes." She looked at the piece of foot art in her hand and back at Olivia.

"I promise, I don't usually lose my temper. I think this was the last straw in a hellacious morning with all these tourists around." She leaned in conspiratorially toward Olivia. "I can't even flash myself where I want to go without being seen; there's just too many of them."

Olivia felt immense relief wash through her. Of course, she thought, anyone would be frustrated with this crush of sightseers in town. This witch said so herself. Olivia still felt horrible about Donna but better about herself.

Then Olivia realized she was simply staring awkwardly into the woman's face, and neither of them were talking. At the same time, the other witch realized she was still holding the napkin against Livy's leg. They both started to laugh.

"I guess I could have let you wipe your own leg." She rolled up the napkin and set it on the table. "Here's a dry one for you." Surreptitiously she conjured a fresh napkin and gave it to Olivia. "Can I buy you a drink? I really don't want you to think I'm crazy." She caught the waiter's eye and then introduced herself to Olivia.

"I'm Malila Davalos."

"Olivia Phalen."

"Oh! You're Alejo's friend." At Olivia's startled look Malila said, "I used to report on polo matches and knew him when he was Juan Gutierrez. I've seen pictures of you with him in Town & Country recently."

Now Olivia remembered Malila from the few rare shots of both her and Alejo in polo magazines half a century ago, but those didn't capture the startling color of her eyes or her exquisite cheekbones. Malila knew Alejo...it was nice for Olivia to hear of their common connection.

"I'm going to fix this shoe–do you mind being lookout? I'll put my napkin over it and maybe pretend I'm getting into my purse or something. She opened her handbag, grabbed the napkin off the table and fiddled with it while Olivia looked around. Malila had her shoe, the napkin, and her handbag all in her lap, camouflaging what she was doing, and in seconds she was done. She snapped her bag shut and displayed her strappy shoe.

"All fixed." She buckled it back onto her foot as the waiter placed a glass of chardonnay before each of them. She raised her glass to Olivia's.

"Apologies again."

"That's okay. Where are you staying?"

"The *Hermitage*."

"Oh, I love that hotel–that circular lobby with that stained glass rotunda is amazing. Like a Victorian summer house. So beautiful. Their rooms are nice, too."

"I always stay there when I'm here; the hotel staff knows me."

"Yeah, I know what you mean. I usually stay at the *Metropole* for the same reason. Always had good experiences there."

"You know, they serve drinks and do tea on the second floor lobby." Malila wanted to enhance her connection with Olivia. "You should come–my treat."

"Oh, that sounds great! I have an apprentice and I'd like to bring her if that's okay, or at least offer to. Lately she's been out on her own more, but I want to introduce her to as many of us as possible."

"Absolutely yes; I'd love to meet her. I assume you're here for the Grand Prix? I have Paddock Club passes for both days."

"Oh, I've heard those are fabulous. We have reservations at the *Virage*. This is my first F1 race, but we have friends driving in it."

"Witch?" Malila lowered her voice on the word.

"Of course." Olivia lowered her voice as well and then leaned toward Malila. "Doesn't it seem that most witches crave that dangerous edge? It's like having powers and being nearly immortal ... I can't explain it very well, but it's like we need more of everything to really feel it. Even danger."

"Oh, absolutely. People need a little risk in life. It feels good, especially if you succeed. Witches just need more. I mean, if you're magic and all, why do anything ordinary?" She laughed. "You know, some mortals are like that, too. Can you believe those people who fly in wingsuits along those sheer cliffs?"

Olivia was right with her. "Oh, yeah, one little bounce against a rock and they're done." She took a sip of her wine. "I know a few witches that do that, just for fun. I guess we're all the same except for the magic."

Abruptly Malila looked at her watch and gathered her purse. "Oh! Hey, I have to be somewhere in twenty minutes, but let's get together soon with your apprentice. I'll put my number in your phone, or I can leave you a message with the *Metropole* front desk."

"That sounds terrific. Make it this week." Olivia pulled out her phone and Malila touched it.

"In the next few days, I promise." Malila got up to leave. "Tell Alejo I said hello."

"Oh, that's right–I'll do that." Olivia watched Malila as she walked away. Well, that was nice, she thought. The last twenty-four hours had been such back and forth, feeling good, then horrible, then slightly better and then plain rotten, finally ending up good again after meeting Malila. Olivia was glad she had bumped into her.

Malila waited until she was well away from the café before she looked in her purse; in fact, she had turned several corners and was almost at her hotel before she undid the clasp and looked inside. Nestled amongst the lipstick, iPhone, and credit cards was a small glass vial filled with blood. Olivia's blood. Malila had pressed it against Olivia's leg under the napkin she'd used to blot the white wine.

Malila couldn't risk taking it out and looking at it on the street, but she couldn't resist a little confirming peek to make sure it was there. Ah, yes. It was there. And it was full.

A few minutes later, Malila was in her hotel lobby. As she crossed it she stepped around a blind corner, flashing herself to her hotel room with her purse still open and the vial out now so she could get a better look at it.

"Locke!" She spoke the name into the logos as she appeared in her suite and then held the vial to the sun coming through the window. What was its color?

It was dark red ... Like hers.

Malila conjured a small glass saucer and poured the blood onto it, inclining her head to see its color. The tiny dome of blood had both a navy haze and a faint silver sheen on it, similar to 3D car paint. From one angle it had a silver hue, from another it was metallic blue, and underneath it all was a vibrant red. Yes, exactly like hers.

Around her, her suite was darkening, the sun from the window shadowed as if in solar eclipse. The atmosphere in her suite became a thick, cloudy greyish-black as the logos emerged into the mortal world, obscuring the sun, the furniture, and everything else. It closed in tightly around Malila and she welcomed it, comfortable and confident in these turbulent surroundings.

Touching the blood with one finger, she stretched out her other hand, speaking some True Name syllables into the logos and using those sounds to connect with the power out there. Then Malila took the fingertip with Olivia's blood on it and smeared it across the air, carving a glowing blue path in the churning grey haze. She could see energy come in from the logos, sucked toward the blood, illuminating as it touched so the blood lit with cerulean fire.

The pale blue stream of glowing blood told Malila that Olivia was both Blue/Black and Silver-Tint. But she wasn't turning darker, Malila could tell, otherwise the glowing blue would be darker than the blue blood itself. The logos knew the future, knew the truth of the person whose blood this was.

While Malila was observing all this the room had continued changing. Now it opened up, an endless black vista into the logos where magical ley-lines ran through it. They looked like rivers of molten fire stretching into infinity, endless and volcanic in the black void. The ley-lines connected with other dimensions, other realms, other places of nothingness out in the logos.

Malila turned to watch as another presence emerged from the volcanic black inside a churning column of grey. She came closer to greet it, stepping inside the column to be with the demon there.

"Hello, Locke..." She smiled as she raised her arms up into the seething column that curved around her, encompassing her, and she ran her hands along the demon form inside it to caress and welcome him.

Locke was her Necromancer, a demon bound to her by past circumstances. Sometimes it was violence, sometimes love, sometimes a tragedy that locked the witch and the demon together by shared experience. Whatever locked them together would manifest in their powers.

For Malila and Locke it was love. They had fallen in love once, long ago when he was witch, but Locke had been killed in a horrible tragedy. Malila had been devastated. And desperate. She made an agreement with a dark lord to bring him back, but as always, there was a price.

Locke was no longer human. They could be together forever but never quite touch. That created their curse: desire so strong that it manifested through Malila. She carried the power to control love and lust and could use it to bend others to her will–but could not always control it. Sometimes, as with Alejo, it came unbidden and captured both parties unexpectedly. Usually Malila stayed away from Alejandro; she risked being controlled by her own curse if she stayed close too long.

But the curse also made Locke and Malila a formidable pair. Because they were eternally separated by the different worlds in which they existed, because he was not bound by mortality, Locke could go where Malila could not, out in the logos, and use powers she could not, while Malila held sway in the mortal realm.

Malila gestured to the glowing blue of the blood still etched in the logos. "Do you see it?"

"Yes."

"Is it the same?" Malila asked about the blood. "I need to be sure."

"The same." Locke regarded the glowing blue emanating from the living fluid. "I can feel it."

"And Dantin? Is he here?" Malila wanted to know: Why had she felt Dantin in Olivia's hotel room? He was much darker than this.

Locke was silent for long, agonizing seconds while Malila awaited his answer.

"I cannot tell for sure." He finally said, "I will discover what I can, but we will need a place like this, where ley-lines converge, to have the greatest power. You will need to bring Olivia to me."

Malila nodded.

"I told you *La Brisas* was the best place to have lunch. Isn't this view fabulous? You can see the lagoon, and the ocean, and almost everything else from here." Olivia swept her finger across the vista around them.

Alejo had just arrived with Jaden and Michael, his friends who drove the Formula One racing circuit and introduced them to the two women.

"Taylor and Olivia, this is Michael Roswell," he gestured to the one closest to him, "...and this is Jaden Sharpe." He pointed to the other.

The four witches greeted each other and then Michael nodded approvingly at Olivia's choice in restaurants.

"I like that they serve lunch until three. It's thinned out in here, and I am really glad to be out of the crowd." Michael looked at the few remaining diners on the terrace.

"And I'm glad we're outside so I could bring Lexie." Taylor had ahold of the leash and her dog was standing patiently by her side, waiting to follow wherever they went. They still couldn't tell what breed she was since her hair hadn't grown out yet, but she was so patient and sweet that people loved her no matter what she looked like. And she was clean and sweet-smelling, thank God.

The *La Brisas* outdoor terrace was a favorite in Monaco. The smooth white tile and white patio umbrellas gave it the look of a tropical white sand beach. They followed their host to a table next to the railing where they could look down on the Mediterranean tossing its waves against the limestone cliff, and while Lexie lay in the shade under Taylor's chair the host passed out menus.

Olivia already knew what she wanted so she put her menu off to the side.

"Chef Marcel is a wizard of cuisine here. You should try the grilled swordfish."

Taylor turned to Jaden while they looked at their menus. "How long have you known Alejo?"

"Not long–about twenty years." For some reason the combination of Jaden's dreadlocks and British accent threw Taylor at first. Both he and Michael had accents although Jaden's was a shade more cockney. She would have thought he was a soccer player, not an F1 driver.

"How did you three meet?"

"The usual. Alejo was here for Grand Prix and we ended up at the same party together after the race. We knew right away we were all witch, so of course we introduced ourselves."

"Are you two on the same team?" Olivia wanted to know. "There are only two regular drivers per team, right?"

"That's right, but we're not on the same one right now. We have been in the past."

"Which is easier? I hear you have to help each other out as well as compete against each other if you're on the same team."

Taylor was fascinated. "How does that work?"

"Drivers win races and gain points for both themselves and the constructors. There's two different championships each year."

"Constructors?" Taylor didn't know what that meant so Michael explained.

"The constructors are the whole team. F1 cars are the only ones built entirely from scratch, with the exception of the engine. There are engineers and other professionals on the team that construct the plans for the car, build the car, run all the tests for it, everything. I'm with Sagenhaft and Jaden's with Caponetti."

Taylor nodded. "Okay."

"A driver can be instructed to do something to help the team, maybe even to help your teammate gain a better position but it's hard to put that in front of your own win. We're really competitive." He looked at Jaden. "The last time you and I were on a team together I could hardly talk to you by November."

"Yeah, that was brutal." Jaden nodded. "Hey, remember years ago, Vince Tenderril from Whitestone? His teammate Raukken had taken the pole position and was in a spot to win it all and gain more points for Whitestone, too."

"What happened?"

"Well, Tenderril had pushed it hard and come up close to Raukken. He was in second place but was having tire problems and had no pits left so they told him to keep the rest of the field off Raukken and let him win with a bigger lead. That would also take less chances with the car because it's especially dangerous to push a car that's not running top-notch. Instead, Tenderril took advantage of Raukken's thinking that he wouldn't try to pass him, and did just that at the last second for the win. Not only did it cost Whitestone those extra points, but it caused a lot of tension in the whole team–the pit crew, everybody. He could have killed someone and he didn't take proper care of the Whitestone's investment. Tenderril was such an ass–he was so unapologetic about it."

"I remember hearing about that," Alejo said.

"Yeah," said Jaden. "Man, what a dick that guy is."

Michael raised his drink to Alejo. "Hey, Baquero–thanks for coming out to watch and for bringing such beautiful company." He smiled at the two women and then took a sip of his beer.

Taylor asked, "So why haven't you all made this a regular thing, getting together? I can't believe you've never met Olivia until now."

Michael answered her. "During season we're all really busy. Alejo has the polo circuit with a match almost every week and in F1 we have a race every few weeks. We were just at the Spanish Grand Prix a week ago, and we'll drive in the Canadian Grand Prix first weekend in June."

"Oh." Taylor realized they had careers. They couldn't go where and when they wanted; even through magic it would be too exhausting. She thought of Alejo and how he didn't use magic when he played but instead preferred to work hard and practice with his teammates.

"Do you use magic when you drive? I've been looking at the Monaco course online. Any little error and you're toast."

Jaden answered her. "We used to be able to, but nowadays every single thing on the car is monitored and transmitted to the engineers. It's all telemetry so we wouldn't be able to get away with much. You really have to try and drive a perfect race like everyone else. I like that, though."

Just then the waiter came to take their order, and after he was gone, Jaden addressed Olivia offhandedly.

"Canadian Grand Prix's in a couple weeks, love. Why don't you ditch Alejo and lob over to Montreal to watch us?"

"Hey," Alejo cut in, "you don't just take someone else's vacation partner and say, "Come over here with me instead.'"

"She's witch–she could pop over there for a couple days and be back again before you even missed her," Jaden said.

Alejo clenched his teeth. He knew Jaden was challenging him, trying to pull her out from under him, just to see if he could. He felt possessive towards Olivia, but it was bitingly true that they weren't a couple. Just as irritating, he didn't like the way Jaden was talking so casually about her, as if she were property. And he knew Olivia wouldn't appreciate his approach, either.

Sure enough, as if on cue, Olivia broke in smoothly. "Jaden, I think if you had invited all of us politely," she put just the slightest emphasis on *all*, "instead of saying I should ditch Alejo, you wouldn't be the one looking like such a dick right now." She looked him in the eye for a long second and then turned pointedly away from him.

"Damn, Jaden–she just *iced* you!" Michael was grinning broadly and laughing at his friend. Even Alejo and Taylor smiled after a moment.

Olivia shrugged her shoulders. "I don't believe in putting up with any bullshit."

"Oh, he's full of that." Michael laughed into his glass as he took a sip of his beer. Taylor decided right then that she liked Michael better than Jaden. She liked the quiet of Michael's voice better than Jaden's blustery persona. And she couldn't stop staring at how his mocha skin set off his grey-blue eyes. He caught her staring and smiled warmly at her.

Meanwhile Jaden was still trying to regain his dominance, like a frat boy trying to one-up Alejo in the conversation.

"Oh, Olivia, I wouldn't have left Alejandro here alone without you. In fact, I was going to try and talk him into taking up F1 driving." He turned to Alejo. "We'll put some real horses under you instead of those polo ponies you ride. I've got eight hundred horses to your one."

"Yeah, but I only need the one between my legs to get the job done," was Alejo's retort. The others were shocked for a millisecond and then burst out laughing. Alejo was hardly ever so crass, but it was the perfect response; it shut Jaden's mouth on the subject and he ended up laughing, too. In fact it broke the ice with all four of them and they spent the rest of lunch chatting easily and getting to know each other. Jaden turned out to be pretty nice after all; he made sure the waiter brought Lexie some water and even fed her the rest of his steak.

By five o'clock they had to go; there were team meetings for Jaden and Michael to attend, and they each wanted to put in some simulator time, explaining that like airline pilots, they spent time practicing each race in a simulation model that was an exact mockup of the course and the F1 car's cockpit. The races were too dangerous to come into cold.

They all said their goodbyes, and the two drivers headed west across town while the others walked north to *The Metropole*. As they made their way home, Alejo noticed that Olivia seemed perfectly composed now, unlike last night. She didn't make a reference to their discussion or act any differently than usual. She told them both about her day, saying it was uneventful, only relating her morning at the beach, stopping at the café, and meeting Malila. That surprised Alejo; he thought he would be introducing her and Malila.

Alejo thought about Olivia and Malila. For the first time in his friendship with Olivia, he felt awkward about two women in his life meeting each other and didn't know why. He'd always had girlfriends come and go, and some of them witch, but that had never been a problem since he and Livy weren't dating. It wasn't the sex with Malila, either. He'd had plenty of that in his lifetime while he and Olivia had been friends. So had she, for that matter, and it had never fazed either of them.

Then he realized it was because he'd never told Olivia about Malila, especially that Malila had found her in Paris for him. Malila knew so much about Olivia, but Olivia hadn't known of her until now, and he'd always been completely open with Olivia. Well, Malila had made him promise not to tell. For some reason the fact that he hadn't been the one to introduce them felt dishonest too, although he had already planned on doing it.

He knew he hadn't done anything wrong, but it still grated on him, these secrets. And he still had to honor Malila's wish to keep the Paris thing secret. You'd better have a good reason for it Malila, he thought.

When they got back to the hotel Taylor had a plan.

"I'm going to watch some movies and hang out with my girl." Taylor took Lexie's face in her hands, rubbing her ears and kissing her head while they waited for the elevator. "Do you two want to come?"

"I like that idea, but your room is too crowded for all four of us," said Olivia. "Why don't we go to my suite for movies?" She turned to Alejo and Taylor. "Aren't there some of those Oscar winners we've been meaning to watch?"

"Yeah, Olivia, you're right. That sounds perfect," said Taylor.

"Fine with me," said Alejo. Obviously Olivia didn't want to talk about the previous night with him, or she'd have let Taylor go and gotten him alone right then. If it's not a problem to her, he thought, I can't make it one. He knew they wouldn't be discussing it.

The next day Malila called Alejo.

"Hi, there," she said. "I wanted to tell you that I bumped into Olivia yesterday so I introduced myself."

"She told me already. You actually fell on her?" In spite of himself, Alejo laughed at Malila.

"Hey–my shoe broke. It wasn't my fault." Malila defended herself.

"You're hardly ever that clumsy. I'd love to have been there."

"Yeah, I'll bet you would have. Listen, I'm going to invite Olivia and Taylor out to lunch or something. I wanted to let you know so you wouldn't be surprised, especially after I'd asked you to introduce us and then did it myself since I was right there in her lap. Literally."

"I appreciate you telling me. Will we see you at Grand Prix as well?"

"Yes. Olivia said you have a ground floor suite at the *Metropole*, but why don't you take her to the Paddock Club? That's the only way to really experience an F1 race."

"Michael and Jaden have arranged pit passes for us."

"Yes, but that has limited access at limited times and you'll need to go somewhere else for food and a place to sit. I realize you can flash yourselves anywhere, but The Paddock has more of everything in one place than anywhere else.

And I mean everything. I'll see if I can pick up three more memberships so you have that option if you want it."

"Thank you, Malila. That's nice of you. I know both Olivia and Taylor would love that. I'd like you to meet Michael Roswell of Sagenhaft and Jaden Sharpe, too. He's with Caponetti. But Malila, this time let me arrange it so I can introduce you the way I want to, yes? Sometime later this week."

"Oh, of course Alejo. Just let me know." Then Malila's voice turned sly. "And Alejandro..." She paused for effect. "Try and keep your hands off me when we're with the others, will you? You're on vacation with Taylor and Olivia, not me."

That startled Alejo. He had been wondering how to deal with that very concern, and she had brought it up first. This woman never ceases to amaze me, he thought, making it so simple like that. Most of his girlfriends would compete for attention when Olivia was around but of course Malila wouldn't. She was too confident, and she was nobody's girlfriend or property. And she liked her privacy, her independence. She was really something.

Dios, he thought, if there were no Olivia, he might be falling in love with Malila instead. Why did he always want the ones that were hardest to catch?

Jaden handed the pen and Grand Prix program back to the smiling fan with a wink as the *maître d'* shooed them away. He and Michael had been signing them off and on throughout the evening, but at least during dinner they had only been interrupted this one time. *Le Grill* at the *Hotel de Paris* prided itself on being a place celebrities could go to be undisturbed, but Grand Prix was a time of excess, even in a city of celebrity and excess, and there was an incredible saturation of admirers in this one tiny country.

"You know, I thought Alejo had fans, but this is unbelievable," said Taylor.

"Oh, thank you very much, *mi niña.*" Alejo faked annoyance at her.

Michael was quick to jump in before Jaden did. "It's only because everything is squeezed so tight here and the race is held on the city streets. The other Grand Prix are usually on courses outside of town where you pay to get in, but here it's pretty easy to find us unless we spend the whole time in our hotel rooms. It's not like we're world-famous movie stars; it only happens at Grand Prix time."

"Well," Olivia observed, "there were a few of those stars asking for your autograph if you remember."

"I know–I couldn't believe it. I didn't know what to say to them, and here they were asking for *my* autograph." Even Jaden was almost humble about it.

"Well, everyone's got their own little corner of fame, I guess. Just depends on who's around you." Taylor was looking around the room and recognized several celebrities, big and small.

"Wow," said Michael. "That's pretty smart."

Taylor looked at Michael quickly, thinking he was making fun of her but he wasn't. He was smiling at her, holding eye contact until she smiled back.

"Thanks," she said. Silently she tapped into a little fantasy she'd had about him the other day. Good thing he couldn't read her mind.

The Monaco Grand Prix was only five days away and there wasn't a room or a reservation or a venue that wasn't sold out to race-goers. Only the wildly wealthy and famous or the supernatural crowd could get reservations to places in town like *Le Grill*, and even Malila had had to do some conjuring to get a table for six there. It was a good thing they'd been regulars for the last two months.

And then there were the parties surrounding the Grand Prix. For the last two weeks revelers had filled the bars and hotels with their festivities and now, in the last few days before the race, the party spilled into the streets, people drinking and dancing and staging entertainment where the actual race would be run. They stayed out all night, Michael told Taylor, and in the morning you would see a few tired carousers wandering up the sidewalks to find their way home while street crews came in to clean up the mess.

Taylor was astonished. "Isn't that dangerous? What if there's debris left on the track for qualifying and race day?"

Jaden grinned at her from across the table. "Yeah, you literally put your life in their hands, going out there a few hours later."

Michael cut in. "Jaden's being dramatic for his own benefit, as usual. The marshals always make sure the course is as pristine as possible. There's dozens of them all along it for safety reasons, before and during the race."

"It's still damned dangerous, though." Jaden was more serious this time and Michael nodded his head in agreement.

"Yep. Well, high speed will do that." He changed the subject, lowering his voice and speaking only to Taylor.

"Taylor, Olivia tells me you're a bit in love with the yachts here."

Taylor felt foolish for a second; she didn't want to seem naïve. Michael's expression was so open and honest, however, that she decided to tell him.

"I am, I guess. I'd only seen them in pictures before I met Olivia. They're sleek and mysterious, you know, and even after we rented one for a day and took a cruise I still feel that way. I can hardly imagine what it's like for other people to live on one or travel around the world in it."

"Well," said Michael, "I've got a pass to the Force India party on a three-hundred-foot yacht the night before qualifying laps. Do you want to go?"

Taylor's eyes widened. "Really? I'd love to."

Michael took what looked like a credit card out of his pocket and gave it to her. "Here."

"What is it?"

"It's an entry card. Only invited guests get them and they scan them at the door so only card-holders can get in."

"Aren't you coming with me?"

"Of course. I want you to hold it for us, though. Keep it in a safe place until Friday night." Saturday was qualifying day.

Taylor looked at the white card in her hand and fingered the gold chip embedded in the surface before putting it into her purse. After a second she changed her mind and slid it into her bra, explaining to an amused Michael, "What if I lose my purse? I'd better keep it close by."

Michael smiled and nodded his head. "I can't think of a better place for it."

Across the table, Malila was holding Jaden deep in conversation. She'd noticed how he kept trying to flirt with Olivia, and there was no mistaking her lack of interest, so Malila thought she'd help Livy out by throwing a bit of her infatuation spell his way. She also made sure to keep some distance between her and Alejo, usually by putting Olivia between them, but trying to stay out of the grasp of both men was a little hard to do all the time. She was glad Alejo was so close to Olivia. He didn't seem to be as ardent with her when she was around. Thank you, Olivia, she thought.

As it turned out, Olivia and Malila had much in common: opinions on multiple subjects, likes, dislikes, similar powers, their taste in clothes, and their sense of humor. They'd gone a few places together in the last several days, but Malila hadn't been able to bring her close to the ley-line convergence for Locke. Malila was becoming more apprehensive by the moment. She was getting attached to Olivia and that made what she had to do much harder.

She sturdied herself against her feelings; don't worry about what she'll think when she finds out, she thought, just do what you have to. Don't think about what you'll have to do to her if Dantin has taken hold. Just get her to your hotel where Locke can assess her, and then you'll know for sure. She got Olivia's attention across the table.

"You said you have reservations to watch the race at *Virage*. That's a great view of the cars as they come out of the tunnel and round the chicane onto *Le Piscine*."

"And Alejo has a ground floor suite with a terrace next to *Avenue des Speluges* so we can watch from there as well. It's just before *Mirabeau*."

"It's nice to have those options, but I love F1's Paddock Club. It's right next to the pits and has a gourmet grazing buffet, a bar, champagne that flows day and night, access to the drivers when they come in to schmooze, and anything else you could imagine, like visiting the pits. It's luxurious, too. You can't beat the service and exclusive access."

"You're kidding. That sounds fabulous." Olivia loved anything that gave her an inside view of whatever she was attending.

"Well, look then." Malila pulled out three large carbon-fiber badges on black lanyards and handed them across the table. "I have Paddock Club VIP passes for you, Taylor, and Alejo. If this is your first F1 then you need to go all out."

"Oh, Malila, this is wonderful." Olivia, Taylor, and Alejo each took a badge and looked them over. They were sophisticated, high-tech examples of Formula One wealth at its finest. The event, date, name, and all the other details of their access were etched into the carbon fiber with a chic design underlying the print.

All three of them expressed thanks for Malila's generosity and Olivia was first to offer payment.

"Just let me know how much and I'm happy to pay you back." She knew it could cost twenty thousand for the three of them, and that might be an understatement, but it didn't matter. They were perfect.

"Oh, no, please. My treat. It'll be fun."

"Thank you, Malila." Olivia accepted the offer easily; she was often as generous with her money and her desire to give others an experience like this. She also loved the kind of special treatment Malila was talking about. Very, very nice, she thought, as she looked at the treasure dangling on its ebony cord.

It turned out that Malila was familiar with the F1 world; she'd been following the circuit since the early days in the nineteen-fifties. About the same time she quit reporting on polo, she had discovered Grand Prix racing and it was her kind of fun: fast, hot, different, and it was nice to be in on the early days of a sport.

They talked of the race, hearing strategy from Jaden and Michael and of course more driver gossip. That subject bounced around the table until talk returned to the crush of people and the parties, and Olivia shook her head.

"I think there are just too many people in town right now for me. I sleep like a rock at night, but I'm still tired when I wake up in the morning; I don't know what the deal is. I'm going to go back to Seattle for the next few days and get some rest. I want some quiet, some sleep, and to see my greyhounds. Anyone else want to come? But fair warning: it will definitely be a low-key trip." Olivia looked around the table.

Jaden and Michael shook their heads; it was too close to the race and they needed to practice, rest, and concentrate. But Alejo, Taylor, and even Malila were all in. Taylor wanted to introduce Lexie to Doobie and Bailey, Olivia's greyhounds. Malila had never been to Seattle, and she also wanted to keep an eye on Olivia. She did look tired, Malila observed.

"Where should I stay while we're there?" asked Malila.

"Oh, definitely The Sorrento," said Taylor. "If you like old money or a boutique hotel with a lot of character it's perfect. It's not very big, either. Alejo and Olivia know a charmsmith named Schmidt who stays there whenever he's in Seattle."

"When do you want to leave?" Malila asked.

"Tomorrow, but I'm not taking the jet; I'm going to flash there. I don't want to waste ten and a half hours plus a layover when we only have a few days."

Michael reminded Taylor, "We have a date on the Force India yacht Friday night, remember."

Taylor smiled and nodded at him, secretly pleased. A date with Michael. She looked at Olivia. "I have to be back here in time for that."

Livy winked at her apprentice. "Tomorrow it is, then. Wednesday morning. That gives us the afternoon, all day Thursday, and then Friday morning before we need to come back." She turned to Malila. "We'll all meet at Alejo's suite in the morning?"

"Wait a minute." Malila was doing some calculating. "Monaco's nine hours ahead of Seattle so right now it's"–she looked at her watch–"eleven this morning in Seattle. So if we meet at eight a.m. tomorrow we'll get there at eleven p.m. Seattle time. That means if we go home now and sleep so we can meet in the morning, we'll just end up sleeping there, too, since we'll arrive in the middle of the night."

They all stood there, trying to wrap their heads around the time difference. Malila sighed.

"You know what? I'm going to spell a reservation at The Sorrento from here and flash as soon as I pack a few things. That should get me there around noon or one and I can take a nap and adjust to the time difference. You can call me when you get in. Olivia and Alejo, you both have my number."

That will be perfect, Malila thought; she would have time with Locke to look for a ley-line convergence in Seattle since she hadn't been able to get Olivia close to the one here in Monaco.

Olivia turned to the others. "You know, she's right. Let's go to Seattle tonight, sleep in our own beds for a few hours, and then go from there. I'll call JaneAnn on the way back to the hotel so we don't just drop in on them."

Jaden shook his head. "Man, you guys make me time-lagged just listening to you."

Michael touched Taylor's hand. "If you're going to go right away I'll take you back to your hotel. We can walk Lexie together before you leave." He put money on the table–enough to cover everyone's evening–and left the restaurant with Taylor.

The others stood up to leave. "Thank you for the Paddock passes," Olivia said to Malila. "I'm happy to return the favor anytime I've got special access somewhere you'd like to go."

"Oh, don't wait 'til then–I like anything unusual, so when you find something like that give me a call." As soon as she said it, Malila felt false. She realized Olivia might not be around much longer. That would depend on what Locke found out about Dantin, and the fact that Olivia was constantly tired was not a good omen.

Malila appeared across the street from the Sorrento and assessed the building. It was a cozy "L" of brick and carved limestone maybe seven stories high. Taylor was right; it was boutique, vintage, and intimate. Gangsters might have stayed here in the nineteen-twenties if this were

Chicago. Even the circular pull-around for cars had a fabric *porte cochère*, like a New York apartment building with a doorman. She liked it so far; now she just had to check in and go to her suite where she could confer with Locke.

After signing the register she peeked in on the octagonal-shaped lobby at the suggestion of the concierge. He was right; it was a sight to behold. The Victorian room and its substantial supporting column in the center was wrapped entirely in rich walnut panels that extended to the ceiling. Several wing chairs covered in emerald green brocade were set up for maximum comfort next to the fireplace and around the lobby.

The concierge had said they served Victorian tea here in the afternoons, describing a luxurious ritual where time slowed down for a while with a pot of tea and pastries in the lobby with its welcoming hearth, green palms, and velvet furnishings. Lovely, Malila thought. In the eighteen hundreds she had split her time between London and colonial India as a guest of the British Empire and had lived it for real. Having tea here would mimic some nice memories.

Malila rode the elevator to her room on the seventh floor. She had a corner suite, of course.

She could enjoy more view that way and Seattle was reputed to be beautiful. But she also felt safer when she could see all around her. Sometimes she hated being Blue/Black.

"Locke?" She opened her suitcase and arranged her toiletries in the bathroom while she waited for him. He wasn't long in arriving; Malila had just changed clothing when the room darkened and he appeared.

"Any luck?" Malila was hoping he'd found a convergence.

"Not yet. I do know where JaneAnn and Olivia live, but that gained us nothing. If we go out, I'll check for convergence wherever they take us. For now, I will track the ley-lines and hope we can get Olivia to where we need her."

"I understand. Thank you, Locke. Will you stay with me until I fall asleep?" Malila held out her arms to him and he draped over her as closely as he could, but it was maddening for them both, this almost-but-not-quite being able to touch and feel each other. Love never requited, passion constantly inflamed but never consummated between two magical beings; no wonder it expressed so strongly as Malila's curse.

Locke stayed with Malila until her breathing became soft and rhythmic and he knew she slept.

Then he left, following the ley-lines in Seattle to find the convergence they needed.

Across town Olivia, Taylor, and Alejo had just brought Lexie into the courtyard of Olivia's townhouse where JaneAnn was waiting with the greyhounds and they could meet on neutral ground. Outside of Olivia's townhouse where the other dogs played, it was no one's turf. It only took five minutes to move from cautious staring and sniffing to playing on the lawn like littermates, and when JaneAnn opened the door they bolted into the house as if they'd known each other all along.

JaneAnn cocked her head to the side as she stared at Lexie, now drinking water in the kitchen. "What is she, anyway? She's shaped like a hound but has kind of long hair, although not really. I can't figure out what breed she is."

"You know what? Don't ask," said Taylor. "There's nothing to do but wait a few more weeks and see what she looks like when her hair grows out." She looked at Olivia. "I am so tired of hearing that question."

JaneAnn laughed. "The good news is that Doobie and Bailey don't care what Lexie is. Look at them." They were following Lexie all over the house as she explored, and it was hard to get any of them to settle down, which was maddening because Alejo, Taylor, and Olivia were still on Monaco time and wanted to sleep.

"I'll take them to my house and they can play together while you get some rest," said JaneAnn.

Taylor shook her head no. "I haven't left Lexie before. I don't want her to think I'd do that." She remembered Lexie, filthy, abandoned and hungry in the park where they had found her.

"Are you kidding?" As usual, JaneAnn was the sensible voice. "She doesn't know you exist right now. She's happy to have dog friends."

Taylor still hesitated and JaneAnn gave her an option. "Okay, look. Why don't you come over to my house and sleep in the guest room upstairs with the door open. Lexie can play with the greys, and she can find you anytime she likes."

"That's a deal. Alejo, you can have my room while I'm gone." Taylor reached out her hand and Lexie came over to her.

Olivia kneeled on the carpet and patted her thighs. "Come here," she said to Doobie and Bailey.

The two dogs came over immediately and laid down in front of her, rhythmically tapping their long tails on the floor in happy expectation.

Olivia reached out to pet them both and kissed them on the noses.

"I know I just got home, but I need some sleep, okay? You guys go play with Lexie at JaneAnn's, and I'll see you in a few hours." She hugged them and massaged their soft fur for a full minute before she stood up. The greys jumped up with her and Olivia walked them over to JaneAnn, loving them up one last time before backing away so that JaneAnn, Taylor, and the dogs could fade out, on their way to JaneAnn's house.

Alejo was already on his way upstairs to Taylor's room and Olivia followed him, saying good night as she passed him on the way to her room, but neither stopped for discussion. It was after midnight in Monaco and they were both happy to close their doors and get some rest.

In a very short time Olivia was asleep, dreaming.

It started out well enough, with her and Alejo and JaneAnn at a tropical resort. Then suddenly they were gone, and she didn't know where they went, but she was unconcerned, the way things were in dreams sometimes. She was suddenly without them in a grove of palms waiting for whatever came next. Strangely, what happened next was Dantin; he was with her under the canopy of Tahitian palms. Stranger yet, she was still unconcerned. She lay back in the sand, looking up at him and the palms over his head, feeling adored and romantic. She knew there was something wrong with this scene, but she knew it was a dream so she didn't fight it. Instead she wrapped her arms around Dantin and pulled him to her, to feel his arms around her and his body touching hers. She felt his arms encircling her back and she looked into his eyes...

At home in her bedroom Olivia stood up, still asleep. She walked to the mirror and lifted her eyes to her face. Two faces stared back at her. One was mortal; Olivia's full lips and doe eyes within a swirl of auburn hair was real and touchable, but she was fascinated by the other face, a ghostly apparition that overlaid her own. She knew those features in the apparition, knew them very well. She lifted her fingertips to touch her reflection in the glass.

Olivia didn't control her own movements; the apparition did. It stared at Olivia and itself as it looked in the mirror.

How many times, thought Dantin, as he looked at his ghostly self embedded in Olivia, had he wanted to own her? How many times had he craved her physically, wanted to dominate her, beat her into submission so she would be his alone and bend to his will? Now he was with her in the most intimate way possible. He knew her thoughts, her fears, her desires...

He ran her hands over her form, over her breasts and down her ribs to curve behind her and feel the roundness below her hips. He had spied on her before, when he was alive in his own body, and he had captured and tortured her occasionally when the urge had taken him. But she was never his the way she was now. He could make her do anything willingly, even feel the way he wanted her to, in dreams. He particularly loved making her dream about him, of course. He moved her hand down her stomach and then between her thighs. Now he knew what she liked...or could make her do what he liked. Oh, this was delicious.

Not only that, he knew her secrets. Everything she'd ever done in the last five hundred years–what she knew, who she loved–he felt it. And he felt the pain he'd caused her. He relished those memories of hers. He even knew about Taylor and the memory spell. Oh, the damage he could cause her once he figured out how to move past her dreams. He was getting stronger all the time.

It had taken him a while to figure out where he was at first. The last thing he had remembered was Olivia killing him with that damned charmed sword, that bitch. He hadn't seen that coming. When his death was final, and the logos pulled on him like a tornado, he hid inside her and she hadn't known. He chuckled. Well, that was one advantage of a violent death– any spirit wanting to stick around might get lost in the fray.

He was learning how to operate on this plane, though. He'd learned to control her through dreams and would learn to move past her dreams, too; he was positive of that.

That evening they all had dinner at Palisade, where JaneAnn thought Malila would get the best view of downtown since it bordered Elliot Bay.

"Since this is your first time in Seattle you need to see it from across the water." JaneAnn pointed to the glass-encased skyscrapers of Seattle glittering in the setting sun on the other side of the bay. Golden fire painted the buildings, making it look like a city of the gods. The water reflected the sun in a dazzling blue. The contrast was breathtaking.

"How could I have missed Seattle? I've been all over the world and had no idea." With a flick of her fingers, Malila threw a protection spell over the table so they wouldn't be heard by people nearby. "There's a huge power vortex here, too; I can feel it. I'm surprised more witches don't live here."

"Oh, I know," said Olivia. "Everyone thinks we're still rural, off in the corner of the world with no plumbing, I'm sure. Most witches want to live in Paris, or New Orleans, or San Francisco, or Rio de Janeiro, or Shanghai where it's exotic and sexy."

"I like it," said JaneAnn. "I don't want a zillion people moving here and making a mess of it."

"It's really changed in just the last twenty years," said Taylor. "I've lived here all my life, and I remember the only thing here before they built Palisade was the marina and that jetty." Taylor pointed to the rows of sailboats parked at the docks in the marina, surrounded by a wall of huge black rocks that kept out the rough water.

"Yeah, I remember when this place first opened, but now it's been here a long time." JaneAnn looked around her at the restaurant. Then she turned to Olivia.

"Do you remember the first time we walked in here?"

"Oh, yeah," said Olivia. "This huge pavilion of a room with all the art glass hanging from the ceiling and a hundred feet of windows facing the water? And that grand piano perched over the bar? Yeah, I definitely remember my first time."

"I remember going over that bridge on our way to the table and looking down at all the starfish in the water thinking, 'Wow–this restaurant has a tide pool and a waterfall right in the middle of the floor.' That's still my favorite thing whenever we come here." JaneAnn looked over at the ledge that spilled ocean water into the tide pool. "I love the sound of that rushing water."

She turned to Malila. "This is your first time at Palisade; what do you think?"

"It's a great place to bring out-of-towners, that's for sure. Very impressive when you first drive up, with those huge supporting columns and broad stairway. I felt like I was ascending into some sort of massive Chinese palace."

Malila could feel the vortex was denser here, too. Lots of power. She could feel Locke nearby right now, scoping out the ley-lines.

"You know, if more witches aren't coming here and you have this much vortex, lucky you. It's always nice to have something special to yourself."

"Amen to that." Olivia clinked her glass on Malila's.

They finished dinner just after the sun had set. Taylor asked Alejo if he would walk Lexie and the greys with him. The Palisade was nestled in a park that ran along the waterfront and gave access to the Elliot Bay Marina. It was perfect for the dogs.

"I thought it would be fun for them to go somewhere different. I'll even tell you why I named her Lexie if you keep me company." Taylor remembered Alejandro was curious when she first named the dog.

Alejo smiled. "I'd go with you even if you didn't tell me." He teased JaneAnn as he helped her take the dogs out of her Escalade. "You spoil Olivia's dogs. This thing is a palace inside and they're not even yours."

"They are right now, for a whole year. I get to fuss over them any way I want." JaneAnn knew Alejo felt the same way about animals; he indulged his string of polo ponies with elegant stables and the best food and veterinary care he could find.

"If one of you wants to take Malila back we'll just flash ourselves home." Alejo knew they'd only brought two cars.

"Oh, I'm going to stay here and look around," Malila said. "I'd like to go through the marina and walk to the other end of the park. Don't wait for me; I'll flash myself back to the Sorrento." She wanted to get time with Locke while they were both here, and she thought she'd better get some distance between her and Alejo before Olivia left.

They all said their goodbyes, agreeing to touch base in the morning and then Malila headed for the marina while Alejo and Taylor took the hounds in the other direction. As they walked along, Taylor had a question she wanted to ask him.

"You know, Alejo, I've been with you every day for the last six months, and I still don't know much about you and Olivia in the past. Sometimes you talk about places you've lived, like Saint-Domingue, and I know about London and the witch-trials, but how about after that?"

"What do you want to know?"

"Tell me about Paris. When we were there you both mentioned that something had happened, and you had to come and get her. What was that?"

Alejo watched the dogs play while he riffled through his memories, deciding where to start. "Come on." He walked them both to a knoll in the grass and gestured to it. Taylor sat down and Alejo joined her.

"You know about Tristan, right?"

"Yes, JaneAnn told me the story. Olivia and Tristan were a couple."

"They weren't just a couple; they were perfect together. The same sense of humor, the same skill with a sword or a spell, the same craving for adventure, how they looked at things, what they wanted from life and how they got it. Perfectly aligned."

"JaneAnn told me Dantin was jealous of Tristan. He also hated them both for ruining his set-up with the Inquisition. He hated you for that, too."

"That was an ideal Blue/Black masquerade he had crafted, hiding in plain sight as an Inquisitor where he could have all the power and torture and wealth a Blue/Black could ever want. That he was a witch, burning mortals for being witch, and crusading against witches was the ultimate in Blue/Black deception, and he felt like a king. *Dios*, he was furious that we exposed him and ruined his sadistic, lurid little empire. But revenge is a powerful and favorite craving for a Blue/Black. Somehow he found the one time Olivia and Tristan had their guards down. He ran them both through with a magical glaive, killing Tristan immediately. It cleaved his heart and thrust into Olivia's back as she stood in his arms. There was no way she could save herself and him, too. He was dead before she could pull herself off the blade."

"I hate hearing that story. It always gives me the wiggins." Taylor couldn't bear to think of how grisly a picture it painted. "I'm glad Dantin's gone."

"Yes, *niña*, me, too." Alejo continued the story, feeling a little bizarre as he did so. He hadn't said it aloud in over two hundred years.

"Olivia was devastated by Tristan's death. Nothing assuaged her pain. There was no time, no thought, no corner of her mind that wasn't consumed by her grief as she tried to move on. She tried to get over it, finally asking Schmidt for a charm to help her. He did, but not even that gave her relief. She told me she'd rather die than feel this way." He reached over to Bailey, who had just lain down next to him, and rubbed his back as he continued.

"It got to where Livy wouldn't talk to anyone, not even me. Then she disappeared one day. She didn't tell me she was leaving; she didn't tell anyone. She was just gone. We all scryed for her but she'd blocked us, so we knew she was alive at least. We just couldn't find her. We searched,

asked anyone who might know... but nothing."
He paused, remembering.

"When was that?"

"Around sixteen-seventy. Europe was in so
much chaos at the time that I didn't even know
where to start looking for her."

"How did you find her in Paris then? When
was that?"

"That was seventeen ninety-one. The
Revolution in France had just happened and the
Terror was next. And Olivia was sitting there
waiting for it to swallow her. A friend of mine
told me she'd seen her there, in with the
Aristocracy, not taking care of herself, living a
decadent lifestyle to dull the pain, drinking
herself unconscious nearly every day, sex with
anyone who offered it–or took it from her."

He paused. Taylor waited silently.

"Dantin had found her, too, and was giving
her a slow, miserable death one poisonous spell
at a time, piling infections on top of each other
and keeping her alive to endure the torment. He
was relishing that she was a living corpse, and it
was all his doing. I went and got her, now that I
knew where she was, and took her into hiding.
The only person who knew where we were was
Schmidt, and he put every kind of protection and
hiding spell he knew around us."

"Where did you go?"

"Prussia. He knew a nobleman with a small castle, nothing that would attract attention, and we took her there. I needed Schmidt to help me heal her. Not only was she wasted away, and poisoned by too much alcohol, but she had syphilis, and tuberculosis, who knows what else, and several magical diseases Dantin had given her that were nearly impossible to cure. I had to give her part of my essence, and thank God for Schmidt's prowess with magic. It was over a year before she was well again."

"You said she told you she wanted to die. Was she angry that you came to get her?" Taylor knew Olivia didn't like her wishes subverted.

"No, what she had said was she'd rather die than feel this way; missing Tristan so much. She was so miserable that nothing mattered or gave her happiness. She did go to France intent on immersing herself in grief, hoping that not caring about anything would mean not caring about her pain and hoping she could mask her grief with different horrors, but that never works. What really happened was so bad it was worse than any of that–and far worse than the grief. And when she found out Dantin was behind the worst of it? That's when she got angry. She swore she wouldn't let him win."

"And she got tough. Made herself strong again." Taylor had a sudden epiphany. "No wonder she was so hard on me when she first took me in."

"*Sí*. She doesn't like to show weakness even now, though her vulnerable side is so beautiful when she lets it out."

Taylor smiled. "I think she shows it more now since Dantin's gone."

Alejo was quiet and thoughtful as he petted Bailey's neck and looked out over the water. The streaks of sunset were deep red now against the darkening sky. Now that the most difficult part of the story was over he was more relaxed, and that last glass of wine at dinner was hitting him and bringing a nice glow. Just a nice little buzz, he thought.

"Any good memories from the castle?" Taylor wanted to leave the conversation on a pleasant note. She hadn't realized the story she'd asked for would be so brutal.

Alejo reflected. There was one memory he always thought of.

"When Olivia was better and could get around on her own she used to walk at night, sometimes outside the castle. Neither one of us could sleep. I offered to go with her, but she always wanted to be alone." He paused, massaging Bailey's soft fur in little circles with his fingertips while he remembered. After a moment he continued.

"There was one night when the moon was out. It was full and bright, like the light that comes before dawn when everything is washed with grey and you can see so easily. I couldn't sleep as usual and walked to the arrow-slit to look outside…"

"Arrow-slit?" Taylor thought she understood but asked anyway.

"Castles have narrow windows to protect them from attack, but from inside an archer can see a wide swath of the surrounding country. Through it I could see Olivia walking in the field below. I remember she was wearing that black gown…"

He stopped there, looking down at Bailey while he remembered the story. He didn't speak for so long Taylor had to prompt him. "The black gown…"

"Schmidt had bound healing spells and protection markings into yards of black cotton for a simple gown. She wore that constantly until she was completely strong again and could protect herself. It covered her totally; high on the neck, long sleeves, down to the floor, and it flowed behind her when she walked, even inside the castle. She was beautiful in it. That night she was outside walking in the wheat field and the breeze caught it and moved it, rippling the black gossamer over the golden wheat."

His fingers had stopped moving on Bailey's neck; he was completely lost in thought. Taylor could see in his eyes how powerful a memory this was for him.

"Olivia in that flowing black dress, standing there in those waves of gold, her long red hair lifted by the breeze." He trailed off and didn't say anything more.

Taylor hadn't banked on this when she had asked for a good memory. A sudden truth was in front of her, and she couldn't believe she hadn't seen it before. He was in love with Olivia.

She scanned all their experiences together the last few months. How could I have missed it? she thought. She'd been with them every day for months and been party to their friendship and their sometimes silly behavior with each other. They were best friends, no doubt about it, but in love?

Taylor played back her memories of the three of them. He was always solicitous, always protective, but that was with both her and

Olivia. Sometimes, though, he would look at Olivia with the same look that he had right now. It was the same way he looked at her in Monte Carlo, outside the casino when she closed her eyes to smell the perfumed air. Him watching her, his gaze lingering a little longer than he needed to.

She thought back to the time she'd surprised him in the hallway and remembered Alejo's expression when he kissed Olivia's forehead, and how he'd hesitated a little before he did. A wave of realization washed through her. He had almost kissed her lips! That's where he was looking, anyway. She was absolutely sure what she had seen now. *Her vulnerable side is so beautiful when she lets it out.* Taylor could feel the emotion coming off him as if he were radiating heat. Alejo was in love with Olivia.

"You're in love with Olivia."

Alejo turned a surprised face to her. "What?"

Taylor looked into his eyes and saw his feelings displayed there. She repeated herself. "You're in love with Olivia."

Alejo's first impulse was to deny it. If he were younger, say eighty or a hundred he might have done so, but he knew better now. He could tell Taylor saw it, and it would be foolish to deny what she could so easily see. Not only that, he didn't want to. There was simply no way he would ever be false about his feelings for Olivia.

"Yes."

"Is that when you knew? That night with the black dress?"

"Maybe before that, but that night I was sure."

"Does she know?"

"No. I don't think so."

"Why haven't you told her?"

"Do you really think it's so simple, *niña*?"

"But you're perfect for each other."

"Are we? And how would you know?"

"I can see how you are together."

Alejo sighed. "You've seen us only as friends, Taylor. Love adds a whole new complexity, a different expectation of each other."

"But you have to tell her."

"And why is that?"

For Taylor that question was ridiculous. "Because you love her. She should know about it."

Alejo knew better. "Why, Taylor? Why should she know? Just because I feel it is not good enough reason to burden her with it."

"But if you love her you have to tell her."

"No, I don't. They're my feelings to handle as I please." Her superficial understanding of the situation was frustrating for him.

Taylor looked so confused that he had to explain. "*Mi niña*, think about it. What if she doesn't love me back?"

"But what if she does?"

"And what if she doesn't? Once you say something, it changes your friendship forever if only one person is in love. Even if you talk it through, even if you both agree on how you will be *compañeros*, knowing only one has *el amor* changes how both think and act."

"How? You are best friends."

"For the one not in love, they will always question if they are being manipulated, or worse, they feel sorry for the one in love who is not loved back. For me, I won't put up with that. I may be in love, but I'm no woman's *esclavo*." His tone left no doubt what that meant.

"But, Alejo, it would be such a loss! What if she does love you?"

"*Mi niña*, I'm sorry to be blunt, but you know nothing of love. For you this is a romantic idea, a fairytale, not a reality that could ruin what is most important to me if it goes wrong. I've been in love many times and then moved on when it ran its course, but I'm not willing to give up Olivia forever by taking this chance."

Taylor looked so disappointed that Alejo felt sorry for her. He put his arm around her. "Before you knew this thing how did you feel about us?"

"Happy. I love you and Olivia and our life."

"And what has changed? I had these feelings before you discovered them and we were happy. What is the difference then?"

"But you could be so much happier."

"But we're happy now, yes? Very happy."

"Yes."

"Do you want to chance that for less? *Sobrinita*, anytime you can win, you can also lose. This way we are sure to stay happy instead of maybe yes, maybe no." Alejo's accent somehow made it sound like a wonderful plan.

When Taylor didn't say anything he was suspicious. "And you are not to tell her. Agreed?"

Taylor didn't answer and he pressed more firmly. "Agreed?"

Taylor nodded, but Alejo was still not satisfied. "Tell me you promise not to tell Olivia." He felt a little silly asking it, but he had to make sure he could control this somehow and a promise was the best he could think of. After all, she was nineteen.

"I promise." Taylor looked defeated. Alejo was satisfied at that point; he'd never known her to lie. He helped her up from the grass, but Taylor had one last argument.

"Alejo, Dantin is gone now. There's no need for Olivia to protect others from him by keeping them at a distance. You know she lets her softer side out now; you just told me how beautiful it is. What if another man tells her he loves her and she accepts him when it could have been you?"

That was a stunning jolt for Alejo, hearing her say it aloud like that. He'd hardly let himself think it. He didn't want Taylor to see that she'd shaken him, so he didn't answer her. Ignoring her comment he instead called the greyhounds to him and then turned back to Taylor. He hoped his shock didn't show on his face.

"Let's get back to Olivia's. She'll want to see Doobie and Bailey before she goes to sleep." Taylor and the dogs were still staying at JaneAnn's so Alejo could have her room.

Lexie had gotten used to being transported by this time, just like the greyhounds, but she still liked to know Taylor was with her and she leaned against Taylor's leg to make sure she was there during the ride.

When Alejo said "Ready?" Lexie pressed herself closer, Taylor nodded, and they all disappeared into the darkness.

At the marina, that same darkness camouflaged Locke and Malila. Any of the Palisade diners looking at the massive rocks of the jetty would see only gray fog undulating on the ocean side, but Malila stood on one of the black monoliths that made up the seawall with her Necromancer, protected from the waves and salt spray.

"What did you find?"

Locke's deep whisper breathed into her ear as his mist wrapped around her. "I found Dantin there."

Malila's skin went numb. "In Olivia."

"Yes."

"In what form?"

"In his entirety. If they were close when he died, he could have transferred to her."

"Not just his essence? His whole being?"

"Two souls. One body. There is no doubt of it."

Malila felt a chill as she considered what this meant. A witch could swallow an essence; the memories, the learning, and much of the power from another witch but that wasn't a soul, the thing that had drives and desires and hopes and dreams. There should be only one soul to a body. More than that was an abomination, a continual internal battle with no hope of deliverance until death.

"We need to separate them."

"Such a thing hasn't been done in this plane for a hundred mortal lifetimes." Locke was immortal and Malila nearly so, and they'd seen much in their existence including the fading of magic in this world. Both knew the capability to pull a soul from a living body no longer existed in this dimension.

"Locke, we have to. How could it not kill them both?" Anxiety edged Malila's voice. "Please."

"Of course. I will search where I can for you." Locke wrapped around her, trying to comfort her.

The answer will be out there somewhere, Malila thought; they just didn't know where it was right now. The ability existed, or at least it used to. Perhaps it did now in a different dimension. Locke could travel to many of them, although not all.

"Do we know who is stronger?" The question was critical for Malila.

"It does not matter." Locke reminded her. "If one is stronger, it can't be forever. The struggle is constant and the other soul cannot escape. It will surely fragment the host." The prospect of that made Malila ill. She couldn't let that happen; they had to separate Dantin from Olivia.

"Do we know how long do we have?"

"No." But Locke had still other news for her. "You should know. The apprentice can travel ley-lines."

"How is that possible? She's still a novice."

"She may not know how, but she has the ability. She's more powerful than they realize."

"None of us have been able to travel them in six hundred years. Not since this world moved too far from the others."

"Nevertheless, she can. I'm sure of it." A low rumbling of thunder accompanied his voice.

"I'll stay close to them here while you search, then. We have to separate him from her. We'll work out the rest after we have him."

Reluctantly, she stepped away from Locke and watched him disappear. That was the worst possible news, she thought. Dantin inside Olivia and Locke didn't know how long they could stay alive that way. Everything for Malila depended on Locke finding an answer. She hoped it was even out there.

She flashed herself to the Sorrento and appeared under the trees across the street. This venture of hers was getting worse and worse, and she needed a moment to reflect and plan. It was a nice diversion to look at the hotel as she walked toward it. Looking at beautiful things was always soothing for her, and the Sorrento's red brick façade curving around the valet circle with its fountain and greenery was welcoming and reassuring. Maybe a nice stop for a moment in the beautiful fireside lobby would do her good.

She crossed the valet circle already starting to feel better and had just gained the entrance when Thane stepped in front of her.

"What are you up to?" His face was predatory, intent on intimidation.

Malila looked at him and the Blue/Black next to him, the woman from *La Tremoille* in Paris where they'd first heard the news that Olivia had killed Dantin. Her mental armor went up and her expression turned haughty; she didn't want them in her affairs.

"Well that's really none of your business, Thane, is it?"

He narrowed his eyes, looking her up and down. "You've been awfully cozy with these Silver-Tints lately, haven't you?"

"You can tell us–what's going on?" The other Blue/Black, the woman, had a face full of innocence, but she was as vicious as they came, Malila knew. She used that cast of innocence to get what she wanted, and Malila wasn't at all fooled.

"What in the hell do you think I'm doing? Have you forgotten what you so kindly revealed at *La Tremoille*? I have a score to settle with Olivia Phalen."

"Why don't you settle it then? Why are you spending time with her, coming to Seattle and inviting her to the Paddock? We're wondering what you have up your sleeve. Maybe some amusement that you'll let us in on?" Again, faux curiosity from the woman. She wasn't asking, she was telling Malila they didn't approve, but Malila wasn't about to accept that tone from her. Her expression turned hard and she stepped in close to the other woman.

"None of this has anything to do with you. You didn't know Dantin. In fact you barely know me, you little twit." She bit off the words and spit them at the girl, then turned and advanced on Thane.

"And who in hell do you think you are, asking me anything at all?" She leaned closer to Thane, who tried to stand his ground but had to back up; Malila was within six inches of his face. Malila pressed her point.

"This is my vendetta, my plan, my toy to play with any way I want, and I had better not see you two or any other Blue/Black until I'm done. Dantin was mine, and now his Necromancer is mine, and if you two don't fuck off and tell everyone else to as well, I'm sending him after you!"

Malila was angry and enhanced it with magic to drive home her point. She cast a glamour over her appearance that made her look far bigger to them than she actually was.

Thane put up his hands, backing away, but the woman didn't and Malila turned on her. "Do you know what a Necromancer is?"

"Yes." The Blue/Black tried to act blasé but was unsuccessful; it showed in her eyes that Malila was rattling her.

"You understand me, then. This bird is mine. If I want to play with her like a cat before I kill her, then that's really none of your concern."

She looked at both of them. "And now that I've had to say that twice, I'm just plain pissed off. I expect I will not see you again. I'd better not even hear of you." She turned and strode to the elevator, her dismissal of Thane and the woman complete and a clear threat in her final sentence.

Dantin had always taught her the best defense was a good offense, and he was right. It had always worked for him and sure enough the two Blue/Blacks turned and left, their questions unanswered.

They'd be lurking, though, and Malila knew it. Blue/Blacks were always like that, but Malila knew how to keep her guard up. It was like being friends with the mean kids in high school. Not too mature, but that was how they were.

What bothered her most was that they'd challenged her at all. Probably because Dantin was gone. Now they'd all want to try and reestablish the pecking order, and Malila needed to stay on top. Locke would help keep her there. He had kept Dantin on top, and he wasn't even Dantin's Necromancer–he was hers.

Taylor had long ago left with the dogs for JaneAnn's house, and Olivia was in bed in her own room. With the time difference and only a few hours' rest that afternoon, it seemed everyone was tired and ready for a good night's sleep.

Alejo couldn't sleep, of course. He lay on the bed in Taylor's room, looking at the bronze silk that draped the bedposts but not seeing it. He replayed the conversation with Taylor again and again, knowing that he was on borrowed time when it came to telling Olivia his feelings.

He'd always liked Olivia and admired her smarts, and he thought she was the most beautiful thing he'd ever seen, but Tristan had been his blood brother and closest friend. He never dreamed of coveting Olivia while Tristan was alive; not even a fantasy did he allow himself. After Tristan's death, Alejo was nearly as devastated as Olivia, and it would have been sacrilege to think of her that way, a dishonor to Tristan. His job was to take of her for him. He'd waited over two hundred years before he'd admitted what he was feeling even to himself, and now it had been four hundred years.

How long before it was not an affront to love her? With a sinking feeling he realized that was up to Olivia. He had no control over that and no idea what her thoughts were.

He wanted to tell her so badly. It was a craving he couldn't get rid of that was constant nowadays. It was actually painful, this twisting in the pit of his stomach. He had to have her. No, he thought, that wasn't right. He had to tell her, and hope she would love him back. He wasn't complete without her and he couldn't ignore this unrequited craving, all these dreams and hopes that included her, all this desire.

But if she didn't reciprocate he might lose her forever. He couldn't take that chance, he told himself, and decided for the hundredth time not to say anything. Even if it meant she never knew how he felt, he didn't want to lose her. He couldn't bear to think of being without her.

A sudden realization hit him and he laughed at himself; a week ago he had thought nothing of a single vigorous night with Malila to satisfy his lust–and hers as well, he had to admit–but now he was agonizing over the thought of losing someone's friendship versus not having her intimately. It wasn't just the sex he wanted, though. This was completely different, and he knew that. It was the intimacy, the most personal expression of love he could share with her. He was more in love with this one woman that he was closer to, trusted more, and had known longer than any other his whole life. But he couldn't tell her in case it changed them, and the thought of not having her friendship, not knowing they were connected somehow on a daily basis was not a risk he wanted to take.

He closed his eyes, wishing that sleep would come and relieve his torment, but he lay there for a full wakeful hour. Then the thing that Taylor had said hit him with full force.

What if another man tells her he loves her and she accepts him when it could have been you?

Alejo felt sick at the thought. With Dantin gone it was a real possibility. Olivia had kept others at bay to protect them from Dantin, but now he was gone. He knew she had admirers and many of them. Even Jaden was intent on gaining her affection, or rather attention, but Jaden just wanted to acquire her. The thought angered him; no one held her welfare above their own like he did. They'd want her for their own selfish reasons, not to give her what she wanted. And he sure as hell wasn't going to watch someone else be her lover. He couldn't take the chance of that happening. The pain in his chest intensified and he realized he had no choice but to tell her; it was too painful not to.

He strode to the door, opened it, and crossed the hall to Olivia's room.

"Livy?" He knocked softly on the door, half hoping she wouldn't hear him. He swallowed through the tightness in his throat and stayed planted in front of her door, ignoring every urge he had to step away. This had to be the worst thing he'd ever done, he thought. He didn't even know what to say.

A very small, very sleepy-looking Olivia in blue pajamas opened the door and smiled up at him.

"What's going on, Handy?"

Alejo looked down at her, thinking he might dissolve from anxiety, or excitement, or both. My God, he thought, I am so in love. He took both her hands in his.

"I have to talk to you. It's very important, and I'm sorry but I can't wait until morning."

Olivia blinked at him and pulled one of her hands out of his to rub the sleep from her eyes.

"Okay."

She looked adorable, Alejo thought. Hard to believe this was the same woman he had watched run a sword through Dantin's throat six months ago. She had everything he wanted, everything he needed; he knew that for sure. He couldn't possibly love her more. And no one could possibly love her as much.

The thought gave him confidence and he walked her back to her bed, sitting next to her on the edge.

And then he realized he had no idea where to start. The last thing he wanted was to blurt it at her out of the blue.

"Livy, we've been friends forever, right?" He wanted to start her off thinking about how much they shared already.

"Yes." She nodded.

"Can you imagine not being friends or not seeing each other?"

"No." Curiosity crept into her expression. "Why? Is something going on? Are you..." She didn't know how to finish the sentence.

Alejo was quick to reassure her. "No. Nothing is going on. I mean, I want to tell you something. Like you, I can't imagine us not knowing each other. Ever. Olivia, I promise you that anytime you ever need me, anytime you ever want anything I will be there for you."

Olivia wasn't sleepy anymore; in fact she was suddenly, fully awake. Was he trying to tell her he knew she was turning Blue/Black? And that he would help her if she needed him? She was relieved and frightened at the same time. Oh, it would be wonderful if he knew and didn't care, she thought. But then, what if she was wrong, and he didn't know after all?

Alejo saw her expression change. He scanned her face, her eyes, but couldn't tell what she was thinking. If I'm going to tell her, he thought, it has to be right now. He took both her hands in his again and looked into her eyes.

"Olivia, I'm in love with you."

He watched her eyes widen in surprise. She was caught completely unaware, he could tell. He held his breath, watching her reaction intently. Olivia looked into his face for a few seconds and then down at their hands.

The first thing Olivia thought of was the Blue/Black blood. He didn't know. Disappointment went through her as she looked at their hands, at his handsome long fingers enclosing hers. He doesn't know. And then it hit her: *he just said he was in love with me.*

She couldn't think straight. Two sentences tripped over each other in her head: he's in love with me... and he doesn't know. She couldn't say anything; she couldn't even look at Alejo.

Alejo tried to reassure himself. Of course she's going to need time, he thought. She'd need to get used to the idea. The subject had never come up between them; they'd never even flirted with each other in any serious manner. She would need time to get used to the idea.

He was deeply disappointed, though. He had hoped for even a small gesture of understanding, a fleck of hope. He was sure she would have given that if she had feelings for him. Her silence told him differently, that the thought of loving him was completely foreign to her. That was his worst fear–that she had no romantic feelings at all for him, and after he'd told her this, she wouldn't want to love him back. That had to be why she wasn't speaking or even looking at him, he thought. To save him the embarrassment of a painful discussion.

"Livy…can you say anything at all to me? Did you even hear what I said?"

"Yes, Alejo. I'm sorry–I don't know what to say yet. I'm still thinking." Olivia could only picture her blood with its Blue/Black cast, over and over again. She couldn't let him know about that, and yet she couldn't respond to his feelings without disclosing everything.

"Any thoughts at all?" Alejo wished he could fall through the floor right now. Either that or go back in time.

"Well, this is…unexpected." Olivia was trying to buy time. Normally she would have told him so honestly, but she didn't trust her own words at that moment. Oh, God damn it, she thought, why is it that in the moments we need to be most honest we instead cover up? She needed to think, to sort out her fears.

"Handy, can I have some time? This is big news."

The disappointment was clear on his face. "Of course." He dropped her hands and stood up to leave. He turned away but then changed his mind, turning back to her and lifting her hands to his lips to kiss them. He wanted to make sure she remembered that as the last thing he did before he left her.

He closed the door to her room as he left, going back to Taylor's bedroom alone. Damn! Why did he tell her? Things would be different from now on; he was sure of it. He didn't know if they would still be close, pretending it had never happened, or would they be awkward, again pretending it had never happened? Or his greatest fear–would they drift apart?

Oh, *dios maldita sea*, why in hell had he told her? He shut the door to Taylor's room and sat on the bed, miserable.

Alone now, Olivia ran her fingers through her hair. What had just happened? Five minutes ago she had been asleep and now everything had changed. She would lose her best friend in the world because he loved her and she was becoming Blue/Black. There was no way she could tell him, which meant that she'd have to get used to being without him, especially if they couldn't get past this whole announcement of his. The stakes were much higher now. She wished there was a way to undo what had happened.

She still couldn't believe it. Alejo–in love with her.

She thought it again. Alejo was in love with her. Wow. She thought about their friendship, trying to find a clue anywhere. They were certainly good together, and she wasn't blind to his attributes. He was delectable beyond belief.

Well, she thought, it wouldn't hurt anything to imagine it a little, would it? Just to herself, of course. Alejo was in love with her. She let her mind travel along that path. What would that be like?

She'd seen him with other women: always affectionate, always respectful, always ready with humor and friendship even after the relationship was finished. It seemed he always stayed on good terms with them afterward, which meant he really, truly liked them and no blame was assessed for the breakup. Olivia imagined an affair with him might be even better than that for the two of them. After all, they were already friends and had been through more with each other than anyone else they'd ever heard of. Even Tristan and her.

Thinking of Tristan stopped her abruptly. He had been heroic, romantic, a passionate partner–all that she'd heard love should be from minstrels and sonnets. He had been exciting, daring, erotic, and handsome, and nearly every moment with him had been an adventure. Wasn't that what love was supposed to be? An all-consuming, passion-filled flight that took you beyond reality, beyond this plain life?

Alejo could be exciting as well, but after Tristan's death he had been more serious, more cautious, especially with her. She loved Alejo, but was it romantic? Passionate? Daring? They were tight, close friends that had remained constant, even through the mundane and darkest parts of their lives. She'd never really had mundane with Tristan. Every day had been an adventure. But what if they'd run out of adventures? Would they have stayed together like she and Alejo had? And while she was thinking about it, was the all-consuming flight the poets and minstrels spoke of real love? Enough to survive real life?

Olivia replayed her memories of Alejo, her history with him. Like Tristan, they'd been back-to-back with swords in the past, and he had let her be herself and loved her for it, expecting nothing in return. He'd backed her with Dantin, and though she wouldn't let him do her dirty work, he'd stepped in at crucial times to help her. How wonderful even an ordinary day was when he was around, she realized. Their friendship was solid, settled, permanent, and based on who each other was, not what they did. Trust, commitment, friendship–not just romance and excitement, like Tristan. And she had to admit, she found him damned sexy. She hadn't let herself think about it because they were friends.

Then Olivia realized with shock: with Alejo her feelings were complete. They were full circle, in-every-aspect-of-life full blown adult love, not a romantic ideal. She thought back over all of their time together, comparing Alejo's rock-solid partnership to Tristan's larger-than-life romantic, heroic gestures. I've been through so much since then, and Alejo with me. We've matured together and are way beyond the relationship Tristan and I ever had. Of course I'm in love with him.

Oh, my God, she thought, I am *so* in love with Alejo, and I didn't even know it. She almost laughed aloud.

I have to tell him, she thought; I can't leave him with no answer. He must be feeling awful right now. Well, I can fix that. I can tell him about the blood-tint as well, I know I can. We'll find a way to deal with it together. He knew her most horrible secrets from the past and had come to get her anyway. They'd always handled everything together.

The moment she imagined him knowing her plight, all her fears slipped away and she crossed her room to go to him. She imagined kissing him immediately when he opened the door, and him drawing her into his arms to kiss her in return.

As she reached her own door and opened it, though, she had second thoughts. How could she be sure of him? How well did she really know him when it came to Blue/Black blood? Everything they'd ever lived was in opposition to their darkness, and now she was becoming one. She stood in her doorway, looking down the hall at Taylor's bedroom door, knowing Alejo was on the other side.

I can't do it, she thought. I can't risk him fearing me, or worse, hating me. I'd rather we drifted apart so he never knows.

She stared at his door as she closed her own, unable to pull her eyes away from the sight of it until she finally shut her door and the latch clicked closed, separating her room from his and the chance that went with it. She cast a privacy spell around the room, putting a layer of anonymous magic in the perimeter to blur any emotion that might flow through the walls. She didn't want Alejo to try and read her feelings right now. On that thought she reached out her hand and turned the door lock as well. Now the room was safe from scrys, spells, walk-bys, and mortal intrusion. Then she sank quietly to the floor and sobbed.

That was close, Dantin thought. He'd pushed hard to change Olivia's mind about telling that damned playboy she loved him.

Ewww, he thought. As much fun as it could be to feel sex through Olivia, that particular witch was the last person he wanted her to be intimate with. He'd always hated how close Alejo was to Olivia; she should be Dantin's woman, not Alejo's.

But the great news here? He'd controlled her thoughts for those few moments, even though they were intense. And she was awake this time.

Michael and Taylor could hardly hear each other through the pounding music on the Force India yacht. Belly dancers performing to a Euro-tech beat had given way to a packed dance floor where stage lighting in different colors played over the undulating, writhing crowd.

"Do you want a champagne?" Michael's voice cut through the noise. Taylor simply nodded in return so she wouldn't have to shout. Michael had to take her hand so they wouldn't get separated as he led her to the bar, and once their drinks were secured, they found a lucky seat close by and scanned the crowd. There was certainly a lion's share of gorgeous, coiffed, expensively dressed people here, and Taylor was relieved to find she didn't feel out of place the way she had when she first became Olivia's apprentice. She was even confident enough to be honest with Michael about being poor before Olivia found her.

"No shame in that," Michael had said, "most of us were, too, before magic." They had talked on the way home from *Le Grill* the other night, before Taylor had left for Seattle. Michael had asked about her, and her family, and about learning she was witch and living with Olivia. Taylor had told him all about her sister, Karen, and their mother and life as a family before their mom had died. Then she told him about Olivia coming along and helping them when she and Karen had needed it most. He'd been surprised to hear she was nineteen, saying she must have an old soul, or another life before this.

He'd understood about Karen, too, and how hard it was for Taylor because they were drifting apart when they'd always been so close.

"That happened to me, too. I had a brother. We were inseparable when we were little, but then he discovered money–and the fact that he had no scruples. There was no person he wouldn't claw through in his hunger for wealth. At twenty-two he moved to America and became a scheming, ruthless businessman who abused his workers to pull in millions. They called them robber barons back then. He wasn't witch, though, and I didn't dare tell him that I was; he would have tried to blackmail me, or exploit my powers somehow. If he'd been witch, he would have been Blue/Black, I'm sure of it. Even as a mortal he was a poor example of humankind."

He was quiet for a few moments as they walked along, thinking. Then he said, "Still, it hurt to lose my brother that way, still alive but someone I didn't know anymore. We had so many good memories when we were kids."

"I get that," Taylor said. "Karen's back at Wellesley now. She spent Spring Break with us in Paris the last week of March, and it was fun seeing her, but man, what a difficult week with her talking all about college and everything she was learning. She dropped names like crazy, too. A lot of the kids there are wealthy or have famous parents." Taylor sighed. "I found out by accident she hardly had told any of her college friends about me."

"Do you think that was intentional?" Michael's tone was neutral.

"I don't know."

"You should tell her how you feel. Maybe she doesn't realize it hurts your feelings." Although it was good advice, Michael knew talking about having that discussion was far easier than actually doing it.

Taylor looked morose. "Honestly Michael, the rich and famous stuff didn't bug me so much, but she also kept talking about her classes and using what she learned, like spouting philosophy or history, or classical works she'd read. She made me feel stupid because I couldn't talk about it with her. I wish I could tell her about being witch."

"You know, it could be that she sees you traveling around the world and is jealous of that; you never know. People have insecurities you never see on the outside. Usually they're careful to hide them."

Taylor had stared at him as they walked along, comprehending what he'd said and realizing how much she needed someone she could talk to like this. Looking at him now on the Force India yacht, she felt the urge to tell him how much she appreciated him.

"You're so smart." She raised her voice to cut through the noise.

"What?" He shook his head. "I can't hear you."

Taylor leaned toward Michael, capturing his ear to make herself heard. "Nothing. I wish Karen were here to see this," she shouted over the music. "She'd love it and we'd always talked about doing things together."

Michael smiled his understanding, then turned his face toward hers to give her an unexpected kiss. "We'll find somewhere else impressive to take her."

Before Taylor could respond, one of the other drivers came up and spoke to Michael.

"Roswell! I'm going to beat the crap out of you at qualifying tomorrow. And the race on Sunday."

Michael laughed. "We'll see, buddy. Taylor, meet Kevin Melbourne from Alfani."

Taylor smiled and shook his hand. "Alfani is doing well this year. Got last year's reliability problems worked out, apparently."

Michael turned to her in surprised admiration. "Been studying up, I see." He smiled at her and then turned back to Kevin Melbourne. "Yeah, you guys got a lot of great starts until technical problems took you out. How many races did you actually finish?"

Melbourne ignored the jab. "Yeah, we had a bad patch. It happens. But we're insane this year. Our new engineer is a god, as you very well know because we're in first place so far." He poked his finger at Michael as he said "first place" and was very pleased with himself until he turned to the bar in time to see the last glass of champagne walk away with another guest.

"Well, hell..."

Taylor reassured him, although she had to shout over the din. "No problem—watch. They're already racking them up to pour again."

All three watched as four bartenders quickly staged twenty feet of champagne flutes down the length of the bar and began filling them rapid-fire. It was a decadent dance of upturned bottles, dripping champagne, frothing bubbles, music, and dancing strobe lights that they navigated expertly. They filled sixty glasses in less than a minute and the crowd around cheered and clapped at the spectacle before descending on the drinks.

Kevin hoisted his flute at the bartenders and then turned to Taylor and Michael. "I'd stay but I've got trouble to cause somewhere else," he shouted. "Plus it's too loud here to talk. See you at qualifying tomorrow." He smiled at Taylor. "Very nice meeting you."

They watched him walk away and Michael leaned close to Taylor. "He's right—it is noisy in here. Should we find a quieter place?"

Taylor looked around at the party. No wonder they had to shout; the whole yacht was wall-to-wall people, and now that it was later in the evening the polish was coming off the coiffed, expensive looking crowd. They danced and drank now in tousled, sweaty clothing and streaked mascara. The vertigo-inducing strobe lights weren't helping, either.

"Great idea." She slipped her hand into Michael's, marveling at how natural it felt now that they'd been doing it since the walk home from *Le Grill*. They wound their way through the crowd and up to the deck outside. It was no better up on the deck; in fact it was rowdier. Michael again pressed his mouth to Taylor's ear.

"Is there anything else here you want to see?"

CATHLEEN DUNN

Taylor shook her head. "No, but where else could we go? Look at the street. It's packed there and everywhere else, too." From their vantage point on the bow they could see every yacht, the whole dock, and every street within sight was filled with the same craziness.

"You guys weren't kidding when you said the whole town partied." She thought a moment. "Olivia and Alejo are at a private party; we could go there."

"Or we could go to my place or your place." After he said it, Michael shook his head and winced. "Damn. It is really hard to say that romantically while I'm shouting over this din!"

Taylor's laugh was genuine. She really liked Michael. "Well then, let's start with Olivia and Alejo and leave from there. I don't want to keep you out too late; you're driving tomorrow."

"I'll be fine–don't worry about me. But you'll have to take us there because I don't know where it is."

Taylor looked around. "I'll bet we could disappear from right here and no one would even notice." The people on deck were drunker than the people downstairs, which was saying something.

"Damn, girl, aren't you bold?" Michael grinned. "Let's at least go somewhere less conspicuous than the middle of this crowd to pop out of here."

Together they made their way to a corner behind the wheelhouse and without ceremony Taylor flashed them to a spacious hotel hallway. Michael wasn't at all surprised. It was smart not to assume everyone at a destination was witch unless you knew for sure. Best to get close and then walk in like a mortal. He looked around.

"Which door?"

They knocked on a pair of double doors nearby and were welcomed into a sumptuous penthouse suite on the top floor of *Le Meridien* hotel. A mere fifty guests milled about in the spacious suite, a far cry from what they'd just left. For a second it was difficult to spot Olivia because there was more open area than people.

"I thought you two were at Force India's party," Olivia said when they walked up to her.

"It was too loud." Taylor was relieved at the relative silence in the suite.

"And too crowded." Michael plucked a canapé off a passing waiter's tray. "After that yacht it's almost criminal how much room you have here. What party is this, anyway?"

"It's one of the 'Nights in Monaco' galas, to raise money for the Prince Albert II of Monaco Foundation." Olivia pointed at Prince Albert himself conversing with guests not thirty feet away. The Prince was Grace Kelly's son, the perfect and elegant American movie star who in nineteen fifty-six had captivated the world when she'd given up her acting career to become Monegasque royalty.

And if that weren't enough, she spied a former president and two famous singers on the other side of the room, schmoozing with guests. Honestly, she thought, I will never get used to this life that I'm living.

Alejo arrived and greeted them. "Hi, you two. Did you hear how this fundraiser works? It's actually fun. To donate, we bet money on one of the drivers through the Casino and they donate that to the Foundation. If we win our bet, they donate that amount to the Foundation as well. And the Casino donates an extra million to the Foundation each year."

Olivia cut in. "I made a separate bet that I'm not going to donate–an extra hundred grand on Vince Tenderril to win. He's going to make me some serious cash."

Alejo turned to her. "You're not betting on Michael or Jaden? How about Melbourne? He's got more points than almost everyone this year."

Michael was surprised, too. "I thought you said you didn't like Tenderril's methods."

Olivia looked annoyed. "So what? I don't care about his damned methods. He doesn't fuck around and play nicey-nice, and that's what I need for this bet. He'll do whatever it takes to win, and I'll be the recipient of it."

Taylor was taken aback; Olivia was never this callous. She looked at Michael in embarrassment.

Alejo couldn't believe it, either. Was Olivia being unpleasant on purpose, to distance herself from him rather than tell him she wasn't interested in him? He dismissed that thought immediately; she wasn't that immature. It had to be a joke.

Olivia looked at the others staring at her. "What?" She appeared oblivious to her comment.

No one said anything for a moment until Alejo broke the tension. "Don't you think you sound a little harsh?"

"Oh, for Christ's sake. I was just kidding." Olivia waved it away. "Tenderril's stats are great this year, and I really do think he has a good chance."

Michael tried to help smooth it over. "He has racked up a lot of points this year; he's third overall so maybe she's right about that." He looked at the others. "But he's still behind Melbourne and me. Hajime and Jaden are right behind him, too, and looking to pass him, so he will need to be more aggressive, like she said."

The others nodded, still feeling awkward but glad for the out that Michael had provided. Taylor took his arm.

"We'd better get you home. You have a big day tomorrow and a bigger one after that." Everyone knew qualifying laps were tomorrow and the race was the next day, Sunday, so this was the perfect excuse to leave. Michael nodded.

"She's right," he said to the others and then turned to Taylor. "And you need to walk Lexie before bed. I'll do that with you."

They said their goodnights and left, magically emerging in Taylor's room where an ecstatic beige dog greeted them from atop the bed. They both laughed; Lexie's whole body was wagging. Taylor tried to make amends with Michael as she pulled Lexie's leash from the nightstand drawer.

"I don't know what that was all about with Olivia. She's not usually like that." Taylor tried to explain as she clipped the leash to Lexie's collar.

"No worries." Michael brushed it off. "Everyone gets in a mood sometimes." He gave Taylor a kiss and Lexie a vigorous rub along her back.

"Come on, let's get this girl walked and get you both to bed."

The exclusive access the Paddock membership provided was everything Malila had said it would be and more. Here it was, a race day, and here they were in the pits talking to the teams and actually touching the cars.

It was amazing, Taylor thought, that such powerful engines sounded like angry, buzzing hornets. She'd expected the Formula cars to have a heavy, throbbing sound, but they didn't. A Sagenhaft engineer on Michael's team had explained it to her: Formula One cars revved faster than any other, so their eight hundred horses screamed out of the engines at almost fifteen thousand rpm. It was power bursting at the seams, he'd said. It sounded like it.

"This isn't NASCAR," the engineer told her. "Those things are beasts–heavy engines, bodies that weigh over twice as much and have less horsepower. But these sleek little dreams are high performance like no other. There's nothing as technical or complex on pavement." He ran his hand along the car's glossy surface. "They're perfect."

He went on, espousing his love for the creations and their technicalities, and soon even

Taylor was convinced. They were gorgeous machines; fast as hell, lighter, curvier, sexier, and they didn't waste an ounce of power. They even had a system that recovered kinetic energy lost during braking and funneled it back to the engine. They were a barely controlled tornado in carbon fiber skin. And her Michael was driving one of them.

Malila had accompanied Taylor down to the pit lane where they met the engineer and fallen into conversation, but now she looked at her watch. "We'd better get back. Olivia and Alejo should be upstairs by now." The two had slept in but were undoubtedly now in one of the Paddock lounges that overlooked the pits.

They left the Sagenhaft garage, stopping to let the guard unclip the barrier rope that restricted access to each team's area and then stepped onto the pit lane itself, which was filled with crews swarming around F1 cars for today's qualifying sessions. They weaved their way through the activity to the Paddock and in less than ten minutes they were in posh surroundings.

The Paddock Club was the epitome of techno-luxury design. It was a futuristic world of all white, struck with red and black. A circular white bar was ringed with red Lucite barstools, and the long, white-clad buffet was bursting with red ginger blossoms accenting the chic black trays of food. It complemented perfectly the world of racing they were in. Guests could even sit in a black and red Formula One car in the center to get their pictures taken behind the wheel. Taylor plopped down in one of the white leather armchairs and nearly disappeared into the cushions.

"Oh, crap. Could someone please take these so I can climb out of this chair?" She held up her champagne and plate of appetizers for Alejo to take and used both hands to pull herself out of the seat. After they'd all had a laugh at Taylor's expense, and her along with them, they claimed a cluster of seats close to a wall-sized video screen as their base for the afternoon.

Qualifying laps were surprisingly simple to understand. Three short sessions–around fifteen minutes each–of high speed laps through Monte Carlo determined where the cars would be at the start of Sunday's race. There was a minimum speed limit, and any car slower than that didn't race. Then whoever had the slowest times in the first session would have the last six starting positions in what they called the grid. The same applied for the next session where the middle six spots were assigned, and then the last ten cars vied for the spots at the front of the grid. It made for a field of the very fastest cars.

"Faster lap times mean closer to the front so we want Michael to last until that third session so he gets the pole–that spot at the very front." Malila pointed at the first box painted on the street.

"Michael told me about that. He said if you have the pole position, there's nothing in front of you but open road and all the driver has to do is stay there."

"Yes, but he's got to avoid the other cars snapping at his heels for the entire two hundred and sixty kilometers." Malila informed her. "Make no mistake; driving a race car is a dogfight no matter where you start, and the Monaco Grand Prix especially is like charging a racehorse through the fine china department without touching anything."

Taylor was blown away by the immediacy of watching F1. Every driver had a camera onboard and the video was displayed on one-hundred-inch screens scattered throughout the lounge. It was a jarring experience. The scenery changed every second. Colorful banners and sponsor ads and writing on the safety barriers flashed by, blaring a visual cacophony at a hundred miles an hour, followed abruptly by blips of trees, buildings, hairpin turns, then the darkness of a tunnel. Twisting turns alternated with straightaways and a constant change of noise, direction, and velocity. Fast engine noise, then slow, ascending and descending through gears, braking sharply and speeding up over and over and over again. The whole course was a crash waiting to happen.

Taylor was shaking her head as she watched. "They're going so fast and the course is so curvy, I can't even tell where they're at half the time." She looked at the course map she held. "By the time I find them on this, they're already way past it. I can't keep up."

A Paddock concierge came over to help her out. "Mademoiselle, think of it like so: all you really need to know today is *Mirabeau* is at that end"–he pointed left–"and *La Rascasse* is at that end"–he pointed right. "The rest will come when it comes."

"*Merci beaucoup.*" Taylor smiled her thanks at him and went back to watching with Olivia, Alejo, and Malila. In eighteen very short minutes, the first laps were done and the last grid positions were filled.

Taylor suddenly had a realization and turned to Alejo. "I get it now–from your ground floor suite we can watch the cars go by just before *Mirabeau*!"

"Yes! That's perfect. Look at you, knowing where *Mirabeau* is and all," Olivia surprised them with the sarcasm in her voice.

Both Malila and Alejandro stared at her, unbelieving. Taylor was plainly embarrassed. That's kind of a snotty thing to say, thought Malila. She addressed Olivia coolly.

"Aren't you forgetting this is your first Formula One, too?" She looked Olivia right in the eye, poised for whatever came next. Alejo didn't like what might happen next and jumped in.

"Save it for later. The second laps are about to start." He gave Taylor's hand a quick squeeze to comfort her. What in the hell had gotten into Olivia? Alejo thought. She'd been silent, sulky, or annoyed all week.

Malila knew what had gotten into Olivia. On the spot she made a firm decision. As soon as this weekend is over, she told herself, I'm having Locke capture her. One way or the other, I'll take care of this once and for all.

They turned their attention back to the race, where Michael was still in competition for the pole position. The entire pace was definitely faster, drivers vying hard for advantage, especially at the corners. At one point a car nearly hit the wall when his wheel locked up and he slid, slowing the cars behind him. Another driver took advantage of the chaos, passing two cars trapped at the edge of the jam to continue on and get ahead. They could see one of the drivers pounding his steering wheel in frustration as the other car passed him.

Alejo was standing with his arms folded, staring intently at the screen. "The drivers don't want to press full-out like they will tomorrow, but this is definitely a battle for the pole. Especially between Melbourne, Michael, and Tenderril."

"I met Kevin Melbourne last night," said Taylor. "He said he was going to beat the crap out of Michael."

Everyone laughed. Malila said, "I'm not surprised. You can't race at this level and not really, really want to win. It's not just Melbourne and Michael, either. Jaden's fourth in overall points this year and he really wants to get out of Michael's rearview mirror. He's a very good driver, but Caponetti is having technical problems this season. Still, who knows what could happen, especially in Monaco? You see how tight this course is; it's insane."

Olivia reminded them of her wager. "Yeah, well, I'm not losing that bet. Tenderril's going to take this whole thing. He'll be an animal out there."

Malila noticed Taylor's concerned face; Olivia's attitude was creating tension for everyone and she was definitely enjoying it. Malila tried to smooth over the moment for Taylor.

"Michael and Jaden will be fine," she said to Taylor. "This is what they do for fun." She pointedly ignored Olivia's stare.

Several more laps went by and they were in the last moments of the second qualifying round when one of the cars cut *Mirabeau* corner too close, clipping it with his front wheel and burying the front airfoil in the Tecpro barrier. The impact flipped the car across the track, dashing it to pieces as it rolled. The two cars behind it narrowly missed a collision, and other drivers slammed on their brakes to avoid pieces of spoilers and fenders flying off in all directions. A loud gasp exploded in the Club, and across the room a woman jumped to her feet, hand pressed over her mouth.

"Oh, my God!" Taylor's eyes were wide.

Malila kept her tone calm. "Let's wait and see, Taylor. Hope for the best."

"I can't believe he didn't hit those other cars." Alejo was shaking his head. "He was damned lucky he cut right between them. They all were."

"I can't see the driver." Taylor felt sick. "He has to be hurt."

Everyone in the Club waited silently. After a minute Alejo pointed at the screen.

"No–he's okay, *sobrinita*. See? He's still in his seat inside the roll cage." They all watched the driver unbuckle himself from the seat and climb out of the wreckage. He stood for a moment to look at his destroyed F1, then walked off to the side with his hands on his hips, head down.

"He must feel like shit," said Alejo. No one disagreed with him.

On the other side of the room, the woman breathed a huge sigh of relief and sat down, dropping her head in her hands.

The track marshals brought out the safety car to lead the pack through the last lap while the mess was cleaned up. The second qualifying round ended with the middle six grids assigned to the slowest six drivers, but both Jaden Sharpe and Michael Roswell, as well as Kevin Melbourne, Vince Tenderril, and Raj Hajime had been in front of the accident and had finished the last lap in front. They would be in the next and final round, each vying hard for the pole position.

Seven minutes later, final laps were hitting the fastest times yet, and drivers came frighteningly close to each other during the turns. In the hairpins, where they had to slow down to fifteen miles an hour, Hajime crowded Jaden from behind, giving Jaden's rear tire a little kiss with his front one.

Alejo grinned. "Hajime's just saying: 'I'm here and right on your tail, so you'd better watch out. Or better yet, just let me pass.'"

"Oh, that'll piss him off," they heard a Paddock Club member say from one of the deep leather chairs close to the screen. They turned to see Michael Schumacher, a seven-time Grand Prix world champion sitting there, engrossed in the action. Taylor's eyes grew wide; Michael had told her about him. He was legend in the Formula One world.

"He'd better not try that move at top speed," said Alejo. "That would pull his front tire right up and over the other car's back one, and probably over the whole car as well. I've seen it happen when someone made a mistake and rode too close."

"Really?" Olivia was still intent on the screen. "That must have been a sight. Jaden told me about a few accidents he's seen."

Malila interjected, "Let's not get onto that discussion. It's bad luck on race weekend."

Alejo, however, had a different concern. When had Olivia been with Jaden to have that conversation? And what else were they doing that he didn't know about? The thought made him grit his teeth. Damn it, he told himself; he wouldn't be feeling this way if he hadn't told her he loved her. Or would he? Shit. This was exactly what he'd been hoping to avoid. He wished he'd never said a thing about it.

Qualifying ended for the day with Melbourne at the pole, Roswell next, then Tenderril and Sharpe and Hajime after that. The rest of the field would have to hope for luck, a miracle, or extreme skill in order to be on the winner's podium.

After qualifying was over Malila asked the other three, "Anyone want to come down to the pits with me?"

Alejo and Olivia begged off but Taylor said yes. She wanted to see more of this world that Michael was part of.

They took their champagne and Malila walked her up the pit lane, explaining much of what they saw while the crews prepped their garages and pits for the next day. Most of the cars were already in *parc fermé*, where access was restricted until after the race to prevent anyone from sabotaging them. Now that the pressure of qualifying was off and the teams had more time, Malila introduced Taylor to several of them.

"You seem to know everyone." Taylor was impressed.

"I've been coming to these for so long that I had full access before they started restricting it. Plus I'm witch, right? There are ways to get access–as long as you don't attract attention."

"Thank you for doing this with me and explaining so much," Taylor said. "I really love this and I want to be able to discuss it with Michael."

Malila smiled at Taylor from behind her sunglasses. "I'm happy to teach you. But remember, Michael liked you even when you didn't know anything about racing, so don't worry about that part."

She faced Taylor and spoke seriously. "In fact, don't make yourself over into what you think he wants. Just do what you're doing and especially, just be yourself. The rest will come if you two are a match."

Taylor liked how Malila didn't believe in being this or that for someone else. She agreed with Malila's advice but she really, really liked Michael and wanted him to like her as much. Malila seemed to read her mind.

"You really like Michael, don't you?"

Taylor thought about last night with Michael on the yacht, and then afterward at her hotel.

"Yes." She nodded. "A lot."

There was something about the way Taylor was smiling, thought Malila...

"Is he your first?"

"What? My first boyfriend? No. Jeez."

"No, I mean, your first..." she stopped because Taylor was blushing. "He is!"

Taylor looked in her face, trying to feel mature. "Malila, so what? I'm only nineteen. Just because you guys are all a million years old ... God, you had to start somewhere, too."

"Does he know?"

Taylor couldn't believe Malila's boldness. "Yes, and we're waiting a little longer. But that's our personal business, isn't it, Malila?" She was able to finish and stand her ground.

Now it was Malila's turn to be embarrassed. "Oh, you're right. I'm sorry. I just assume we're all...we all... oh, you get it."

Taylor didn't really know what Malila was trying to say. "Kind of, I guess."

"Look, you're right. For the rest of us it's been centuries since the first time at anything. We don't get apprentices that often anymore." She touched Taylor's shoulder. "I really am sorry, sweetie."

Taylor relaxed. "No, it's okay, really. The apprentice stuff I understand. I get it all the time." She laughed. "You should have seen everyone the first time I went to a witches gathering. I don't know who was more curious: them or me."

At that, Malila decided a change of subject was the best direction. "Come on–let's go back upstairs and get our pictures taken with some of the drivers." They headed back and walked up the red-carpeted stairs to the Club.

A virgin, thought Malila. I'll be goddamned.

Race day weather was brilliant and beautiful. The sun shone brightly on Monaco, peeking out through occasional clouds that wafted by. Monte Carlo seemed to be charmed on its special day.

They now were all familiar with the Paddock. They knew when the Pit Walks would be, when the drivers and constructors would come to share their race strategies, where to find the buffet, and where the celebrities hung out. Television, radio, and sports stations all sent their announcers to cover the event, and one of the anchor desks was set up in the area where the witches were seated. Their pre-race media patter was full of race day events and relaying the drama that surrounded the teams. Anything and everything to set the stage and increase the excitement was fair game as far as the sportscasters were concerned.

Two of them were on air right now, telling the world of the rivalries behind the races in their clipped British accents. One of them was pointing in dramatic fashion to the images of two smiling drivers in their Nomex racing coveralls.

"...the Constructors haven't yet named a Number One and Number Two driver on this team, so these two must duke it out to see who will dominate and win that Number One position. Not only are they teammates, but they are bitter rivals until the decision is made."

His partner at the desk cut in, looking straight at the camera: "And after that, they could shake hands and be friends, or stay enemies all season long. But they'll have to stay professional for the sake of the team." He turned a serious face to the first announcer. "I'd hate to be in their shoes, Neville."

The first announcer, a man with Chiclet-like teeth agreed, nodding. "You're so right, Dennis. We'll see how that turns out." He turned to the screen his producer was pointing at, where a grassy hillside covered with people was being displayed for the television audience. Instantly, he changed his tone from dramatic to festive.

"Just look at all those people! It seems everyone wants a ticket to come here to Monte Carlo and see the Grand Prix. Even though billionaires play here, there's also a bit of free seating on the hill above *La Rascasse* corner for those lucky enough to secure it. Every seat in this tiny country is a good seat." Both announcers watched as the camera swept over the steep grassy hill that was covered with spectators and then pulled back to a larger view of the yacht-filled harbor, which was their cue to announce a commercial break.

"You're listening to coverage of Formula One's crown jewel in the racing circuit, the Monaco Grand Prix, and we'll be back right after these messages." Both announcers relaxed and sipped water while the makeup person dabbed at their faces.

There was easily three times the activity in the lounge than there was yesterday. Not only were the sportscasters here, but it was crowded with people milling about, chatting and posing and trying to impress, and there was extra security for the celebrities and CEO's in attendance. The video screens alternated between views of the race course from all angles, the drivers' camera and audio feeds, and the telemetry feeds from the cars and the engineers they were linked to. Spectators had an inside view of the drama and hype. It was festive and feverish at the same time.

Taylor touched the ring that Michael had given her last night when he found her researching Formula One accidents on the web. She'd started to look out of curiosity and rapidly wished she had not. At F1 speeds, the crashes were violent, horrific, and massive damage happened in milliseconds.

Michael had come over to see her after qualifying and found her on the bed with her iPad and Lexie snuggled up next to her. She was shaking her head, still looking at the aftermath of an accident on her screen.

"Michael, even if you're witch, you don't have time to cast anything to protect yourself."

"Sure I do. I can usually tell when things are going south. And I hardly ever make a mistake, love."

Even his English lilt wasn't soothing her right then. "Hardly ever doesn't make me feel better. Look at this one–I didn't see anything hit his helmet it happened so fast, but they said he was dead instantly."

Michael looked at the screen and had a smack of what Taylor felt. He'd known that driver personally. They'd gone for a drink the night before the race, when he'd revealed to Michael he was going to ask his girlfriend to marry him. Michael pulled himself out of that memory and put his arms around Taylor.

"Here, pet, you can't let yourself do this. You'll be a wreck."

"It's really hard when all I can do is watch it happen, especially on a remote screen with everyone else." Her voice was matter-of-fact instead of plaintive, a thing he appreciated greatly. She did make good sense, Michael thought, and took the ring off his little finger to give to her.

"Here. Put this on." He watched as she tried it on to see where it would fit and then slipped it onto her middle finger. Then he touched it, concentrating.

A wash of images and feelings hit Taylor, confusing her and making her dizzy until they gelled into a continuous stream that flowed through her.

Michael was watching her. "How's that?" he asked.

Taylor looked at Michael, then around at the room. She was seeing it twice–not only what she saw but what he saw as well. "It's a little confusing."

Michael pulled the charm back a little. "How about now?"

Taylor broke into a smile. "Oh! Michael, this is perfect. It's like I'm right with you. I can feel you and tell what's going on, kind of like we're connected."

"So tomorrow you'll know how I'm doing. You'll be right there with me."

"Oh, thank you!" She hugged Michael and Lexie jumped up to get herself in there, too. They both laughed.

"You're welcome." Michael could tell her fears were assuaged. It's always harder to be the one left behind; he understood that.

"If you concentrate you can be with me, but I can't feel you–I can't risk the distraction while I'm driving. Okay, pet?" He added something to make her laugh. "Besides, the car's worth ten million quid; no way am I going to crash it."

"Ha! Okay, deal." Taylor felt immense relief. "This is better than great, Michael. Thank you."

She felt the ring again now as she sat in the Club and smiled, resisting the urge to connect with him just because she could, and turned her attention to the sports desk again where Neville and Dennis were coming back from commercial break.

"And here we are back in Monte Carlo for the Monaco Grand Prix on this beautiful spring day. Just look at it,"–the camera panned over a crowded city where people lined balcony railings, filled restaurant terraces to bursting, anywhere with a square foot of space–"every balcony is packed, every yacht has beautiful sunbathers, every hand a glass of champagne, and we're just twenty minutes away from lights out and the start of the race. The cars have already moved from the pits to their positions on the starting grid and are warming up."

Sure enough, the decibel level was starting to increase with twenty-two, urgent sounding Formula Ones revving their engines on the pavement nearby. The crowd noise swelled, too, filling the air inside the Club. Even Dennis and Neville's dramatics fit perfectly into the excitement.

"You know, Neville, there's nothing in Grand Prix quite like this. No other track has the crowd so close or the course so tight. Racing in Monte Carlo is like threading a needle at a hundred and eighty miles an hour."

"You're quite right, Dennis. And the undisputed master of the Monaco Grand Prix was racing legend Ayrton Senna. He ruled this course. Let's have a look back at the six-time winner of the Monaco Grand Prix–a feat as yet unmatched in the world of racing."

Everyone in the lounge was riveted to the screen as they watched the montage: first, the youngster in the go-kart driving around the track, and then him barely in his twenties but passing car after car in tight places no one else would dare pass. One piece of footage showed Ayrton leaping ahead of an incredible five other cars during a single lap to gain first place in some fearless and frightening driving.

"He was a ruthless competitor," the voice-over said, "and yet he stopped his car once during a race and ran across the track, risking his life to help driver Eric Comas, who had crashed on the track." The footage switched to Senna avoiding cars as he ran across the track and then bending down, helmet-to-helmet with the unconscious driver in the other cockpit. The retrospective ended in slow motion, with a handsome face topped with curly brown hair smiling back at the screen as he held the Monaco Grand Prix trophy over his head. Neville wrapped it up.

"...Ayrton Senna, winner of forty-one total Grands Prix races and three World Championships, along with sixty-five pole positions in his stunning career. He was the Monaco Master, and he will be missed."

A smiling Dennis continued the broadcast. "And if history tells us anything, whoever wins at Monaco has one hand on the World Championship. Let's go to the grid, where Kyle Ashton is in the middle of it all. Kyle, how loud is it down there?"

The camera cut to Kyle, who stood facing the camera with one finger in his ear and the other pressing his headset and microphone tightly against his head.

"Neville, it's a little hard to hear you, as you can see," he shouted into his microphone. "The drivers are now all in their cars and they're warming their engines, revving through different rpm's to make sure they are smooth enough to get a clean start." He walked to his right, the camera following him to the first car in the grid, which was swarmed by technicians and one engineer, who was talking to the helmeted driver.

"Here's Kevin Melbourne, conferring with his team and making sure every detail is perfect for this race. I had a chance to talk to him earlier, and he said he feels confident and familiar with this course. He also said he plans to repeat his victory of two years ago when he won here at Monaco."

He walked away from the car again and the camera panned down the street between the two columns of sleek, brightly airbrushed cars.

"...and as you can see, everyone is behind him, just waiting for their chance to hit the gas and chew up this track."

Neville tried to have a conversation with Kyle, asking, "Isn't that a beautiful sight behind you, two columns of Formula One cars queuing up behind the pole position?"

Kyle pressed his finger deeper into his ear. "What?" he laughed a little self-consciously. "I'm sorry, Neville; I just can't hear you."

"Never mind," said Dennis, coming to his rescue. "It looks like the race marshals are about to shoo everyone off the track anyway."

"What?" shouted Kyle into his microphone, and then moved off the track as two orange jump-suited marshals walked toward him, intentionally crowding him off the track. "Oh, it looks like the race marshals are shooing us all off the track. I'll need to give it back to you."

"Yes, indeed." Dennis chuckled as he looked at Kyle on the monitor. "They are clearing the track, which means we will be starting the Monaco Grand Prix in a very few moments. And then it's lights out, and the race will be on," he finished dramatically as the coverage went to yet another commercial.

"Malila, what do they mean by 'lights out'?"

Malila looked at the TV screen. "You can't see it right now, but when they come back to the start have a look. There's an arm of red lights facing the grid, up high enough for all the drivers to see. When it goes dark, the race starts."

The balcony over the pits was empty now that the cars were on the grid; everyone was clustered around the life-size screens that carried the race track footage. The Paddock was truly the best seat in the house; there was nowhere else they could get this much coverage in this much detail. Even Alejo agreed that this was much better than his *Metropole* suite or their *Virage* reservations. Not only that, the sportscasters kept everyone informed in fine fashion. Right now they were announcing the start, the hype in their voices matching everyone's anticipation.

On the grid itself, the noise from the cars was deafening and the screaming crowd was at fever pitch. Taylor looked for the lights at the front of the grid and there they were, a horizontal arm of red lenses that lit up in succession: one, two, three, four, five, and stayed on a full second before all going dark–and twenty-two Formula Ones leaped off their lines.

Taylor touched Michael's ring and reached out to feel him. He hit the throttle hard, hoping to get an early advantage and close in on Kevin Melbourne before the first turn, but while he closed the gap quickly, Melbourne had started those precious few feet ahead of him and was able to take the corner first and speed up *St. Devote* hill. The rest of the cars tore by the camera and were gone in a second, disappearing up the hillside and around the corner. Okay, she told herself, one chance at overtaking Melbourne lost, but there'll be others.

The coverage changed to Casino Square and she watched the pack flash by in a blur of colors. The crowd in the lounge watched the cars take *Mirabeau* and then on to the hairpin turns where they had to slow to a crawl, but after that they accelerated again into the tunnel and out the other side to the chicane and *Tabac* corner. Okay, Taylor thought, next comes *Le Piscine*, the road by the swimming pool, then around *La Rascasse* and back past the pits where they had started, coming around to *St. Devote* again. This is great, she thought, I've got it now. Not so bad.

The first lap finished without any incidents and the announcers took over.

"We're off to a clean start so far," Dennis was telling the audience. "That doesn't always happen, does it, Neville?"

"No, indeed," answered Neville. "And here's a look back at those." He launched into a retrospective of previous Grands Prix where things had gone wrong on the very first lap, entertaining and educating the audience while the next seven laps passed by.

Taylor connected with Michael to see how he was doing. She was struck by something he'd said the night before: "I can't risk the distraction while I'm driving," and now she knew what he had meant. His focus was intense, his concentration hard on every detail he saw and every tiny adjustment he made. After a few laps she was exhausted from shadowing him. I can't do this for the whole race, she realized. Just then she heard Michael's engineer on the radio in his helmet.

"The safety car's out."

"Where?" asked Michael.

"Accident at the tunnel."

Taylor could feel Michael slow down and relax but only a little. When the safety car was out, rules required everyone to stay behind it and keep their positions until the accident was cleared. But that also meant all the cars would close in on the safety car, and the distance Michael had put between him, Jaden, Vince Tenderril, and Raj Hajime would disappear. They'd be right behind him when the caution flag was lifted.

Meanwhile the sportscasters were analyzing slow-motion footage of the accident. The Radcliffe-Royce car had come out of the tunnel and begun to fishtail. It swept wildly from side to side, causing the cars behind him to brake and almost hit each other as they tried to avoid colliding with the swerving Radcliffe-Royce. Just before the chicane it broadsided the safety wall and, luckily, rolled to a stop off to the side while the other cars passed him.

"Well, one down. He's obviously out of the race." Dennis was looking quizzically at the footage. "You know, Neville, I can't really tell why that happened."

"Neither can I," replied Neville, "but it could have started back in the tunnel; you just never really know. We're lucky the others didn't pile up behind him."

"Right," said Dennis. "You can't lose your focus for even a second at these speeds, and we've still got sixty laps to finish. These drivers will need stamina as well as skill to finish this race."

"That's right," Neville said. "And you've really got to be on your toes to negotiate these courses. You can see in this footage how the car shimmies and flexes as they cut the corner at the chicane." He showed a slow-motion replay of the McLaren car as it drove over the wide marker at the edge of the track. Rumble strips built into it allowed drivers to feel where they were, but they also caused the light cars to bounce across it, losing contact with the track and making the car's front airfoil wobble wildly.

"It's amazing they can keep traction while doing that." Alejo was shaking his head as he watched the footage.

Neville and Dennis were very good at entertaining the audience while the safety car was out, and eight laps had gone by quickly when the accident was finally cleaned up and the caution lifted.

As expected, Vince Tenderril and Raj Hajime were both on Michael's rear spoiler and wasted no time jumping on either side of him after the safety car exited, trying to pass before the next turn, but neither one of them was able to get the advantage. Michael stayed in front and pressed the throttle hard to try and put distance between them, but Tenderril and Hajime didn't give an inch. They stayed crammed behind him, constantly trying to pass and vexing Michael with their pressure.

Olivia clenched her teeth. She'd love to throw a spell on Tenderril's car that would push it and give him the win, but she couldn't figure out how without the others knowing. She wished she knew more about this sport and what she could get away with. She'd never cheated before, and it wasn't the money that meant so much to her; it was her burning desire to win, to take everything, to beat others who had bet against her. She'd have to find a way to take other cars out of the race.

A shiver went up her spine. Thinking that way was so brutal, so unlike her. But she was having these attacks of conscience and feelings for others less often. If that was being a Blue/Black, she didn't want any part of it, she tried to tell herself, but something quickly pushed that down. Why fight it? it told her. If you don't feel bad about it, then what's the problem? She could feel herself changing and caring less and less that she was.

Ten more laps went by with no change in the leaders: it was still Kevin Melbourne, Michael Roswell, Vince Tenderril, Raj Hajime, and Jaden Sharpe with the rest of the field behind them. They had just passed *Mirabeau* and dived into the tunnel darkness. The screen switched to an aerial view of the race. The cars came blasting out of the tunnel toward the chicane, a spot on the track that made a quick jog to the left, then right.

"That seems really dangerous to put that there," Taylor said. "Right after the tunnel they have to slam on their brakes."

"That's exactly why it's there," Alejo said. "To slow them down so the race doesn't get too fast."

"What? I don't understand." Taylor was still looking at the screen.

Malila answered. "What if they left it straight all the way to *Tabac* corner? That's a ninety-degree turn and they'd be almost at two hundred miles an hour. In fact, accidents used to happen there all the time until they put up the safety barriers. Before that drivers would crash into whatever was there–buildings, trees, even the harbor a couple times."

"You're kidding!" Taylor had grown up a world where nearly everything was padded, stickered with warnings, or restricted for safety. She stared at the screen, open-mouthed as she watched.

"Two hundred miles an hour..." she repeated. It was a shocking speed.

As if on cue, Hajime slowed down for the chicane, then accelerated hard toward *Tabac*. He rounded the corner but his timing was off and he drifted into a long sliding skid, pivoting in slow-motion as he scraped along the rail. Rubber stripped off the tires as he tore down the track, leaving a raft of bluish smoke in his wake. He impacted the wall and the car exploded in a burst of carbon-fiber and titanium parts.

Directly in front of the grandstand filled with people.

Behind the protective chain-link fence, spectators ducked reflexively, then stood back up to see the aftermath, which included a two-foot piece of suspension that had impaled itself in the safety fence right in front of them.

"Well," said Olivia dryly, "now you know where *Le Piscine* avenue is, too. He just crashed on it." She was pointed to the street running along the harbor. "I'm surprised those billionaires dock their yachts so close to the action, but I guess if you can afford a yacht, you can afford repair bills."

As the rest of the cars whipped by the decimated F1 the witches overheard a spectator turn to her partner. "I'll bet he lost traction because of all the graining."

"Graining? What's that?" Taylor turned to Alejo.

"See all those black bits on the road?" he said. "They look like gravel?"

"Yes." Taylor nodded.

"They're pieces of tire. When they corner so hard, little bits tear off the rubber and spread across the track. They'll make you lose traction just like gravel will."

"Is Hajime okay?" Malila was focused on the wreckage. "Oh never mind. I see him getting out on his own."

Once again the yellow flag came out and cars bunched up behind the safety car. They saw Melbourne and Roswell in the middle of them.

Olivia was irritated. "Why are cars in front of them? I thought they were the leaders." She pressed her lips together, scowling. "In fact, where are Tenderril and Jaden? Oh. Never mind. I see them a couple cars back."

Alejo answered her. "They're catching up to the slowest ones, lapping them."

Olivia nodded but didn't reply. She seemed anxious, her knee bouncing up and down under the table as if she had nervous energy to burn and couldn't wait for the action to start again. She is acting strange, that's for sure, Alejo thought.

"Are you doing okay, Livy?"

Olivia looked at him blankly and then nodded yes, dismissing him with silence and going back to fidgeting.

Okay, thought Alejo, that's it. I'm done with this. She's hardly spoken to me since that night at her house, and I'm not going to put up with it. After the race tonight I'm sitting her down to settle this one way or the other. She either loves me back or she doesn't, and if she doesn't we'll decide what to do, but this business of acting strangely and ignoring me is *la mierda*. Bullshit.

He stood up. "I'm going to grab a scotch. Do you want to come with me?" he invited Malila. They'd been keeping their distance from each other but right now he didn't care.

Malila smiled up at him from across the table and lifted an eyebrow. "I'd better not, Alejandro."

Alejo smiled back at her. "Stop it. I'm sure we can get to the bar and back without any mishaps."

"Oh, I don't know about that." Malila smiled at him coyly. Alejo made himself ignore his thoughts about her and his desire to get her alone right now.

"You might be right. Do you want me to bring you back anything?"

"I would love a glass of white wine, thank you."

"Taylor?" He smiled affectionately at her.

"Oh! No, thank you, Alejo." Taylor smiled at him as she shook her head and then went back to the race.

"Olivia?" Alejo turned his attention to her. She only shook her head without looking at him.

"I'll be right back." He walked over to the bar, got his scotch and a chardonnay for Malila and brought them back, sitting down and vowing to ignore his annoyance with Olivia until he and she had hashed it out.

By this time the race was back on and Kevin Melbourne had already lapped more of the cars in the field, pulling ahead and gaining lead time on Michael every second there was still a car between them. Taylor could feel Michael's frustration–and his determination to catch up and pass Melbourne.

Once again, cars had bunched up at *Mirabeau* and this time Michael was able to get around them on the outside. The witches knew he could take steep chances because he had preternatural reflexes, but he was still human and he could push only so far without using magic. He had to work to win because Melbourne was every bit as good–and he was mortal, not witch.

The group of cars accelerated out of *Mirabeau* and spread out, but the next minute they all arrived at the two hairpin turns and had to brake sharply. Cars usually took the turn wide to maintain a little more speed, but Michael leaned heavily on his steering wheel to cut the corner tighter than the car ahead of him and he came around first, passing on the inside and accelerating deep into the straight stretch just before the tunnel. He was chasing hard now, directly behind Kevin Melbourne.

At this point, attention was on Michael and his camera feed came up on the screen. Taylor caught her breath, seeing that he came within inches of the left-hand wall of the tunnel at over a hundred and twenty miles an hour. Then he shot out of it, going from darkness into blinding sunlight at the same speed.

Behind him, Sharpe and Tenderril hit their accelerators hard through the tunnel, passing the others in a terrifying run through the dark and now were right behind both of the leaders. They came out at breakneck speed, headed straight for the chicane. No one wanted to slow down.

Melbourne cut the chicane close and battered across the washboard of rumble strips at nearly full speed, a teeth-jarring move that launched the aerodynamic car into the air, covering a good thirty feet before it hit the ground hard, flinging a piece of something unknown off in one direction. The other three followed to almost the same effect, both Sharpe and Tenderril landing slightly askew and raising puffs of blue smoke as their tires skidded for a millisecond. Then they corrected and hit the accelerator again, coming up fast on *Tabac* corner as they chased the two leaders.

"Good Lord!" shouted Dennis into his microphone. "These four are out of their minds." He watched open-mouthed as the drivers braked hard to negotiate *Tabac* corner and then headed down *Le Piscine*. Dennis turned to Neville.

"I can't believe they made that turn!" He caught himself and calmed down a little, struggling to regain his professional tone. "Well, obviously this is a true rivalry. They're taking some awful chances and that's saying something for an F1 race." Dennis rubbed his palms together nervously.

Neville took over for Dennis. "They're going to have to pit soon; their tires have got to be degrading by now. That should give us all a quick breather."

"Yes, they all know they need fresh ones, but the question is," said Dennis, "who's willing to stop first? Let's listen in on the radio conversations."

They could hear the engineers on the radio talking to their drivers, relaying telemetry and advising next steps.

The Whitestone engineer was talking to Tenderril. "Vince, your left front tire reads low pressure and your air intake is down three percent. You need to come in."

"What's Melbourne got on me?" Tenderril wanted to know.

"Four point six ahead of you."

"I'll come in when he does."

"Vince, you're going to keep losing speed if you don't pit."

"Not until one of the other four do."

"We advise against it." The engineer's words were neutral, but the tone was not. They were telling him to come in and pit.

"Damn it!" Vince bit off the words. "You just tell me when the others come in. I'll decide when to pit!" There was no reply from Whitestone.

Jaden was talking with his engineer, too. "Anyone else coming in?"

"No, but Tenderril's speed is degrading. He may have issues."

"Best advice?" Jaden asked.

"This lap. Roswell and Melbourne haven't been in yet so you'll have new and they won't."

"Understood." Jaden would pit this time around for new tires and hope they would gain him enough speed to pass Tenderril and then catch the leaders. He was behind Tenderill by only half a second and couldn't believe his luck when he saw the Whitestone car pass by the pit exit. That meant he couldn't come in until the next lap. Jaden pulled into pit lane, and six seconds later was coming back on the track with brand-new treads. He could feel the difference already, noting his speed was up and he could take corners faster. Now the others would have to come in or risk falling behind. His strategy had worked. He was ahead of Tenderril by three seconds and closing in on the leaders.

The Whitestone engineer's voice was in Tenderril's ear. "Sharpe in and out."

"What? He was right behind me!"

Melbourne and Roswell were informed that Sharpe had pitted. Since they were just coming up on the pit lane, they entered for new tires as well.

Whitestone was in Tenderril's ear again. "Roswell and Melbourne coming in." It took scant seconds to switch tires. "And now going out."

Vince knew he had missed a huge opportunity through his stubbornness. Now he was on the opposite end of the course. On slow tires.

"Goddamnit!" He shouted into the radio.

Back at Whitestone, the two engineers smirked at each other, enjoying the moment and thinking that Vince deserved what he got. He really could be a dick.

Eight laps left in the race, and Olivia was twisting inside. This was getting worse and worse, she thought. Melbourne still in front, then Roswell right on his ass, and Sharpe only two seconds later. How in the hell am I going to win this thing?

The four leaders were still pushing hard but were very aware they were low on fuel. Faster speed always sucked more gas, and the worst possible scenario was to run out before the finish. Radio communication from engineers to their drivers was constant now as they gave them the fastest possible speed to maintain while restricting fuel consumption. The calculation should take them to the very edge of empty at the finish line. It was nerve-wracking for everyone.

Taylor could feel Michael was on the edge, constantly strategizing and looking for an advantage at high speed, watching the road, watching his rpm, and all the time there was the possibility of a crash. It was complex and invigorating and mesmerizing. Suddenly Taylor understood why he loved it so much.

For the second time, they were coming up on the main group of cars and lapping them. By now everyone knew of the showdown and moved out of the way to give them wide berth as the four flew past them. Melbourne and Roswell were keeping their lead with Sharpe and Tenderril three seconds behind.

In the last lap they floored it, knowing it was all-or-nothing this time around. It would be *St. Devote* to *Mirabeau*, the hairpins, the tunnel, then *Tabac*, *Le Piscine*, tight *La Rascasse* corner, and then the sweeping curve to the finish line.

The four leaders were now far ahead of the rest, screaming up *St. Devote* hill to the Casino.

Sharpe was gaining on Roswell and Melbourne, but it wasn't easy. Monaco didn't give many options to pass, and was even less forgiving of mistakes while trying. Tenderril was driving like a wild man as he tried to close the gap between him and Sharpe, coming within millimeters of the wall and barely making the Casino turns.

Kevin Melbourne looked in his rearview mirror to see Michael Roswell matching his every move. I've got to keep him behind me, he thought, calculating all the spots where a pass could happen. Roswell was known for passing cars in the turns, either inside or outside, Melbourne knew. He didn't dare drift the turn to block him; the tires were too sticky and the car too light. Drifting an F1 was asking to crash. He'd have to give up speed and stay right in the middle to prevent Michael from passing. If he could.

Mirabeau was now directly ahead of them. Melbourne stayed in the center, away from the wall but not too far, trying to maintain speed. Roswell came up on the inside, trying to force him away from the wall but the leader wouldn't budge, even when Michael's front tire touched Kevin's back one, making a screeching sound. Barely inches from each other, the two ripped around the corner and into the hairpins beyond.

"What is he doing?" Neville's mouth was agape. "I can't believe the nerve of these two. Any closer, any faster at all, and there's an accident to be had."

Dennis agreed. "Michael Roswell's going to get a penalty if he does that again. Oh, look, they're going into the tunnel–and now Vince Tenderril and Jaden Sharpe have closed in on them."

The video feed showed Tenderril's view of the three cars ahead of him, bunched tightly together in the tunnel as they hurtled through and blazed out the other side.

Again they chattered across the chicane barrier, all four closer together than before and nearly piling up as they came off the rumble strip and headed toward *Tabac* corner. A shocked gasp came from the crowd in the Paddock followed by silence. No one wanted to miss a moment of this showdown. Silent amazement was the only reaction when they made it around *Tabac* intact.

The four shot through *Le Piscine* at a scorching pace, still close together. No one was able to get the advantage on the others, and Olivia was furious about it. Tenderril was fourth. Fourth! For chrissakes, how humiliating to have boasted his win in front of everyone and then come up short. This wouldn't do, but she didn't know how to change it. She watched them come around *Le Rascasse*, just before the long broad curve to the finish line.

"No!" she shouted, causing everyone to look at her in surprise. And then Olivia saw the graining at *La Rascasse*. Clenching her fists, she conjured quickly, flashing a cluster of them from *Rascasse* to the track just ahead of Melbourne, feeling immense satisfaction when he hit them and started to fishtail.

Roswell was so close to Melbourne that he couldn't brake quickly enough and at such high speed, he collided with Melbourne's back tire. The sticky rubber pulled Michael's car up and over as it turned, crunching his rear spoiler and launching both F1's into the air.

Melbourne's car flipped and came down hard on its top, skidding across the finish line and grinding parts, metal, and protective gear away as it slid. Michael's cartwheeled end over end, coming to rest five hundred feet down the track in a trail of shattered parts.

Taylor screamed, unable to help herself. Calm down, she thought. You have your ring. See how he's doing. She closed her eyes and tried to connect with him.

Tenderril and Sharpe hit their brakes as they plowed through the wreckage, but Jaden didn't stop until he got to Michael. There he jerked to a halt and jumped out, running over to his friend's obliterated F1.

Back at the finish line, Melbourne's car had come to rest and the safety marshals were already swarming it, trying to see Melbourne's condition. The crowd grew quiet as they waited for a sign that he was all right. Down the street, another group of spectators had clustered along the barrier to watch Jaden as he tried to reach Michael in the wreckage.

Taylor had her eyes closed, concentrating hard. She could feel Michael but just barely. He was so faint and far away she could hardly feel him at all. And he was getting fainter all the time. She had the sudden, hollow realization that she was feeling him die.

She opened her eyes to look at the screen, where she could see Jaden had wedged himself under the wreckage, stretching his arm through the mangled cage to try and reach Michael.

"No," she whispered. "Please." She closed her eyes again.

In the Paddock, everything was silent. People simply watched and hoped. Alejo noticed Taylor's stricken look and put his arm around her while they waited, watching Jaden's efforts with the others.

He can't even feel me, thought Taylor. I can't tell him he's leaving us. The urge to shout to Michael, to tell him "come back" was overpowering, but she felt helpless. Her heart dropped as she realized: I can't even tell him goodbye. She felt numb, dully replaying her memories of their last few weeks until she realized Alejo was shaking her, trying to get her attention. She opened her eyes to Alejo pointing at the screen.

"Look," he said. The camera had zoomed in tight on Michael and Jaden. Jaden had a grip on Michael's gloved hand.

Taylor touched her ring again, reaching out. Michael was still there. And so was Jaden, with him. It took her a second to understand what was happening, but then she could tell Jaden was infusing Michael with energy to bring him back. Taylor could feel him waking up ... and then the pain started. It was excruciating, the agony engulfing his entire body. She could feel that Michael had massive injuries, and until they were fixed by Jaden they hurt like hell. It was all Taylor could do not to scream with him.

She started to cry. "Alejo, he's so badly hurt."

Alejo held her tighter, trying to bolster her. "*Quedarse con él, sobrinita.* Stay with him. It won't take long."

After a long minute the torment began to ebb, and the first normal thing she felt was Jaden's hand gripping Michael's. Then slowly she felt him emerge from the pain and realize where he was. He couldn't move, though. He was pinned by the car and too weak to move it; he was completely drained of his powers.

"Jaden," he croaked, "get this fucking thing off me."

Taylor almost cried from relief.

Everyone in the Paddock was glued to the image of Jaden tipping the mangled car off his friend and pulling him out of the wreckage. A few spectators clapped, but then remembered there was still an unconscious Melbourne in the other car. Everyone watched quietly as Kevin was extracted and put into the ambulance to be taken to Princess Grace Hospital.

After that, speculation buzzed around what had happened. Dennis and Neville were giving what little information they had, but their dramatic manner was much more subdued than their earlier broadcast. There was no need for it; the situation was serious, not festive. They replayed footage from the accident, commenting on the graining that shouldn't have been in that spot on the road, and then relayed the announcement that the winner would not be determined until a thorough investigation was done.

"Goddamn it," Olivia said disgustedly. "Can I not get a break? When will we find out who won this thing?"

Malila and Alejo turned to stare at her for the second time in ten minutes and not just because of her callous comment.

Olivia had shouted earlier, and was talking now, in Dantin's voice.

Alejo turned an angry face toward Olivia, trying to decide if he had heard her insensitive comment correctly. Malila knew he had no idea what was going on, but whatever it was, he was about to do something about it. She'd have to control this, she realized, and stepped between him and Olivia.

"Alejo, Taylor's had quite a scare—could you take her to find Michael? I'm sure she needs to see him in person. He'll want to see her, too, but he'll be busy with the marshals and Sagenhaft. Start with Jaden; he can get you to Michael."

Alejo jerked his gaze away from Olivia to focus on Taylor. "Yes, you are probably right."

"What's going on?" asked Taylor. She could tell Malila and Alejo, were concerned with Olivia but wasn't sure why, although she could tell Olivia wasn't herself. In fact, Olivia now looked as dazed as she felt.

Malila didn't take her eyes off Olivia. "Taylor, Alejo is taking you to Michael. I'm staying with Livy."

"Okay." Taylor was grateful for the escort.

"We'll call you both later." Alejo said, taking a last look at Olivia before placing his palm in the small of Taylor's back to guide her out of the lounge where they could disappear unobserved.

Malila took Olivia's arm harshly. "What the fuck is wrong with you, doing that in public?"

Olivia didn't answer. Malila knew she could be talking to either Dantin or Olivia at this moment, but there was no way to know which until she could get her alone. Still holding Olivia's arm tightly, Malila steered her through the crowd of Club members and as soon as they were out of sight she flashed them both to her suite at the *Hermitage.*

Once they were alone, Malila pushed Olivia onto the couch in her sitting room. Olivia still looked dazed, but Malila knew Dantin was in there somewhere. He would be suspicious, of course. He wouldn't show himself until he was sure of her intent. Malila stood over Olivia and folded her arms, eyeing the other witch closely.

"Tell me about the race, Olivia."

"I made a bet on Tenderril." Olivia said dully. It was her own voice now that came out, but Malila was still careful.

"Yes. And?"

"I don't know what happened. I mean, I don't know what will happen with the bet. I don't know who won."

"So, the bet is the most important thing to you?" This was sounding more like Dantin all the time, Malila thought, but then Olivia looked up at Malila with wide eyes and whispered the next sentence.

"I made that accident happen." She was horrified. "Oh, my God."

Malila was still stepping carefully. "Yes, you caused the accident. So what? You had to win that bet, right?"

"Yes, but ... No ... No, I didn't have to win. Especially not like that." Olivia's brow furrowed as she fought the dark thoughts welling up. Malila kept pressing her.

"Then why did you do it? Why did you kill Michael and maybe Melbourne, too?" She was purposely brutal with Olivia, trying to make her rattled so she could get the truth out of her.

Dantin would pretend he was Olivia until he was sure he had the edge. He'd made a mistake in letting his voice come out at the race, but he wouldn't repeat it.

Olivia was absorbing what Malila had just said. "I killed Michael?" She was shaking her head. "Oh, no. Michael...and Taylor." She put her head in her hands. "Oh, my God," she repeated.

"Oh, come on, Olivia. Quit acting so weak. What is going on with you?" Malila hoped that her tack would either piss Dantin off and draw him out or get Olivia off balance, get her to tell everything she knew. Maybe she'd even admit she was Blue/Black. Then Malila had a thought– what if Olivia didn't know about her blood tint? Was she even aware of Dantin?

Olivia didn't say anything for several long moments. Then abruptly, she lifted her head and threw an accusation at Malila.

"Wait a minute. You're no better, saying, 'you caused the accident, so what?' How can you say that and take it so lightly?" Olivia was indignant.

Malila wouldn't be distracted. She continued to press.

"I'm not the one who caused it, Olivia. You are. I'm trying to find out what you really are."

She leaned in close to Olivia, her eyes intense. "You act more like a Blue/Black than a Silver-Tint," she finished confidently.

Olivia felt the blood drain from her face. Somehow Malila knew. The name Blue/Black said aloud was a challenge hanging in the air between them. Hearing it stated so confidently by Malila seemed to demand an answer.

Neither said anything for several long seconds. Olivia was thinking hard. If she already knows about my blood-tint, she thought, than why don't I just say it? It would be a relief. I can't stand being alone with my secret anymore, and things certainly can't get any worse. Still, she couldn't bring herself to say the words.

Suddenly Malila grabbed Olivia's wrist. "I'm losing my patience with you, Olivia." She knew that was a risk, knowing Dantin's temper, but she needed to break this stalemate.

"Okay. I'm turning dark!" Olivia stood up, face to face with Malila as she defiantly spit out the words. "I killed someone and now I'm turning Blue/Black!" Then she lost momentum as she realized what she'd admitted.

She lowered her voice again. "My blood's turning dark." She finished the sentence flatly. "Blue/Black."

Malila dropped Livy's wrist. "Well," she said dryly, "that was a little dramatic, don't you think, Olivia?"

"What?" Olivia was unprepared for that response.

"Is that all? You're turning Blue/Black?"

Olivia was completely confused. "Isn't that enough?"

"It's not the end of the world, Olivia." Malila was infuriatingly blasé.

Olivia bristled. "How can you take it so lightly? Blue/Blacks are vicious, jealous, destructive–I don't want to be one! I'd rather die!"

Malila was pretty sure she had her answer now; she was talking to Olivia. Dantin could be sneaky, but he was submerged right now for whatever reason, and that was exactly what Malila needed. She kept Olivia talking.

"I don't believe you're Blue/Black. Prove it. Show me your blood." She conjured a blade and gave it to Olivia, who snatched it from her and sliced her palm, letting the blue-tinged red well up. She held out the hand that was now filling with blood.

"Proof enough?"

Malila bent over Olivia's hand and took a look, then sliced her own palm the same way. She showed it to Olivia.

"Like this?"

Olivia's stared at the blood in disbelief. She pulled Malila's palm to her own, gauging the two colors. It was clear they were the same.

"I don't understand. You're not a Blue/Black. You don't act like one at all."

"Well, not completely. There's Silver there, too, same as yours. Look."

For another long minute Olivia stared closely at the two pools of blood. They were identical.

"You see it, don't you?" Malila said, angling her hand to show how the color changed with the light. "Both Silver-Tint and Blue/Black."

Olivia couldn't grasp what Malila was showing her. "I don't understand."

"I'm both and so are you." Malila stepped closer to Olivia. "Livy, we can control the Blue/Black urges."

Olivia backed away, shaking her head in confusion. "No. That makes no sense at all."

"Olivia, we're the same."

"No." Olivia said firmly. "If you knew how horrible Blue/Blacks are..." She was thinking of Dantin.

"Olivia, I do! I was born into a Blue/Black family; their whole circle is Blue/Black. I've had to hide my Silver-Tint for nine hundred years. Can you imagine what they'd do to me if they found out?"

"But you've been with Alejo and Taylor and me. We're Silver." Livy was more confused by the second.

"I have my reasons," Malila responded.

"But what if some Blue/Blacks saw you with us?"

"Well, I've had to be careful. Very careful."

"Malila, why weren't you just honest with us?"

"Why weren't you honest with Taylor and Alejo and JaneAnn about turning, Olivia? They're your closest friends."

Olivia had no answer to that. She stood still, finally letting Malila grasp her hand and heal the cut on her palm.

Malila went on. "Of course I couldn't tell any Silver-Tints. Or Blue/Blacks. I couldn't tell anyone–no way in hell."

I couldn't tell anyone, either, Olivia answered her silently. Those were exactly the same thoughts Olivia had struggled with for the last six months. Maybe Malila did know what she

was going through. And for nine hundred years–
Olivia couldn't imagine. But she shook her head.

"No. You Blue/Blacks are all liars. It's one of
the things you're proudest of–the skill of
deception. I don't trust you." She was poised to
disappear and then remembered Malila's blood.

"I want to see your blood again. This time I'll
use the knife. No trickery."

Malila held out the knife.

"No," said Olivia, "I'll use my own." She
conjured a blade. "Turn around."

"What?"

"Turn around." Olivia said firmly.

Malila hesitated. Everything in her screamed
not to trust Olivia. She swallowed hard and
turned around, her back now to the other witch
who held a blade in her hand. She closed her
eyes, waiting.

Olivia considered where to cut. It would have
to be unexpected, and she'd need to do it fast.
She paused for several long seconds, knowing it
would make Malila less prepared.

Swiftly she sliced Malila's neck just under the
jaw, opening a florid gash. The bluish-red,
almost purple blood flowed down Malila's neck.
With a sheen of silver. Olivia felt her knees go
weak.

Malila turned back to Olivia. "Well?"

"I can't believe you exposed yourself like that." Olivia reached out to Malila's neck and ran her fingers over the cut to heal it.

"Olivia, letting you do that was more convincing than anything I could say. I've got to tell you, though, I was scared. You act more like a Blue/Black every day."

Olivia looked at Malila, with whom she'd spent every day for the last three weeks and hadn't seen a glimmer of cruelty. The woman who's been so nice to Taylor. The woman Alejo has known for centuries.

"Does Alejo know?"

"Oh! Gods, no. I don't dare tell him."

"And you know I haven't, either. In my world you're either one or the other. In or out."

"Mine, too," said Malila.

Olivia looked at the blade she still held with its trace of blood. "Mixed. I've never even heard of that before."

Malila took Olivia's hand in her own. "Olivia, I've been waiting for you a long time. We're the only two I've ever heard of with both kinds of blood-tint. I can teach you how to master it, I swear. Please, please trust me."

Olivia shot a hopeful look at Malila, and then her face fell. "Oh, no..."

"What?"

"I killed Michael, and maybe Kevin. Oh, Jesus," she put a hand to her mouth, "Kevin's a mortal."

That made it worse; mortals without powers couldn't defend themselves. For a Silver-Tint, protecting the weak and not abusing their power were cardinal rules–and karma punished disobedience severely.

Malila waved away her concern. "No, it's okay; Michael's all right. I said that to prod you out of your daze. But Kevin is at the hospital. I have no idea what condition he's in."

"Jaden and Michael can get in there and help him."

"I hate to give you bad news, Livy, but both their powers are pretty drained right now. You almost did kill Michael, and Jaden had to bring him back. They won't be hot again for a week."

"Oh, hell. I have to do it, then. I need Jaden to get me into Kevin's room."

"Absolutely not. Olivia, you can't control yourself yet. You hardly even knew where you were today." She hoped Olivia would assume that was because of the dark blood. She had no idea yet how to tell Olivia that Dantin was possessing her, let alone how to handle her when she found out.

Olivia was still thinking of how to help Kevin. "You'll have to use Alejo or Taylor, then. I hate to do that to her, but she went through worse with Dantin's chimera last year."

Malila knew about the chimera episode because Dantin had told her, but she didn't tell Olivia. "We should use Taylor, then; she's not as recognizable as Alejo, and Michael's circle already likes her. We'll need to tell her somehow. We can scry her location and then send her a talisman."

Olivia started laughing.

"What's so funny?" asked Malila.

"Malila, she's nineteen. Just text her."

"Oh! Duh, of course. Is she up to it? The Kevin thing, I mean."

"Malila, you'd be surprised at how powerful she is. I'll text her right now." Olivia pulled out her phone and began tapping away.

Malila was deciding what to do next, now that she had gained Olivia's confidence. Obviously Olivia had no clue about Dantin as yet, and Malila still had no idea how to separate them. She knew Dantin would expect her allegiance to him; she'd been with him a long time. Whatever she did, she'd better do it now. She was framing her next sentence carefully, deciding how to tell Olivia about Dantin as she watched the other witch finish her text and put the iPhone away.

"Olivia, there's something else." Malila had a pang of guilt as Olivia turned her now-trusting face toward her. When Olivia saw Malila's serious expression her feeling of dread returned.

"Oh, what now? What could possibly make this worse?" She really didn't want to hear the answer.

"Have you…" Malila didn't know how to proceed. Just say it, she told herself. "I think Dantin–you were talking in Dantin's voice at the race."

Olivia froze. So many thoughts ran through her head that she was completely overwhelmed and couldn't speak for a moment. Then the full meaning hit her.

"No…." She shook her head slowly. "Tell me you're joking." Malila had to hold her up as her knees buckled.

"Here. Sit down." Malila got Olivia seated and sat down beside her. How in the hell am I going to comfort her? she thought. I don't even know myself what to do about her situation. Then she stopped cold at the way Olivia was looking at her. Olivia was glaring at Malila through narrowed eyes, malice clear in her stare.

Dantin was back in the room.

CATHLEEN DUNN

"Clever, aren't you, getting close to Olivia...what I can't figure out is: how did you know it was me?" Olivia's voice was pitched lower, rough, masculine in timbre. It took all of Malila's nerve not to shiver at the sound.

"Hello, Dantin."

"Here to rescue me or are you glad I'm gone?"

"I was planning on getting a few secrets out of her and then killing her on your behalf–until you turned up. What other reason could there be for me to get close to Olivia?" Malila was hoping that Dantin was such a narcissist he'd believe this was mostly about him.

The look in Olivia's eyes was malevolent. "That's quite a story you told her about wanting to be friends, now that she's turned. I know everything she does, of course, which means I know everything you do. I don't trust you, Malila."

"Of course. But how else was I supposed to make her trust me? I was planning a horrible death for her, but then I stumbled across you in there, and that certainly put a change to my plans. I think you're the reason her blood is mixed now, but Locke is finding a way to separate you from her."

"No need. I like where I am."

"You can't stay in there with her, Dantin; it will kill you both. Besides, you're half Silver-Tint now. That makes you weaker than you were in your own body."

Dantin didn't reply and Malila could see in the eyes he was considering what she said. She pressed her point.

"Wouldn't you rather be in a Blue/Black? I could find you a powerful witch, or one that has enhanced their power with additional essences." Blue/Blacks were known for killing other witches to consume their powers; Dantin himself had done it hundreds of times.

Dantin was silent as he thought that over. Then he reached out swiftly, grabbing Malila by the throat before she could avoid him. He augmented his grip with magic so she couldn't break away and put his cheek against hers, his voice rasping in Malila's ear.

"Nothing has changed. I'm still here, one way or the other. I control Olivia and like before, I can tell your little Silver-Tint secret to every Blue/Black that exists. You don't have enough powers to keep them all off you. Not even Locke could protect you," he said as grey haze filled the room and Malila's necromancer appeared. Dantin kept his hold on Malila as he spoke.

"Keep your distance, demi-god. I still own the entrapment spell, and I'm the only one who can unlock it. You touch me, and Malila will suffer sevenfold."

Locke seethed with fury but kept his distance. He couldn't take action without hurting Malila while Dantin had them both ensorcelled. In addition, he couldn't hurt Dantin without hurting Olivia. With burning eyes he watched Dantin sharply, waiting for an opening he could take advantage of, but he knew Dantin, as usual, held all the cards.

Dantin was a bastard of the highest degree. He found weaknesses and exploited them, gathered information and blackmail fodder, bartered or stole unusual powers, and then used it all mercilessly against everyone. In the Blue/Black community he was both reviled and adored. It was the highest compliment.

Dantin still had Olivia's cheek against Malila's and Olivia's voice, tainted with his own, filled Malila's ear.

"As much as I love being inside Olivia," he chuckled thickly at his double-entendre, "I think I'll just use her up. Then I'll find flesh of my own to inhabit for the next several centuries. But until then, now that I know everything about her, I am going to own this bitch. She won't like it, not at all … and that makes my victory sweeter. If she doesn't bend to my desires, I know exactly what will scald her until she does. Oh, I'm going to love dominating her and abusing her body."

At this point Malila gathered her thoughts; time to reassure Dantin of her pure intentions and get out of this chokehold she was in.

"Dantin, no one likes to be blackmailed but of course we all do it to each other; after all, we're Blue/Blacks. You just do it better than the rest of us. So whether you believe me or not, I got close to Olivia because I heard she was the one who made you disappear. I wanted to see if she got the key to the entrapment spell from you and if so, I planned to take it from her and then kill her. We can't let a Silver-Tint get away with killing a Blue/Black, now can we?"

There, she thought, he should believe that. He would know it was a lie if she said she was going to avenge him after all he'd put her through for the last four hundred years.

Dantin considered that, but he didn't change the pressure on her throat. "Nonetheless, I don't need you to find me a witch to possess. I can do that myself now that I know how. I did it with Olivia, and I can do it again."

He had a sudden burst of realization. "Oh, this is marvelous," he laughed. "If I don't like where I'm at, or pile up problems, I can simply switch bodies. No one will know who I am if I don't want them to. Oh, my God, I could make Olivia everyone's enemy and then abandon her to them." He was practically sparkling with glee. Then he looked at Malila suspiciously.

"How did you know about her blood?"

Malila tried to act nonchalant. "Dantin, everyone suspects that she killed you. I wanted to see if the legend was true; that Silver-Tints turn when they kill for revenge, so I acquired her blood. I only found out about you when I spied on her."

That seemed to satisfy Dantin. He loosened his grip but then tightened it again.

"I might look like Olivia but nothing has changed. I still hold leverage over you and Locke."

Malila shrugged, still feigning unconcern. "The same as it's been for four hundred years. It's no big deal, Dantin; I'm used to it by now." As soon as she said the last sentence she regretted it; the thing Dantin loved most was when people feared him. He drew back and slapped her, a brutal backhand that cracked through the room when it hit her, knocking her to the floor.

"You don't ever say "it's no big deal" to me!" He was nearly burning with rage as he stood over her. "And you, demon–stay right there," he said, pointing at Locke.

It was all Locke could do to hold himself in check, and Dantin could feel his hate scorching the room and prickling across his skin. He laughed at the Necromancer's fury.

"Oh, how I love this. You're a demi-god and I'm just a witch. And yet you can't touch me."

He looked down at the subdued and unconscious Malila. "I'll see you later, you weak bitch. Count on it." He disappeared from the room.

Locke was immediately at her side, tending to the bruises that were already forming and surrounding her as closely as he could. Locke threw his head back and roared in frustration. It was agonizing not to be able to protect her, or touch her, or comfort her. Using magic, he healed the broken cheekbone and suspended her in a cocoon of his warmth.

He considered waking her, knowing she'd want to go help Olivia, but he delayed. Let her escape her concerns and fears in sleep, he thought, just for a short time while I watch over her.

The sun was an hour lower in the sky when Malila awoke. She was still drowsy at first, and it took a few seconds to orient herself and recount the day.

Locke was miserable, knowing her plight and his helplessness. "My love, I am so sorry."

Malila reached up to caress his cheek, knowing full well neither could feel it, but the gesture comforted them both.

"There is no blame, Locke; we're both in the same trap." Malila was patient with him, reassuring him of her affection, but then she turned anxious.

"Locke, we'd better find Alejo and the others quickly. I can't help Olivia on my own."

"I found them already for you. They're at Princess Grace Hospital." He showed her the exact location.

"Can you try to find Olivia? I'll be back as quickly as possible with Alejo."

"Of course," Locke nodded. Then he added as Malila postured to disappear, "I hope for all of us that Alejo is the Silver-Tint you think he is."

Malila found Alejo and the others at the hospital where Kevin Melbourne was in intensive care.

"How is he?" she asked Jaden.

"Melbourne's doing fine. They're calling it a near-miracle. Right now they can't figure out how they could have misdiagnosed him with critical injuries at first, because he's expected to be out of ICU after only one night of observation. Taylor's a hell of a witch for an apprentice."

Alejo came over to them. "Where's Olivia?" He looked anxious.

"She's in my hotel suite. She doesn't feel well." Malila stepped away from Alejo. She didn't need her accursed infatuation spell interfering with them right now. Although she needed to take Alejo with her as fast as possible, she was concerned about the others.

"And how are you, Michael?" she asked as Michael and Taylor came up to them.

"To be honest," said Michael, "I feel like I have a massive fricking hangover. I imagine you feel the same way, buddy." He bumped a fist with Jaden. "Thanks, man."

Jaden shrugged in response, but the message was clear; they would both go the distance for their friendship.

Michael put his arm proudly around Taylor's waist. "You should have seen her, Malila. She managed to get a moment with Melbourne's trauma surgeon and pulled all the information she needed from him by just a touch on his arm. Then we slipped into invisible mode, visited Kevin in triage, and she went to work. I've never seen anything so slick."

Taylor smiled humbly. "Well, I can't take total credit. Olivia and Alejo taught me that little skill over brunch one morning."

Michael looked around them. "Where is Olivia, anyway?"

"Back at my place." Malila said. She fixed a pointed look at Alejo. "Alejandro, I need you to come back with me. Now." She left no doubt that the problem was serious, and private. Taylor picked up on her cue.

"Alejo, I'll stay here with Michael until we know Kevin's all right. You can catch me up later."

"*Gracias, niña.*" He turned and left with Malila. When they got to Malila's suite, Alejo looked around for Olivia.

"Where is she?" he asked. Then it hit him; he and Malila were alone together for the first time in days. Unbidden, he felt the warmth travel up his thighs to his belly and he had to restrict himself from reaching for her. He shook his head and stepped away from her, trying to ignore it.

"Malila, where's Olivia? You said she was here in your suite."

Malila took a deep breath. I'll start with the worst part, she thought, and just blurt it out.

"Alejandro, Olivia's not here. Dantin took her."

"That's impossible, Malila; he's dead. I watched her kill him." Then he realized what he'd revealed to Malila. *Mierda*, he thought.

"Alejo, he was right here, in Olivia's body. I spoke to him."

Alejo didn't believe her. "That's not possible. What do you know of Dantin, anyway? Why would you assume that it's him?"

"Alejo, every Silver-Tint or Blue/Black knows about him." Malila tried to avoid revealing her connection with Dantin.

Alejo was looking at her suspiciously. "But we didn't tell anyone what happened. How could you possibly make that connection?"

Malila tried to turn the conversation back on him. "You told me she killed him, so I assumed..."

"No, I only just said it now, and the first thing you said to me was that Dantin took her."

"Alejo, since you admitted she was the one who got rid of him, I'll tell you what I think. I think he stayed with her when she killed him. After all, hasn't she been acting different lately? More sarcastic and standoffish?"

"But Malila, what does that have to do with..." he lost his train of thought. It was nearly impossible to think when he was alone with her, and he didn't like it. He also didn't like that she was being evasive, and it was not her usual independence. She was working very hard to keep something a secret.

He stepped farther away from her to try and clear his head. He was getting fed up with the layers of secrets between all three of them, Olivia included. He was fed up with Olivia being unpleasant to him, fed up with feeling led around by his lust for Malila, and most of all, fed up with feeling stupid for revealing his feelings to Olivia. And where was Olivia, anyway? And how did Malila fit into all this?

Bullshit, he thought. I don't have the inclination or the patience for any of this. He clenched his fists, trying to keep his voice low.

"Malila, whatever it is you're trying to do here, be honest and say it. It is obvious that both you and Olivia aren't telling me everything, which is really, really pissing me off."

Malila watched him with some trepidation. She knew her spell was making him aroused and aggressive and he would be hard to control if she didn't give him what he wanted. In addition to that, she knew he was right. They were wasting time, and the truth would come out sooner or later. All she could do was be honest with him and try to do the right thing. She put her hands up, surrendering.

"Okay, Alejo. I'll tell you everything I know, but it's a little complex so please bear with me. I know Olivia has Blue/Black blood. I don't know if she got it because karma's punishing her for killing Dantin, or because he stayed with her instead of dissipating into the logos. But I know she's got it."

"And how do you know that? And why pick Olivia to look at?"

"I heard she might be the one who got rid of Dantin, so I got to know her because I wanted to see if it really would turn a Silver-Tint into Blue/Black. I thought if I got close enough I could get some of her blood."

"And?"

"I did and I was right; she's not just Silver-Tint anymore."

"Well, I know she had some dark right after it happened, but they were only streaks."

"It's more than streaks now; it's all dark–almost purple. But it still has silver in it, Alejo. I don't think it will get darker because I tested it with a logos charm."

Alejo nodded. He'd heard of such a thing. "All right, Malila. So it's dark. Why would you need to know? And why not just karma taking its payment and punishing her actions? Why are you so sure it is Dantin inside of Olivia?" He knew he had another question to ask her, but he felt his head swim again, and lustful urges swept down his chest to his loins. He gritted his teeth as he resisted. He had no tolerance for any distraction right now.

"Goddamn it, Malila, if this is a spell then remove it immediately. There's a time and a place for a *hechizo mágico* like that, and it is not right now."

"I can't."

"Why not?"

"I don't control it." Malila felt positively stupid saying so.

"What? *Mierda*. Shit. We'll discuss that later. Right now we solve one problem at a time. What makes you think that Dantin possesses Olivia?"

Malila didn't answer right away. Fear hammered in her chest at the thought of admitting she'd known Alejo all these years without telling him the complete truth. He would hate the deception, and would hate even more that she was associated with Dantin, Olivia's nemesis. But how could she have told him anything at all? He wouldn't have understood.

"I'm waiting, Malila." Alejo said.

"Let me tell you about the spell first, Alejo. They're all tied together."

Alejo folded his arms. "*Bueno.* Go ahead then, Malila."

"Locke? I need you, please." Suddenly she wanted Locke with her. She wanted to show Alejo that she wasn't alone, that there was someone else who believed her and loved her, that she was worthy of love.

The familiar, cloudy greyish-black turbulence emerged in her suite as the logos entered the mortal world and swirled around Malila. Alejo watched without expression. He recognized the logos; he'd seen it before in various forms.

"Wait. Before you tell me about the spell, show me what the logos told you about Olivia." He wanted that confirmation first.

"All right." Malila stretched out her hand, speaking True Name syllables into the turbulence and then called for Olivia's blood. The same glowing blue that had lit up the blood the first time came through the haze and this time the cerulean fire settled in Malila's hand.

"Tell me," Alejo ordered.

"The color of this fire means Olivia is both Blue/Black and Silver-Tint, but she's not turning darker. If she was, then this blue would be darker than her blood but it's not; it's lighter." She flexed her hand and the azure glow danced around it. "This color tells me–the logos tells me–that Olivia will not turn darker."

Alejo's expression was unchanged. "Both Blue/Black and Silver-Tint. Okay. Now tell me about the spell between us."

Malila had never seen Alejo like this. He was usually laid-back and easy-going, open with his feelings and smiling instead of the stern manner he had now. And he was really tall, she realized. She felt like he was towering over her while he assessed everything she revealed to him.

"Right. The spell. I'll show you." She turned to watch Locke's form intensify and define as the room opened up to the endless black vista with the fiery ley-lines running through it. Locke didn't have to emerge this dramatically, but Necromancers were known for this kind of attachment to the logos, and Alejo would know right away what he was. It certainly helped in this situation to have a formidable ally, and she was grateful to Locke for showing it.

Malila went to Locke as he emerged from the black void. He enclosed her protectively.

Alejo nodded tightly. "A Necromancer. So that kind of spell between us. But why me? What did you hope to gain from me in the three hundred years we've known each other?"

"Nothing, Alejo," she said simply. "I don't control this one." She stopped there; he'd either believe her or not.

Alejo's look softened. "Then why all the secrecy? It is nothing to be ashamed of if the spell came unasked." He obviously knew what that meant. It meant there was real affection underneath the spell; otherwise it couldn't come on its own.

Malila bit her lip. Locke could tell she was apprehensive and he reassured her. "Honesty is best. You've done nothing wrong except try and avoid trouble in both worlds. I can tell him if you like."

Malila shook her head. "No. I have to do this." She stepped away from Locke and faced Alejo. "Alejo, there's much more, but there was no way I could tell you until now."

Locke added his rumbling voice to Malila's. "Make sure you heard what I just said, Silver-

Tint. She has done nothing wrong except avoid trouble in both witching worlds. Listen to her with innocence."

Alejo unfolded his arms. "I'll assume innocence on her part. Go ahead, Malila."

You do remember I found Olivia for you, in Paris, right?"

"Of course."

"So you could rescue her."

"Yes."

"From Dantin."

"Yes, I remember." Alejo knew this was not easy for Malila. "I couldn't have found her without you. But you wouldn't let me tell her about you. Does that have something to do with this?"

"Yes," Malila whispered.

"Go on."

"If Dantin had found out I told you her location he would have killed me. Or worse."

"But how did he know you?" Alejo was not following.

She swallowed and pushed down her fear. "He knows me because my parents are Blue/Black, and he holds leverage over me because I'm not."

"You're a Silver-Tint born to Blue/Blacks? But they kill Silver infants when that happens."

Malila shook her head. "My blood was mixed and they thought it would turn darker, so they waited. When it didn't they were too embarrassed to tell the others, but they kicked me out of their circle. Of course no one questioned it; Blue/Blacks are naturally mistrusting and family ties mean nothing."

She paused at the memory and Alejo could tell it was painful for her. He waited until she went on.

"Both Blue/Black and Silver-Tint; hated by both groups if they had known. When Dantin found out he used it against me. He wanted Locke to control as his own, and I was the perfect leverage, of course. Dantin holds an entrapment spell over me. Anything that Locke does to hurt him, it happens to me." She waited so that could sink in for Alejo.

"So you had no choice," he said. "I can see why you were so secretive with me. But Dantin is dead now, so you are free, right? What has this to do with Olivia?" Then it dawned on him. "Her blood has both tints. Your blood has both."

Malila nodded. "Alejo, she's the only person I know who is like me. No one else would understand. Except for her I have nowhere to go that I'm not deceiving someone or they won't accept me. I'm not even sure of you, now that you know!" She was almost in tears.

"Malila, do you not know me at all? After three centuries?"

"But how could I tell you? How could I take the chance? I've always lived around Blue/Black deception and cruelty, and you were the only honest affection I had. Alejo, that's not a lie; the spell simply feeds off our friendship."

"I know how it works," Alejo smiled at her. "Malila, don't worry. I trust your actions and what you have done for Olivia and me. I've never seen you act like a Blue/Black. Nothing is different because of your blood."

Malila broke down in tears, and Alejo was confused. "Now what is wrong, *mi belleza*?"

"Nothing. I'm so glad to finally tell you. It's a relief."

Alejo stopped himself from moving closer to her. He wanted to put a comforting arm around her but couldn't afford to be distracted. He was concerned about Olivia.

"Olivia must be terrified of turning Blue/Black. For her there would be nothing worse than becoming like Dantin. She would do anything not to. Oh, why didn't she tell me?"

"Alejo, how could she? Silvers and Blues are mortal enemies and you are a Silver-Tint."

"That is how she would see it, yes. I've got to talk to Olivia, tell her that I know and it makes no difference to me. I don't believe she will turn like Dantin. Where is she?" he asked Malila, looking around the suite.

"Alejandro, I don't know."

"What do you mean, you don't know?"

"I told Olivia about our mixed blood, and of course that upset her horribly, but when I told her about Dantin she nearly lost her senses. Then Dantin took over her; he emerged right in front of my eyes. And then he disappeared with her." She stopped there, not wanting to tell Alejo of her humiliating episode with Dantin

Alejo felt his body go numb. "You're telling the truth–Dantin is not gone?"

Malila nodded.

"*Oh, Dios mío!*" He grabbed Malila by the arms. "Tell me what happened. Everything."

"You heard Olivia at the race; she wasn't herself. I brought her back here to see exactly what was happening and Dantin emerged. Alejo, I don't know how he did it, or exactly when, but I saw with my own eyes that he's possessing her." She turned frantic. "Alejo, he is going to use her up, humiliate her, and kill her. He says that now he knows how to go from body to body.

That means he won't be careful with hers, even if he's in it."

Alejo let go of Malila. "I have to find her right away."

"Yes, but what are you going to do once you find him, Alejo? He's in Olivia's body. You can't stop him without it hurting her."

Alejo ran a hand over his jaw. "Let me think."

Malila went on. "And she's partly Blue/Black, so she's stronger than a Silver-Tint, and she doesn't have to pay back the logos as quickly for using magic. That means she'll last longer than you if you two were to fight."

Alejo nodded. "And again, I'm not going to hurt Olivia."

Locke interjected. "I can capture her. As long as I don't hurt him, I can capture her without hurting Malila."

"And do what?" responded Malila. "We don't know how to separate them."

Alejo turned a disbelieving face to her. "You don't know how?"

"Alejo, why would I? Do you?"

Locke defended Malila. "To cleanly separate two souls from a living body is an art lost for nearly a millennium. Malila has sent me to the far edge of every dimension I can touch to try and acquire the answer, so I suggest you tread lightly with your judgment, Alejandro."

Alejo apologized to Malila. "I realize it's not your fault. We have to find a way to get her back, though."

Malila looked at Locke helplessly. "Alejo, I don't know what to do if Locke can't find the answer."

Alejo was adamant. "We have to find a way, Malila." Oh, please, he thought, let this be the reason Olivia has been so cold to me. Please let it be that she loves me back.

"I have to find her," he finished vehemently, clenching his fists. "I have to."

Locke moved closer to Alejo, looking into his face. Then he looked at Malila and back at Alejo for a few more seconds before speaking again.

"Alejo, you are very fond of Malila, maybe something close to love. But not nearly as much as you love Olivia."

Alejo nodded. "Yes. I actually think I love her more than my life." He smiled tightly. "How does everyone know? Is it inscribed over my head?" He turned to Malila. "I'm sorry, *belleza*."

Malila reassured him. "Why are you sorry? I'm so in love with Locke that it turned into magic, remember?" She touched his cheek.

"Alejo, I have no complaint with true love for anyone, especially yours for Olivia."

"I don't even know if she loves me in return. But that doesn't matter; we have to find a way to get her back." He looked absolutely miserable.

Locke spoke. "There may be a chance. Olivia's apprentice can travel ley-lines."

"She can?" Alejo was impressed.

"But that's far too dangerous," said Malila. "She doesn't know how to do it, first of all. Even if Locke took her, she wouldn't be able to go anywhere he can't. And he's looked everywhere he can go. Even if he showed her and we let her go on her own, learning to navigate them is beyond her knowledge; she would get lost and never find her way back because the paths are amorphous. And if that's not enough, every dimension is different. How would she find the right one?"

Alejo had an offering. "I know who to ask. Schmidt knows more about magic than any of the Silver-Tints, and no one knows how old he is. Maybe before the skill left this plane."

Malila knew exactly what Alejo meant. "Maybe Taylor could find what we need, if he accompanies her. She has the ability; he has the knowledge."

"Yes!" said Alejo. He looked up at Locke. "You two go get Taylor and explain it to her."

"Fine," said Malila, "but where do we find Schmidt?"

Alejo knew Schmidt owned an old castle in Austria, far away from the urban centers. It afforded him two things he loved; privacy and extensive magical connections. Both were also very necessary for his charmsmithing business. He agreed to meet them at his home the very same night, and now they all were standing before the massive stone hearth in his living room as they finished their story.

"So let me get this straight. Locke, you are her Necromancer," Schmidt pointed to Malila. "Your curse is the *liebestod*–the love-death."

Locke didn't answer because the situation was obvious. Next Schmidt looked at Malila and smiled indulgently.

"Of course you love him back, or you wouldn't be in this situation with him."

Malila nodded solemnly.

"And you, Alejo, are completely in love with Olivia,"

Alejo nodded yes and Schmidt continued.

"...and," Schmidt continued, "since Olivia is the only other witch like you, Malila, you are hoping to be close friends with her."

Malila sighed. "Yes..."

"But you two," he pointed at Malila and Alejandro, "can't help having rambunctious sex anytime you get a moment alone together."

Malila looked sheepish and Alejandro squirmed uncomfortably. "Well, there's a spell involved..."

"And we really are friends," Malila interjected, feeling sophomoric.

Schmidt shook his head as he tapped out his pipe on the stone hearth. "Somehow, you four have gotten this totally jacked up." He turned to Taylor. "Where do you fit in this quartet?"

Taylor backed up a step, eyes wide. "I'm just the apprentice. Olivia's my mentor."

Alejo was getting impatient. "Schmidt, we don't have time for this–we need to get Dantin out of Olivia."

"Alejo, do you want this done fast or done right? I don't want any surprises that could affect our success."

Locke regarded Schmidt sharply. "True, but there's no need to pass judgment. How was Malila to know of Alejo's love for Olivia? And how was Alejo to know of her Necromancer? I don't insist that she tell; the fear and suspicion she would receive would relegate her to a life without friends or affection. I love her too much for that."

Schmidt looked at all of them. "That wasn't my intent. Let's take look at all of this. Aside from what we'll call the 'interpersonal activities' of Malila and Alejandro, we have the entrapment spell, the mixed blood in two of you, Dantin's unsavory proclivities and now his new abilities, and he's mixed with Olivia. We also have a Necromancer in all of this, and Taylor's supposed strengths with the ley-lines. I'm pretty sure I know everything I need to. Do you know where Olivia is now?" He looked at Alejo.

"No, we've been looking, but we can't scry for Olivia because Dantin is blocking us, and we can't scry only for Dantin because he's mixed with Olivia. We don't know where they are."

"Then you'll need to think like a mortal. Where would Dantin go? Where would Olivia go? And you said it was Dantin in control the last time you saw her?"

Malila clapped her hands together. "Oh, I know! Dantin had this twisted fantuy that Olivia would somehow love him and they would live in his Paris *appartement* together. He's owned it over two hundred years and his corporation would still be paying the bills since there's no proof that he's gone."

Schmidt pointed to Alejo and Malila. "You two go there and see if that's where he took Olivia while I prepare a place that will hold them–and don't get sidetracked, you two," he warned. "Taylor, you come with Locke and me to my workshop. We have a whole hell of a lot to teach you before traveling those ley-lines, and I have to research all the different dimensions that are thought to have extraction spells."

"Wait," said Alejo. "Schmidt, I need to talk to Olivia alone first. And I need something from you." He held out his hands and a shimmer of magic appeared in the air between them. It became a cloud of glittering dust that intensified, and then coalesced into a long, slim box with obscure markings etched into the wood.

"I know that case." Schmidt looked from it to Alejo. "What has that to do with any of this?"

Alejo cradled the box in his left arm and lifted the lid to look inside. The sword it contained lay nestled in creamy satin, its edge gleaming in the firelight. Alejo grasped the hilt and drew it from its bed.

"I want a charm, exactly like the one you made Olivia. How quickly can you do it?"

"Why would you need that charm? It was unique to Olivia, to block Dantin's curse on her. What could it possibly do for you?" Schmidt couldn't fathom where Alejo was going with his request.

Neither could Malila. She turned to Taylor, asking in a low voice, "Why would he want that?"

Taylor answered under her breath. "I don't know, but he must have a reason."

"What's with the sword?" Malila whispered.

"That's the sword Schmidt made for Olivia– the one she killed Dantin with. He also made a charm to protect her out of the same metal."

Malila stared at the sword Alejo held. Looking closely, she saw it still had navy smears of blood on it and she felt surreal, knowing it was Dantin's. This was the sword that had killed him. Well, almost.

Alejo insisted on his request. "Just do it for me, Schmidt."

The charmsmith looked at him a long moment, and Malila felt she had to help somehow.

"Schmidt, I don't know what Alejo is thinking, either, but I know Dantin. He's extremely clever–and ruthless. We are going to need every advantage we can get."

Schmidt relented. "All right, Alejandro. It will take me a day if nothing goes wrong. But Locke and I still need to train Taylor, don't forget. We can't afford wasted time."

Alejo nodded and set the box on the floor. Then using both hands he hefted the sword over his head, swinging it downward with all the muscle he could put behind it. It dashed against the stone fireplace and the blade shattered, casting off shards of the blood-smeared metal. With a gesture, Alejo commanded the shards to gather in the air before Schmidt, who captured them in his hands. Alejo reinforced his need for the charm.

"As fast as you can, Schmidt. I'll be back for it, I hope."

Schmidt inspected the shards as he nodded and then had a thought. "Alejo, wait a minute before you go. Dantin had a familiar, correct? Where is it?"

Malila shrugged. "No one knows."

"Olivia's familiar fought with it, and they disappeared into the logos together." Taylor looked at the others.

"That's the last time I heard from it, too, but they're both chimera; they go off on their own without telling anyone sometimes," Malila said.

Schmidt was strategizing. "Still, they could come back at any moment. My worry is who would they recognize in Olivia's body."

"I don't understand," said Taylor.

"I do," said Malila. "Both the witches and their chimera are mortal enemies. Would Eidolon attack Olivia if Dantin is dominant? Or would Dantin's chimera attack Olivia if unprotected by Eidolon–and would Eidolon even try to protect her? I don't know if either one would recognize their witch while they're blended."

"We'll have to protect them from both chimeras until we can find out how to separate them."

Locke was confident. "I can capture Olivia and Dantin and bind then both so they can't escape, and I can cast a second shell around all of us, but I will need to focus inward. If there will be unknown threats from the outside, I suggest a third layer that can adapt."

Alejo turned to Taylor. "We'll need Daphne and Chloe. And see if they can find Eidolon out in the logos and let him know what is happening."

"No problem," said Taylor. "I'll drop off Lexie at JaneAnn's and let her know what's happening, too." She looked down at her dog.

"You'd rather play with the greys than be bored here with me anyway, huh?"

Schmidt was figuring out the logistics. "While you're doing that, I'll work on the charm. Locke, after Taylor returns with our allies, you'll need to introduce her to the ley-lines so we don't lose too much time."

"I'll go with Taylor," said Malila. "I'll do whatever you need me to do." She looked at Alejo, who was posturing to disappear with the broken sword. It was far sharper than before, the blade now sheared into a stiletto-like weapon. *Please let us all come out of this alive,* she thought.

Taylor had to touch Malila's arm to get her attention. "Are you coming?"

Malila came back to her surroundings. "Yes– I'm sorry. Let's go."

Alejo stood at Dantin's Paris *appartement* door, looking at the dainty gold filigree that adorned the carved wood. It was bizarre to think that that bastard could choose such a beautiful place, all cream-colored and gilded and light, but Malila had said he had dreamed of living there with Olivia, so undoubtedly he had purchased it especially for her. That thought increased the anger he already felt at knowing Dantin had her trapped in there with him on the other side of this door.

He'd planned multiple ways to get into the *appartement* unobserved, but it was encased in several layers of spells. Dantin relied heavily on witchcraft to do nearly everything, Alejo knew, so he decided that the best way to get inside was to simply knock. He had no clue what state he would find Olivia in and he took a breath to calm his emotions. A clear head would be best for what he needed to do.

Sure enough, the housekeeper answered the door. Alejo immediately spelled her to sleep, catching her silently and slipping her into the hallway chair before he crept through the main floor to look for anyone else. He didn't dare use magic to locate Dantin in case he'd set up some sort of alert. Those were not unheard of, although difficult to acquire, and Alejo wasn't about to find out the hard way.

There was no one else downstairs so he ascended the curved staircase to the second floor, going from room to room but finding no one. This makes no sense, he thought, the place is heavily fortified with magic. He was trying to figure out where else they might have gone when he heard Dantin's voice, mixed with Olivia's, behind him.

"Lose something, Baquero?"

Alejo whirled, putting up a protection spell, but Dantin shook his head.

"There's no need for that. I have what I want: Olivia. The worst thing I could do to you is keep you alive to be tormented by that knowledge." He smiled. "Oh, yes. I know about your little confession to her." He adopted a falsetto, mocking tone: "Olivia, I'm in love with you."

Alejo pressed his lips together and tried to control his increasing anger as Dantin kept talking.

"She didn't love you back though, did she? Oh, that was my finest moment." He smiled delightedly. "She doesn't love you because I talked her out of it. Yes, I did indeed. And Alejo, I will make sure you stay alive to watch what else I do to the two of you. But especially to her."

"Let me talk to her."

"Why should I?"

"Why not? You hold all the aces. What would it hurt, and perhaps you'll end up with another humiliating memory about me in the process." Alejo was willing to take that chance in order to see Olivia again.

Dantin-Olivia shrugged. "You're right—why not? I'm so strong now she can't emerge unless I let her. And by the way, I know you have that accursed sword in your possession; I can feel it. So you may as well show it."

Alejo removed the invisibility charm and the sword in its sheath revealed itself at his thigh. He pulled it from the leather.

Dantin regarded it with casual interest. "Hmmm. Broken. I don't remember that happening, but then again it was a hell of a fight." He looked back at Alejo. "Just what did you expect to do with that? I know you're not going to hurt me while I'm in Olivia's body."

"I'd rather kill her than let you have her. You know it can do it; it has both yours and Olivia's blood in the metal along with some powerful charmsmithing."

Dantin narrowed his eyes, gauging Alejo's resolve.

"No," he said finally, "you won't kill her. Not unless you think you're out of options. Well, it will be a fun game between the two of us, won't it, Baquero? Who gets to kill her first?"

He came right up to Alejo, putting Olivia's face within inches of his. Alejo stood perfectly still, not wanting to give Dantin the satisfaction of backing down. He watched Olivia's lips curl into a sneer as Dantin closed the space between them, brushing Olivia's lips against Alejo's, knowing how he felt about her–and about him. He could feel both Alejo's desire and revulsion mixed together at his touch. Olivia's touch.

Dantin laughed in his combination Olivia-Dantin voice, and the sound made Alejo's skin crawl.

"You know," said Dantin, his feminine voice low and husky, "I could take that sword and kill you with it instead. I'm stronger than you are, now that she's Blue/Black." He was talking with Olivia's lips still close to Alejo's, almost touching him. "With so much magic in that sword I wonder what it could really do, don't you? For all I know, it's what made Olivia's blood turn. Or maybe karma really does punish Silver-Tints who kill. Ah, well … who cares at this point?"

Dantin ran Olivia's fingers lightly down Alejo's chest, stopping at his belt. "You know, humiliating her sexually wasn't quite as much fun as I thought it would be. I paid good money for two great big brutes to come in and violate every inch of her, but I forgot to take into consideration that I'm in here, too." He made a sour face at the memory. "Well, live and learn. They won't be doing that again to anybody."

Alejo closed his eyes, trying to avoid the vision that gave him. It was hard to ignore Olivia's touch and the scent of her perfume.

"Just let me talk to her," he said through clenched teeth.

Dantin backed away from Alejo and put up his hands. "Sure, you can talk to Olivia. Why not?"

Alejo watched Olivia's eyes carefully, looking for any change that would confirm it was really her and not Dantin. It was obvious when she emerged; the terror in her eyes was unmistakable and she immediately broke down in tears.

"Oh, God. Please kill me, Alejo." Her lips were quivering; her whole body trembled at the knowledge that she was living this ordeal. "Please," she whispered.

Alejo was immediately at her side, arms around her. "I will find a way to get you out of this."

"No, you won't," Olivia said, defeated. "He has spells you've never heard of, Alejo. He can work True Name sounds that we thought were nothing. No witch can break what he's got wrapped around me."

"We'll find a way. Don't let him kill your spirit, Livy. You didn't let him beat you in almost five centuries of torment, and I'm not going to let you now."

"That was different, Alejo! He wasn't fucking living inside of me! Alejo, he's more disgusting, more evil than I ever thought. You don't know how depraved, how putrid..." she tailed off into a soft moan that dropped into silence and she curled up in Alejo's embrace. Her voice was muffled when she spoke again.

"Alejo, it doesn't matter anymore, anyway. Even if there was no Dantin, I've become Blue/Black. We can't..." she cast about for words "...nobody would want..." she looked at him with despair. "You're a Silver-Tint."

Alejo took her hands in hers and kissed her forehead. "Nothing has changed, Livy. You're still the woman I love more than anything, and we'll find a way to get you free."

Olivia put her arms around his neck and buried her face in his chest. "When you told me you loved me I wanted to say yes, I love you, too, but I couldn't...and everything is so horribly screwed up now. I'm not even me anymore."

Alejo held her tighter. "Yes, you are. You're still yourself, and I still love you, Livy."

She lifted her head and looked into his eyes, and in that very moment Alejo felt he would die from love. No one could possibly feel this much love for another person and survive it, he thought, feeling the passion crushing his chest. He kissed her hair and held her tighter, wishing he could rescue her, take her away from here right now, right this second.

"Alejo, I don't see how you could possibly help me," Olivia said. She was quiet and still for a long minute as they held each other. Then suddenly her hand darted out to grasp the hilt of the broken sword. She pulled it from the sheath and turned it toward them both, but Alejo caught her hand in his, grappling with her while she tried to jab the blade into her chest. He finally wrested it from her, but not before she had run it through her thigh. He pulled it out and pressed his hand to the wound to heal it.

"Stop it!" He held the blade as far away as possible while he held her tight. "You know I can heal almost any wound you give yourself; why would you even try?"

"Alejo, just let me do it. Even if Dantin didn't have me, you're a Silver-Tint and I'm Blue/Black. What would life be like for us?"

"I don't care, Livy."

"Alejandro, you're not thinking straight." Olivia shook her head.

"No, Livy, I'm thinking more clearly than I ever have."

"No! You have no idea what you're saying." Olivia melted into sobs. "Just leave me alone."

Alejo tried again. "Olivia, look at me."

She turned her face to his.

"I didn't bring the sword for you or Dantin."

"I don't understand."

"It's for me."

"What!" Olivia jerked to attention.

"Listen to me," Alejo said urgently, "I don't know whether you turned Blue/Black from getting cut with this sword, or killing Dantin, or from that charm that Schmidt made you, but I need to be stronger to take on Dantin."

"But how are –"

"And I will never care that you're Blue/Black, Livy. I want you to know that without a doubt, no matter what I have to do." He shifted the sword in his hand so that the blade was pointing at them both and with a swift movement ran himself through with it, just below the ribs, while Olivia cried out in horror.

"What are you doing, Alejo!" She pulled out the blade and pressed her hand to the bleeding incision. "What if it really was this sword that caused me to turn?"

He put his hand over hers. "Exactly. If it leaves Blue/Black in me, then we'll be the same– and you'll have no more reason to be *estúpido* and tell me to leave you or to kill you. "

Olivia looked in astonishment from his face to the wound, which now healing under her touch, to his face again. "And you call *me* stupid? You are out of your mind to risk becoming Blue/Black."

Alejo held her face in his hands and kissed her deeply. "If you are Blue/Black, then I am as well. I'm never leaving you."

He looked into her eyes and was rewarded with her absolute love there. In the next second the look turned to poison, and Dantin came back.

"Yes, Alejo, you are leaving her." The horrid double-voice was unmistakable.

Alejo instantly drew back, but not before a blast of magic knocked him across the room and into the plaster fireplace. He regained his footing and postured to fight but then dropped his hands. He couldn't hurt Olivia. He couldn't capture her, either; Schmidt and the others weren't ready for her yet. He saw the smirk on Olivia's face as Dantin watched Alejo surrender.

"A very touching, albeit cheesy declaration of love, Alejo. But you won't keep your promise." He gestured with a flourish toward Alejo and launched him to the other side of Paris, where he landed face down with painful impact. Alejo groaned as he lifted his head, sensing the taste of blood in his mouth. He felt his teeth with his tongue. They were all there at least, although his cheekbone and some ribs were probably broken. He'd landed on some sort of structure made of granite. He spat out the blood and stood up, looking around him to find he was in the crowded *Montmartre* Cemetery, amidst the thousands of vaults and crypts that had accumulated over the centuries. A grey City of the Dead. One of Dantin's thinly-veiled threats, no doubt.

Well, at least I did what I went there to do, Alejo thought. He put a hand to his aching side, not yet healed from where he had run the blade through, and felt an all-over bruising from the magical blow Dantin had given him as well. He was about to flash himself back to Schmidt's and then stopped abruptly, cursing himself angrily as he realized: Dantin now had the sword.

"What the hell happened to you?" Malila came over to inspect Alejo as he appeared, half bent at the waist with his hand pressed to his side. Daphne and Chloe came over, too, trailing Will-O-Wisp embers as they darted across the room.

"Just let me sit down first," Alejo grunted as he dropped into the closest chair. He nodded to the two Will-O-Wisps. "Good to see you."

"How can you see at all, with your eye swelling shut like that?" Chloe pointed at his face with an interested finger.

"How can anyone see with you shining on him so brightly? Dial it down, flame-girl." Daphne was annoyed that Chloe would be so cavalier with Alejo and pushed her away from him. Both Will-O-Wisps darkened until their usually white-hot forms were just a soft glow, allowing the others to gather around. Alejo was surprised to see Lexie following Taylor as she came over to him. He looked down at the dog.

"So you're here, too?"

Taylor nodded. "She didn't want to stay at JaneAnn's; in fact she threw a big fit about it and wouldn't leave my side so here she is."

Chloe was rubbing Lexie's neck and ears. "You're here to make sure nothing happens to them, aren't you?" She gave the dog a warm kiss on the top of her head.

"What happened?" Taylor took the lead while she fixed Alejo's injured face.

"Olivia's still alive and undamaged physically, but she's terrified, of course."

"Dantin let you talk to her? What happened?" Taylor was surprised, but Malila answered her.

"Oh, he knows the most hurtful thing he could do to Alejo was to let him see her like that. I'm sure Dantin had some vile things to say about the situation as well." Malila didn't want Alejo to have to recount what she knew must have transpired.

Taylor tried to lift Alejo's shirt and see where he was obviously in pain, but he pushed away her hand. "It's nothing. Come on, we have lots of work ahead. Where is Schmidt?"

Michael answered him. "He's down in the workshop." He had come up the stairs just then and clasped hands with Alejo.

Alejo returned the greeting. "Hey, Michael." He held still as Taylor finished removing the swelling from his eye and then stood up. "I can do my own ribs."

Michael looked at Taylor. "Locke and Schmidt want you back downstairs. I'll go with you." He took Taylor's hand and they disappeared down the staircase with Lexie following. Malila turned to Alejo.

"Where's the sword?"

"I had to leave it."

"Did you get done what you wanted to do?" Malila wasn't exactly sure what that was, but she had a good idea.

Alejo nodded. "Now if we can just get her back." He turned his attention to the two Will-O-Wisps who sat perched in the air nearby, their ember flames gliding over their willowy bodies.

"Thank you so much for coming to help. You're the only ones fast enough to protect us if Dantin's chimera tries anything, and I don't know what else he might have control over."

Chloe answered him in her velvety voice. "You know we love to do this..."

Daphne finished for her, "...especially for Olivia and Taylor."

Chloe added her own two cents. "But you know we've always liked you, too."

Daphne nudged Chloe with her shoulder. "Well, who wouldn't? Just look at him." She made a big show of admiring Alejandro's assets.

"Okay, you two," Malila put a defending hand between the Will-O-Wisps and Alejo. "That's very flattering, but I suspect he'll change his womanizing ways when we get Olivia out of this."

"Really?" Chloe said in surprise. "Olivia?"

"See?" said Malila to Alejo, "There are some of us who haven't heard the news. Come on, let's go downstairs and see how we can help while they get back to guarding the outside." She started toward the stairs and Alejo followed, leaving the two Will-O-Wisps to gossip about the news of Alejo and Olivia.

"Can you believe that?" Chloe said.

Daphne answered her as they started to fade away. "Oh, but they're perfect. You know, I suspected it all along."

"Oh, you did not," Chloe retorted. "You always..." But the last of her sentence disappeared with her.

Malila and Alejo arrived downstairs as Schmidt was finishing Alejo's charm. Alejandro looked it over appreciatively.

"*Dios*, Schmidt you do some truly masterful work." He showed Malila the inch-long shard of metal from the sword, gleaming within its cocoon of spells. The translucent symbols and True Name syllables encircled the metal and traveled over the shard, like a snake slithering around a tree branch.

"How will you carry it?" asked Schmidt. "You damned sure don't want to lose it."

"A leather cord is fine, but I want it charmed so the shard comes off when I want it to."

"Easy enough." Schmidt produced a thin length of leather and pulled it through a closed fist as he spoke foreign-sounding words to enchant it. "Here." He held out the cord.

Immediately, the shard came to it from Alejo's hand, suspending itself below the cord that Schmidt held. He handed it to the other witch and Alejo put it around his neck, jerking the knots tight. Then they went to the other side of the workshop where Taylor and Locke were training and Michael and Lexie were off to the side watching.

The Necromancer turned his hot mercuric gaze on Taylor. "Show me."

Taylor extended her arms and the workshop dropped away into blackness. Alejo could see her concentrating hard, brows knitted as she commanded the logos. This level of magic was beyond an apprentice's usual experience level, and he could see the effort it was costing her, but they had no choice right now. Taylor closed her eyes and Locke upbraided her sharply.

"Open your eyes! You can't waver in any of your focus. You must be able to concentrate and pay attention to your surroundings at the same time."

Taylor opened her eyes again and refocused, making the effort to take in everything around her. The black void began to change slightly and faint orange streaks began to emerge, but then Taylor's efforts gave out and the void disappeared, leaving them in the workroom again. Lexie, who had lifted her head off the floor in interest, laid it back down again. Nothing happening yet, obviously.

Locke rumbled, sounding impatient, and Malila came over to them.

"Locke, why don't you flow your magic through her? If she can feel how it should be, that may help her." She stepped aside and Locke moved behind Taylor to wrap around her.

The other witches watched as his power flowed through Taylor, warping her image as it called to the logos. The familiar grey cloudiness that accompanied Locke came up but was replaced in seconds by the black void and this time it clearly showed the rivers that looked like molten lava running through it. Taylor was stunned and ecstatic.

"I can feel it! The heat, the magical force." The effect was like a wind, blowing her hair back from her face. "This is incredible."

She pointed at the burning rivers. "Are those ley-lines?"

Locke answered her. "Yes. Those are the ley-lines."

"And those lines connect the dimensions?"

"That's one use for them. They're concentrated rivers of magical power."

"JaneAnn told me about opening doors to other dimensions, but she said it took a lot of witches nowadays to open a door. She also said they weren't very stable."

Schmidt came up and joined the conversation. He had been talking earnestly with Alejo off to the side, but now Alejo took Locke aside for a quiet conference while the others continued.

"Opening doors like that nowadays takes that many witches because they're trying to open it indirectly, without tapping into a ley-line," said Schmidt." They have to combine their powers but you, my dear, don't need to do that. You can just use those." He pointed to the rivers. "We'll use them to go get what we need. The ley-lines themselves are stable, but you must be able to read them, and that's where I come in."

Malila wondered how ready they were. "And do you know what we need?"

"We need a Vessel of Nyrra and its countercharm," said Schmidt, "and I need a refresher in using it while we're there. It's been a long time for me."

"And Dantin–do we have a way to contain him?"

"Yes, it's all ready. Locke will help us with that, and he's our safety net in case we fail."

"Meaning what?" asked Malila.

Alejo turned away from his discussion with Locke and answered her. "He'll take Olivia somewhere through the ley-lines and imprison her there. Either that or kill her if absolutely everything goes wrong. They can't survive combined like they are for long, anyway, and I'd rather give her a quick end than put her through any more of Dantin's hell."

The others fell silent. That was a step no one had dared think about.

Alejo went on. "But that means we have to do this right, and we don't let it fail." He looked at the others, and they nodded soberly.

Michael brought them back to planning the job. "So let's see where we're at. We have the Will-O-Wisps outside to ward off Dantin's chimera but what about everything else? Do we even know what to expect?"

Taylor answered him. "The Wisps can take care of almost anything magical in this dimension. They found Eidolon, Olivia's chimera, but he's not able to distinguish between Dantin and Olivia while they're combined so he'll help Daphne and Chloe outside the barrier. Schmidt's conjuring should take care of everything else."

Schmidt turned to Taylor. "I'm sorry, but we don't have time to let you practice with the ley-lines. It'll be learn as you go and hope for the best."

"That's okay. Let's get on it and get this done."

Schmidt gave her an approving nod. "All right, then." He turned to the rest of the group. "You will need to find Olivia again and bring her here. I can hardly imagine where she is now." He pointed to a broad table on the other side of the workshop that was topped with a reflective, undulating substance. "You can use my scrying pool. It's enhanced with spells that will show you more than a plain scry can."

The other witches looked at the scrying pool, impressed with its obvious power. Schmidt caught their look. "Yeah, well, when it's your business you tend to have all the best toys."

"So," Michael asked him, "where do you need me?"

"Since you're not anywhere near re-empowered yet, I want you to stay here and make sure our efforts are in place." Schmidt answered. "And keep an eye on everyone from the scrying pool to alert the others if something goes wrong."

Then he looked at Taylor again. "Ready?"

"Do we need to take anything?" Taylor asked him.

"Just us. And my journal," was the answer.

"Can you give me a boost?" Taylor asked Locke.

"Yes, but after this I cannot help you. You will be off this mortal plane, and my efforts will be needed with Olivia."

"I understand."

Locke wrapped around Taylor once again, and she raised her arms to call in the logos. It emerged immediately this time, casting its scorched air over all of them.

"Come on," said Schmidt to Taylor, walking toward one of the ley-lines. The others followed to see what would happen; none of them except Schmidt and Malila had seen this before. They all stopped at the very edge.

"Now what?" asked Taylor over the noise of the rushing ley-line. The fiery, luminous river was reflecting its glow on her face.

Schmidt pulled her hand down to the ley-line. "Go ahead; put it in there." He extended his arm and swept it through the magical river up to his shoulder.

The others caught their breath, thinking there would be fire but were shocked to see the river was clear; they could see Schmidt's arm through the rushing torrent. Something made it glow from the outside in, as if fire flowed underneath the river and painted it molten orange.

No matter how many times I see it, I'm still mesmerized," said Malila. The others agreed.

Taylor swept her arm through the river as well and her eyes grew wide. "Oh, my God." She looked up at the others, smiling in wonder at how it felt. "I can't even describe it." She held out her fingertips for Lexie to inspect with curiosity.

"Come on," Schmidt stepped into the river and Taylor did the same, stiffening at the jolt of power that rushed through her.

She looked at Schmidt. "Now what?"

Schmidt touched her forehead with his fingertips. "Here's where we're going first."

Taylor nodded her understanding as she absorbed the location. She looked at the others and caught Michael's expression of concern.

"I'll be careful," she told him.

He nodded. "I know."

Schmidt prompted Taylor. "Come on, kiddo. Time to go."

Taylor concentrated, furrowing her brow, and they disintegrated into the fluid that rushed into the void. Then they were gone into darkness.

Malila looked at Alejo. "We have to figure out a way to capture Dantin."

"I've been thinking about that," mused Alejo.

"He's not going to let us without a hell of a fight, you know," she said worriedly.

"And I have to get that sword back, too," Alejo replied. "It belonged to Olivia, and it's the last, most significant thing of hers that I have. I'm not giving it up. Not to mention that it's charmed six ways from Sunday, and there's no way I'm leaving it in Dantin's possession."

"We have a lot of planning to do if we're going to anticipate every defense he has or trap he could set for us."

"Yes," said Alejo with a hint of a smile, "but I have an idea."

Thane and his companion looked at Olivia with admiration and awe.

"It's like you're unkillable, Dantin."

"That's exactly what I am and don't forget it; I can't be killed." Dantin wanted them awestruck. He wanted his dominance to be total in the Blue/Black world and this situation he had fallen into would make him legendary. And feared. It was absolutely ambrosial for him.

"What do you need us to do?" Thane was a fawning sycophant; he'd wormed his way into a friendship with Malila to get close to Dantin, eager for the chance to meet him and make his mark. That had never happened, but he had stuck close to Malila after Dantin had disappeared, hoping to hitch a ride on her status with the Blue/Blacks. Now he was furious at Malila for the way she had blasted him and Marissa, the other witch, at the Sorrento. Both of them wanted revenge for how she had humiliated them. Well, following Malila had certainly reaped them some golden benefits. Here they were with Dantin himself, or rather Dantin-Olivia, and he was looking to spy on Malila, too, and wanted them to help.

"Find her, follow her, and report back to me. And find my chimera. I haven't seen it for six months, and it probably thinks I'm gone forever. Tell it where I am, but be sure and tell it what's happened. I don't need the damned thing thinking I'm Olivia and jumping on me."

"Dantin," said Marissa, "no one has seen your chimera since you, uh, left."

Dantin turned a scathing look on her. "Well, that's not really my problem, is it? It's yours. Just find it. I want it done fast, too. Thane, you and Miranda split up."

The woman corrected him. "Marissa."

"What?" said Dantin.

"My name is Marissa."

"Whatever." Dantin was uncaring. "Now get out of my sight."

He turned away from them as they disappeared to accomplish their errands, but then was surprised to feel them come back before they were completely gone. There was no mistaking that magical buzz of a witch in proximity.

He turned impatiently. "My directions couldn't have been simpler; just find the –" he stopped when he saw it wasn't Thane and Marissa, but rather Alejo in the room. And Malila appearing right behind him.

Damn it, he thought. That was a smart move on their part, coming in at the same time the others had left and foiling the spell he had cast. It had to open for a moment to let the other witches out, and they had taken full advantage of that crack to slip inside.

"I imagine you are coming with some pathetic entreaty to give up Olivia–maybe looking to trade me something for her. Another body perhaps? I told you I'm not doing that, Malila. Not until I've used her up."

Alejo shook his head. "No, I came for the sword."

"Oh, and I'm just going to give it to you?"

"No, I'm going to take it."

Alejo walked toward Dantin and the dark witch backed up a step, gauging Alejo's intent. The Silver-Tint could be tricky, he remembered. He hadn't forgotten the time Alejo had bypassed his magic defenses and punched him in the face like a mortal. But then Dantin relaxed, remembering where he was now. No way would Alejo hit Olivia.

Dantin called the sword to him and it materialized in his hand. He showed it to the two witches. "This sword, right?"

Alejo was next to Dantin now and could easily converse. "Yes, that sword. Of course, I could try asking for it first and avoid a magical fight." He held out his hand. "How about it?"

Dantin threw back his head and laughed. "Alejo, I like you. I never know what you're going to do. And you have brass like I've never seen. Too bad we can't be friends."

He'd hardly gotten the last word out when Alejo reached out swiftly, punching him right in Olivia's face and knocking him out cold. Olivia crumpled to the ground and Alejo was immediately on her, wrapping her in his arms and checking to make sure nothing was broken.

"I'm sorry, honey," he said to the unconscious Olivia, lifting her tenderly in his arms and standing up with her as Locke arrived to wrap a binding spell around the both of them.

Malila came over and picked up the sword. "You know, I just met Olivia a month ago, but I've watched her and Dantin battle for decades. I can guarantee you she'd be thrilled you did that."

Alejo smiled grimly at her. "Come on, let's get back to Schmidt's and pull this bastard out of her."

"Are you sure that will hold her?" Alejo and the other four witches were looking at the unconscious Olivia, suspended in her magical prison. Taylor and Schmidt had finally arrived with the Vessel of Nyrra after a four-day absence in the magical domain.

Schmidt nodded as he puffed on his pipe. "Oh, yeah. No problem. It only looks delicate."

The prison cell was a barely visible cube of golden evanescence surrounding Olivia on all sides. It held her in the very center, cutting off her ability to touch anything, either physically or magically. Dantin wouldn't be able to cast any further than this cube, and since he was trapped in it, throwing an aggressive spell of any sort was unwise. He'd tried it when he'd first arrived and was very sorry he'd done so.

They all watched Olivia a few moments longer and then followed Schmidt to his workroom.

"I still can't believe I was able to hit him," Alejo said to Schmidt as he arranged a few magical items on the table. "You'd think he would know better since I've done it before."

"Yeah, well arrogance is his biggest weakness," said Malila. "Always thinks he's the smartest one in the room and can outthink everyone. The problem is that he usually can but lucky us this time."

"And lucky us to have found the Vessel as soon as we did." Schmidt was perusing the item in his hand. "I thought we'd have to try twenty or more places, but my journal notes were still pretty accurate."

"I'm surprised it looks so mortal." Alejo touched the translucent surface and it sparked under his finger. "Almost like an Arabian glass lantern. If I wasn't used to magical objects I'd hardly believe it could do the job."

"Believe it," said Schmidt. "This will definitely contain him."

"What do you mean, contain him?" Malila didn't like the sound of that. "Aren't we just pulling him out of Olivia? Getting rid of him?"

"We can't pull him out generally, to nowhere. The Vessel of Nyrra is what pulls on him, if that makes sense." Seeing their quizzical looks, he explained the Vessel to them.

"Right now, Olivia is one container that has grains of two different people in it. You have to have something that separates the individual bits from each other completely and cleanly; you don't want to leave anything mixed. The Vessel of Nyrra is like a magnet that pulls iron filings out of sand, only it pulls grains of one soul away from another." He looked down at the Vessel. "It's not very pleasant, I'm afraid."

He glanced back at Olivia, floating in the cell. "You know, she used to come to my shop when she was a little witchling and watch me work. She sat on a stool, quiet, absorbing everything, watching. Her feet didn't even touch the ground, she was so little." He sighed. "I hate to do this to her."

Alejo put a comforting hand on his shoulder but said nothing. Schmidt put his hand over Alejo's in quiet thanks and then continued.

Well, come on; let's get prepared so we can wake them up and get this thing done."

"Why does the prison keep them unconscious?" Taylor wanted to know.

"It's not the prison; I had Locke do that," Malila told her. "I wanted to shut him up. One of the most destructive talents Dantin has is his use of cruelty. He will use any piece of information he has to get leverage, and humiliation is his favorite method."

"That's too bad," said Schmidt, "because we need them both completely conscious so the Vessel can identify each of them clearly." He picked up a tiny spot of light off the counter and handed it to Taylor. It looked like a miniature star in her hand.

"Here's your countercharm for the Nyrra, Taylor. Your job is to encase Olivia in its field. It's meant to keep her in her body but let Dantin out, so keep it going and don't let it fluctuate." Then he turned to Alejo.

"Alejandro, I want you to hold the Nyrra and face Olivia. Even though I know how to work it better than you, you are the person she's closest to. Plus, I need to be outside the cell to keep it intact or in case something goes wrong."

Taylor looked at the shining charm in her hand. "I wish we'd had time to bring JaneAnn and show her how to use this. I'm not as experienced as she is."

"None of you are in this situation," said Schmidt. "Taylor, it's better that you do it; you got it firsthand from that demon we bought the Nyrra from. By the time it passed from him to you to JaneAnn it would weaken, and Dantin is not someone to take a chance with."

He patted the apprentice on the arm. "You can do it–no worries."

Malila asked Schmidt, "What do you want me to do?"

"You stand by and be ready to help either Taylor or Alejo if they need it. Okay, let's go down the list: Daphne, Chloe, and Eidolon outside Locke's shell that surrounds the house to keep out Dantin's chimera and any other magical thing that gets thrown at us."

"They're out there right now," said Alejo.

"Michael, you and Malila and I right outside the cell."

Michael and the others nodded, and Taylor finished the roster "...and Olivia, me, Alejo, and Dantin all locked inside the cell."

Schmidt nodded, looking around at the others. "Anything else?"

No one said anything.

"Let's get on it, then ..." he called to the Necromancer to drop the somnambula spell over Dantin-Olivia.

"Locke, wake him up!"

He turned and went to the other room where Olivia's prison shimmered around her and the other witches followed. Except Alejo and Lexie.

Alejo hung back until the others were gone. Then raising his hand, he flicked his finger quickly over the palm, cutting it open to see the blood that rose to the surface. Not very dark. Still bright red with its familiar silver sheen. Alejo looked down at Lexie's curious face.

"That's a hell of a thing for me to be worried about, isn't it? Worried and disappointed that I'm not Blue/Black." He closed the wound and petted her head, then followed the others to where Dantin was already conscious and taunting them.

"You Silver-Tints are pathetic. What is that thing, some sort of jerry-rigged orb you're using to get me out of Olivia? I'm not stupid. I know separation spells don't exist anymore so whatever you've cobbled together isn't going to work."

"Dantin, we're busy. No one's going to answer you." Schmidt purposely kept his voice neutral. He wished he'd given some instruction to the group on this front, but it was too late now with Dantin aware of everything they were saying.

Dantin ignored Schmidt. "I've got disciples rounding up the rest of my followers so go ahead, take your best shot until they get here." The other witches didn't answer him, or even look at him, so he fell silent for the moment, observing what was going on.

Lexie was observing, too. She lay quietly in the corner between Schmidt's workroom and the great room where Dantin's prison cell evanesced. She knew the importance of what was happening because Chloe had told her exactly what it was. She liked the Will-O-Wisps because they talked to her like she was one of them.

Now she watched Schmidt caution Alejo before he handed him the Vessel of Nyrra. "Alejo, this will bind you to it so don't be surprised. It makes you both one and primes it with the imprint of what you want to draw into it. If you need to cast, do it by thought or voice because you won't be able to unclasp your hands from the Vessel until we're done."

Alejo nodded and grasped the Nyrra, feeling some trepidation as its magic clamped down on him and bound him to it. He had no idea what to expect in this venture. Schmidt moved to Taylor and worked swiftly, checking to make sure the countercharm was activated and all the necessities were in place before he gave them both a last once-over and stepped out of the cell.

Taylor nodded her readiness to Alejo. He met eyes with Olivia and called on the Nyrra to extract Dantin from Olivia, feeling its immense power when it jumped to life and encompassed the three of them. Schmidt had been right; it knew exactly what they were doing and carried out their intent. They just had to stay focused on it.

Olivia's image began to blur in the grip of the Nyrra and its countercharm. Taylor and Alejo could feel Olivia's presence but it was not very strong, more of a passing whisper in an empty room. Nonetheless, they were rewarded with Dantin's shocked face that appeared out of the blur, separate from Olivia's. The Vessel of Nyrra was working.

Alejo backed up a step as if to pull harder, but Schmidt cautioned him: "Don't try to force it. Let the Nyrra do its job. It's critical you give it time to separate them cleanly."

Both Taylor and Alejo nodded, realizing at the same time how connected they all were by the Nyrra. Being wrapped in the same enchantment meant they shared emotions, and both Alejo and Taylor felt how dangerous Dantin's thoughts were that emerged through the blur. Even worse, they could sense the tearing that both Dantin and Olivia were going through. Both images were grimacing–Dantin resisting, and Olivia simply trying to withstand the pain as they separated.

Dantin lashed out at the both of them, trying to alarm them into stopping. "That's right, we're all connected. If you pull me from Olivia you will pull me from the binding spell she's wrapped in, and I can cast again. I will throw a horrible spell on you all that will be magnified inside this cell."

"Can he do it?" asked Taylor, worried.

"Focus!" Schmidt barked at her. "You're letting it falter!"

Everyone could see the countercharm dim as Taylor asked her question. Taylor saw it, too, and caught her breath. Concentrating again on Olivia, she pushed her doubt away and pressed her powers into holding Olivia tight.

"Don't listen to him," Schmidt told them all in a controlled voice. "Don't get distracted."

Dantin was elated. He was sure Taylor was the crack he needed to fracture this spell. Now that he was pulled far enough out of Olivia, he could cast a weak image spell, and he turned on Taylor, revealing what he knew about her past and Olivia's amnesia charm.

"Well, Taylor. Aren't you the child whore, now... let's look at all those vigorous nights with your stepfather."

"What?" Taylor was confused. "I don't have a stepfather."

"Don't you? Here he is." Dantin cast the image of a lean, unshaven man with pockmarked cheeks and a sweaty stench that came toward her with a lecherous expression. Taylor stared at him, wide-eyed and shocked.

"You know who that is, don't you?" Dantin showed her more memories of her tormentor. How he'd caught her in the hallway one night, pressing against her as if by accident when she tried to pass him in the dark. How he'd grabbed her and kissed her, forcing his tongue into her mouth.

"Uggh!" Taylor winced with revulsion. "That's not true–that never happened!"

"Didn't it?" purred Dantin, "Don't you remember his disgusting, dry lips vibrating on yours as you ran to your room? His slimy tongue? You could feel it for days afterward." Dantin sneered at her.

"No–you're a liar." Taylor accused him through clenched teeth. But her lips prickled now at the memory that was washing over her.

"Am I?" Dantin kept showing the images. Images of the man choking her when she resisted the first time he came to her in the dark until she relented, barely conscious. Him forcing her arms up and over her head to hold them tightly in one hand while he fumbled away at her with the other. All while her sister Karen slept in the next bed.

"No!" Taylor shouted. She tried to be strong, but the countercharm began to waver.

"Look at you," said Dantin, drawing out the words slowly, "you're not even trying to push him away." He showed another vision, this time Taylor a few years older, staring up at the ceiling, bruised and unresisting as the man in the filthy undershirt crawled onto her. More images rushed by, disgusting visions and feelings, his rutting form draped over Taylor's night after night.

"Stop it!" Taylor screamed at Dantin, "Stop it!"

The countercharm she was holding dimmed further. It couldn't hold Olivia back from the pull of the Nyrra. Olivia's warped image flowed toward Dantin's until again they became one and Dantin was back in Olivia's body.

Malila tore through the edge of the cell to rush to Taylor. She held her tightly from behind, her dark hair spilling over Taylor's shoulder as she hugged her close.

"Don't you listen to him, Taylor. He's a liar–
he'll say anything if he thinks it will get him
what he wants."

"No," Taylor wailed, "I remember what he's
showing us, and even more. Oh, my God." She
tried to turn away from everyone, embarrassed.

Malila held her tighter, her cheek against
Taylor's as she spoke. "Then get mad at him,
hate him for making you remember this! Use the
strength in that anger to help Alejo separate him
from Olivia!"

Taylor didn't respond and Malila shook her
by the shoulders, trying to get through to her.
"Don't give up! Punish Dantin for bringing that
monster back into your memory!"

But it still didn't work. Taylor was shocked
at the revelation and ashamed. She tried to hide
her face from the others, but Malila turned her
toward Dantin roughly, pointing at him.

"Don't let him do this to you! Look at him,
so smug there. Do you want him to win, to take
Olivia? Are you weak like he thinks you are?"

Taylor looked where Malila was pointing. It
was hard for her to hate; it was one of the things
that kept her from becoming like her stepfather
all those years. But weak she was not. Being
strong was her core; it was what had helped her
get through all he'd done to her. She set her

teeth against Dantin's flood of images and the countercharm strengthened again. Once again they saw Dantin's image begin to separate from Olivia's.

"Yes," Malila whispered in her ear. "Don't let him win, Taylor. Beat him." She couldn't help that her own feelings of anger and hurt were coming through, but Taylor felt it and used it to bolster the countercharm.

Dantin, however, was not giving up. He had more torment for Taylor.

"Where is your mother, Taylor?"

Taylor whispered the answer. "She died before Olivia found me and Karen. She–she was sick."

But Dantin had heard her. "Was she? Are you sure?"

Apprehension filled Taylor; she didn't trust her memory now, though she struggled to feel sure of herself.

"Yes, I ... She was sick. The bank took the house after she died, and Karen and I ... Olivia found us and..." she stopped, feeling two different memories in her head as the amnesia spell crumbled further.

"This house?" Dantin showed her, and Taylor nodded hollowly as she recognized it. Dantin expanded the vision to bring them inside, through the bedroom where they'd seen the stepfather rape Taylor, then into the kitchen where he was beating Taylor's mother, calling her worthless and stupid and other vile names as he slammed her into the kitchen floor.

Taylor was helpless and horrified as she watched her mother's violent death at the hands of her stepfather. He smashed his fist into her face again and again, and then kicked her all over until she was pulpy and bloody and perfectly still. All the witches watched in stunned silence as the scene played out and then disappeared. Dantin had slipped back into Olivia again.

Taylor was numb. She tried to concentrate, to focus her powers, but all she could think of was her mother and what she'd seen, over and over and over again.

Malila held Taylor tightly, trying to comfort her as she poured her own magical energy into her, adding her Blue/Black strength to the countercharm. Once again, Olivia's image blurred and they could hear her give an agonized scream as the two separated for a third time.

"Alejo! You've got to finish this now!" Malila was horrified at what they were doing to Olivia.

Alejo shook his head and tried not to hear Olivia's anguish. He could only push what magic he had into the spell; otherwise they would rip Olivia into pieces. If he could match Malila's Blue/Black power, they would balance out and feed the Nyrra, but he was at his limit. Alejo wished that if that sword was going to turn him Blue/Black, it would hurry up and do it. If it was even going to.

Michael asked Schmidt, "Can't you go in there and add your power to Alejo's?"

"Absolutely not." Schmidt said. "You see how Dantin can read everyone's secrets in there once they're all connected? The last thing we need is for him to read me and figure out the weaknesses in our little venture, or even worse, pull a counter-spell out of me."

"I'm going in there," Michael started to push his way through the curtain of magic, but Schmidt grabbed him.

"No! He'll use your relationship with Taylor against her–don't give him more to hurt her with. Besides, your powers are only half back."

Michael looked on helplessly. "How about Locke?"

"He's the only thing holding our protection shells in place. Both the outside one and this cell they're in." Schmidt shook his head. "No, they're on their own in there."

The rest of the group was on their own outside Schmidt's, too. Eidolon, Daphne, and Chloe were waiting for Dantin's chimera to strike again. It had appeared and immediately disappeared nearby, seeming to know where they were stationed even though they were invisible. It had brought others, too. After a few appearances by Dantin's chimera, they were suddenly overwhelmed by a dozen or more of them flashing in and out all over Locke's protective shell.

"Why would they do that?" Chloe was looking below her, right and left while Daphne looked up and all around them in confusion.

"What could they possibly hope to achieve by flashing here and gone?" Daphne said. "They're not doing anything."

"Or trying anything." Eidolon burst away to try and catch one of the other chimera.

Suddenly there was no one else there; it was bizarre, the silence and lack of activity after the commotion of a few moments ago. The Will-O-Wisps and Eidolon swept over the surface of Locke's shell as swiftly as possible, trying to anticipate the other chimeras' movements.

"Wait! Stop. This makes no sense," said Eidolon. They all held still, observing and waiting and more than a little on edge. The

Wisps were formidable guardians, able to capture magical creatures that appeared with the intent to harm, but that meant they stayed long enough to do damage. These chimera just flashed in and out.

Just then they saw Dantin's chimera appear again. Both Daphne and Chloe were on it in an instant, but it was gone already.

"Unless it's brought something magical that we don't usually see." Daphne looked around.

"It has to be a diversion," Chloe finished Daphne's thought as they were suddenly swarmed again by chimeras flashing in and out in a frenzy.

Eidolon cautioned them. "Keep a sharp eye, especially now that night is coming on."

The sun had just set. The three of them continued sweeping the area and looking for anything unusual. Dantin's chimera and the others appeared almost constantly now, barely leaving the three sentries enough time to patrol the perimeter.

"I'll be back shortly." Chloe disappeared for about thirty seconds. She returned in a flash of flame, but dimmed quickly and became invisible again.

"What did you do?" Eidolon asked.

"I don't want to reveal that in case we're spied on. Let's keep doing what we're doing and be extra alert. Something is entirely wrong here."

As the sun set, the cooling night air mixed with the warm moist ground around Schmidt's home, creating an undulating mist that licked at the castle. Deer and voles and other animals browsed their way through the mist, coming out from their daylight hiding spots to get to their feeding grounds and creating little eddies in the brume as they moved along.

There was always animal activity at twilight and sunrise, when it was light enough for them to feed in the lushest fields without seeing too many humans, yet not dark enough for nocturnal predators in the open meadows. Eidolon and Chloe and Daphne inspected every creature for evidence of a glamour, but all the animals they encountered were as they appeared. It was difficult to do with all the chimeras in the area. Still, they kept track of every single one of them just in case.

The three guardians inspected the swirling mist as well, but it was the same as appeared every night, some even flowing down the dank stone steps into the castle's vault as usual. As the ground cooled, the mist disappeared, leaving only a few pockets here and there. No intruders.

"I don't like this," said Daphne, turning to Eidolon. "How long did Schmidt …"

"…say this would take?" Chloe finished for her, as usual.

"You know magic," said Eidolon. "It will take as long as it has to."

Long after the sky grew dark outside and the land cooled, taking the mist with it, the undulating pool inside the vault evaporated to become Thane and Marissa. Dantin would have been impressed, albeit begrudgingly, with the amount of patience they had shown, becoming part of the mist and slipping out of the way whenever Chloe, Daphne, or Eidolon came by to inspect it.

Slowly, inexorably they had flowed with the rest of the brume, not rushing ahead or calling attention to themselves, until they finally flowed into Schmidt's underground rooms and no one was watching for them anymore. Quietly they became human again and began making their way to the workroom. They had to find their way without magic since the Silver-Tints were sure to have put magic-detecting spells in place. They would operate as mortals until they found the others.

Dantin was foiled for the moment by Malila adding her powers to Taylor. He was balanced partially out of Olivia and partially combined, still between Malila and Alejo. And becoming increasingly annoyed at the standoff.

"This is ridiculous," he sneered at them. "You're obviously not going to succeed. You're wasting my time." He watched their reactions for any sign they doubted themselves but saw none, so he knew that tack wasn't going to work. The misery of being pulled out of Olivia was wearing on him, too. It was getting harder to think and harder to cast. It were as if someone had a charm that interfered with his powers.

If he was going to do something, he thought, he'd better do it soon before all of them were exhausted. If that happened he could only hope he was the last witch with any power left. He knew it might very well be between him and Malila since they were both half Blue/Black and half Silver-Tint. She might win, too, if her goddamned Necromancer decided to help and his chimera wasn't around.

He gritted his teeth against the pain and concentrated on Malila to see what chink she might have in her armor. And then laughed because the answer was right there in front of him.

Now that they were all ensorcelled together, Dantin could feel Malila's infatuation curse linking her with Alejo. I should have felt it before, he thought, but I was too busy torturing Taylor. No matter, he smiled to himself, immobilizing Taylor had better odds of success and had been more fun, anyway. It hadn't worked though, and now Dantin focused on Alejo, putting a few erotic thoughts in his head to turn his attention to Malila. He saw him glance past Olivia to look at her and then suck in a breath. The man looked a little dizzy, Dantin thought with satisfaction. He added a few more subtle visions–some nakedness and slippery warm sensations–and let the curse take its course.

Desire lapped at Alejo's thighs, pushing its way up through his belly and chest. Ah, *madre de Dios*, he thought as a wave of vertigo disoriented him. He shook his head hard to clear it. Why was this coming on now? He looked away from Malila, determined to ignore it. She wasn't that close to him; it must be because we're connected by the Nyrra.

The Nyrra. The thought of it helped him back into focus, and although it was difficult, he kept his eyes on Olivia. Dantin immediately taunted him, trying to distract him again.

"Something wrong, Romeo?" His look left no doubt that he knew the situation exactly.

Another wave of eros pulled on Alejo's focus and he felt himself succumbing to it, which really alarmed him. I can't let this happen, he thought; time to use the charm. I've been itching to, anyway.

Alejo knew the charm Schmidt had made was a wild card–in fact it was a wild-ass guess on his part–but he hoped it could do what he thought it might. In his lustful haze, it was all he could do to call on the object that hung around his neck, but it obeyed and tugged at the leather cord to position itself between Alejo and Dantin.

"Do you recognize this, Dantin? The charm Olivia used to block your last hex on her?"

Dantin's eyes narrowed. "That's impossible. I shoved that down her throat." He considered a second. "And she has no memory of removing it."

Alejo smiled wickedly at him. "Just because you have no memory of her doing it doesn't mean it didn't happen. You also don't know whether it was one of a pair–and that makes for a *grande hechizo mágico*."

Dantin looked at the charm suspiciously, trying to decide if Alejo was telling the truth and if so, what damage the charm could do to him.

Now it was Alejo's turn to use the connection that the Nyrra created.

"So, Dantin, do you really want to risk leaving this in my possession? I think you know what I'm willing to do for Olivia."

The charm was taut on its cord between them, straining toward Dantin and taunting him with its proximity, and Dantin could not take the chance he would lose it. No way would he leave anything out there that could be used against him. He stretched toward it, moving farther out of Olivia and making her howl with pain.

"That's right, Dantin," said Alejo, trying not to hear Olivia's agony. "It's right here. So close."

Dantin stopped, suspicious. Alejo wanted Dantin to keep coming toward him, obviously, but it felt like a trick. He damned well wasn't going to do whatever Alejo wanted, not until he knew all the angles. He ticked off his concerns: maybe the charm could do everything Alejo thought it would. He couldn't let anyone use it against him, so he had to have it. And Alejo had possession of the charm. But what about Olivia, now that he possessed her?

Then he had a thought. Could he jump to Alejo instead? What would Olivia be willing to do for him if he possessed Alejo?

Alejo saw Dantin stop coming toward him. He could sense him thinking about Olivia and gauging his options, which included jumping bodies. Oh, thought Alejo, I would love that. The closer the better, you bastard. He thrust his chin out at the other witch.

"*Quiere romper las mi pelotas, eh?*" He smiled at Dantin. "You want to take me on? Do you think you can do it? Come on, then."

Dantin looked at Alejo, who was obviously spoiling for a chance to get him close and do him some real harm, and faltered. No, he told himself, he'd waited years to own Olivia and the situation he was in was too sweet. He enjoyed knowing her every thought and being able to make her do what he wanted. And make Alejo suffer knowing it.

"No," Dantin said, "I'll stay with Olivia. I love making her my bitch." Dantin hoped Alejo couldn't feel how afraid of him he was.

"Well then you'd better take this charm from me, because I will use it to destroy you, Dantin." Alejo left no doubt he was serious.

Dantin looked at the charm, so close between the two of them, and calculated his chances. He had to have that charm. If Alejo didn't have it, Dantin was sure he couldn't harm him. The Silver was strong, but not as strong as he was now that Olivia was half Blue/Black. And right now Alejo couldn't move away from him either since they were all trapped by the Nyrra, so the charm was within reach. Perfect.

Olivia gave out a tortured, guttural shriek as Dantin separated further from her to grasp the charm, but it eluded him, floating back toward Alejo. Dantin reached further, gritting his teeth against the pain and grunting as he stretched out his hand toward the charm that now pressed itself against Alejo's throat.

Just one more inch, he thought, and I'll have it, but was astonished to see the charm disappear into Alejo's flesh, becoming part of him. The leather cord now hung naked against his skin. Dantin looked up at Alejo's face, barely a foot from his own now.

"What the hell...?"

Alejo held Dantin tightly, suspended in the Nyrra's field, and whispered to his hated rival. "I will never let you have Olivia, no matter what I have to do."

He pulled on the Nyrra with every ounce of magic he had while Dantin fought against it, trying to reintegrate into Olivia. As hard as Dantin fought, though, he couldn't back away.

But Alejo couldn't pull him any closer, either; he was at the max of his power and it was all he could do to hold Dantin in place while Malila fed only enough power to center Olivia between them. They were deadlocked.

Michael grabbed Schmidt by the arm, "I need to do something! I don't know how much longer they can hold out. Can't you think of anything that would help them?"

"There is nothing," said Schmidt. "If we go in, he uses it against us. If we disrupt the Vessel with any other magic we ruin it. Olivia would be torn to bits or both would end up separated, but mixed with pieces of each other. There's nothing to be done except wait."

Resignedly, they both watched the four witches play out their stalemate, unable to help.

Malila called to Alejo. "I need more from you!"

Alejo looked at her and gave a tiny shake of his head, letting her know he had nothing else to give. He hoped Dantin hadn't seen it but it didn't matter; Dantin could feel Alejo's frustration as well as read it in his face. He smiled maliciously.

"So, after all this you've got nothing. I just need to wait you out. And then I will kill you."

He turned to face Malila and Taylor. "And you two, as well. I am going to stretch out your misery first though; count on that, Malila." He delighted in the fear he saw creeping into their faces and he grinned at them with hate. He looked absolutely malevolent.

Alejo was on the edge of despair. He had used up his arsenal of ideas. He'd brought nothing else with him into the cell and didn't know what else could have helped anyway. The sword, the charm, they were both gone. He was out of options.

He was wondering what his next move would be, trying to create something from nothing, when he felt a burn creeping through him, spreading from his shoulders to his arms. It made him pull in a breath as it expanded in his chest, making him feel bigger, more alive. Whatever it was, it felt invigorating, scintillating ...powerful.

A different kind of power coursed through him that was coming in from the logos, unlike any he'd ever felt, something aggressive, more potent. It made him uncomfortable, the thoughts that came with it, but there was a confidence to it, too, and he accepted every bit of it.

Dantin could see the change in Alejo's face; it was more dominant than he'd seen in him before, and he knew what it was. He tried to back up, frantic to return to Olivia, but Alejo held him fast with the additional strength he now had.

Malila saw the change, too. Her eyes widened as she looked around them; there was no mistaking the cerulean energy that exploded around Alejo in the magical confines of the cell. She pushed more of her strength through the countercharm, just a little, to see if Alejo could match it. He did so easily, and she broke into a huge smile.

"Oh, hell yes." she murmured, releasing more magic. "Alejo!" she shouted, "let's get this done!" She opened up, letting her power rush into the countercharm.

"Remember, not too fast!" called Schmidt, "You both have to pour equal power into it." He narrowed his eyes, watching, and finished under his breath. "The Nyrra will do the rest."

"Taylor," Malila was ecstatic. "Look! The Vessel is separating them–if you help we can get Olivia back." Although she and Alejo didn't need Taylor's power, Malila wanted to make sure Taylor was part of making this happen.

Taylor lifted her eyes to see Olivia's and Dantin's blurred images moving apart again. A wave of hope ran through her and she took a deep breath, pushing a magical wave into the countercharm. It accepted easily without resistance, and Taylor could feel the power on both sides of the spell being used up to separate

Dantin and Olivia. She was elated and cast more, pushing as much as she dared into the two images.

But her elation was dampened when Olivia let out a long, agonized scream with the torture of being separated. Taylor stopped sending her power and Alejo stopped, too, slowing his push, but Olivia called out to him.

"No!" She forced the words through gritted teeth. "Just do it!" It was the first time they'd seen her in charge of herself since the race.

Schmidt and Michael watched the aurora around the four become denser as they continued to cast. It deepened in color and fluctuated, obscuring their view occasionally, but they could see Olivia and Dantin becoming two figures again. More and more, she became solid and he grew transparent and moved away until they no longer touched. Now Dantin was a ghostly prisoner, his writhing image suspended by the aurora.

The Nyrra pulled on Dantin as he fought against it, narrowing and twisting his visage while he continued to flail. Then it consumed him completely–and Dantin was gone.

Alejo looked at the Vessel in his hands, then at Olivia standing in a daze in the center of the cell, staring at him. He watched her look around cautiously, as if testing to see that Dantin was really gone, and was exhilarated to see her break into a smile and run toward him.

He set the Nyrra on the floor and caught her up in his arms, holding her tight and spinning around for the sheer joy of it as she hugged him and laughed, and then cried, and then laughed again. He never wanted to let go of her.

"I'm never letting you go," he said.

"Good–don't," said Olivia, looking into his face and beaming radiantly.

Locke's prison cell dissolved as the others came to cluster around them and welcome Olivia back. Schmidt fussed over her, telling Alejo to put her down so he could examine her, which he refused to do. Michael enveloped Taylor in his arms, telling her he was proud of her and thought she was fabulous, and accidentally kicking the Nyrra so that it spun across the floor to rest against the far wall where Lexie sniffed it distastefully.

"Better be careful with that thing," said Taylor to Michael.

"Oh, who cares? Let him rot in there," said both Olivia and Malila at the same time, and the others burst out laughing. Then Olivia turned sober.

"Thank you all so much." She looked at the circle of very relieved witches. "I can't tell you enough how grateful I am." She turned to Taylor and put her arms around her. "I'm so sorry he did that to you. You weren't ever supposed to remember that horrible stuff."

Taylor let Olivia hug her for a moment, trying not to cry, but it didn't work. She burst into tears and Livy held her tightly, trying to comfort her as the others looked on, unsure what to do.

Lexie was watching them with great interest when she heard a tap, just the slightest sound down the stairs to her right. Quickly she turned her head and looked into the darkness, but it was too late. Marissa and Thane charged through the doorway past her and toward the Nyrra.

Michael was the first to react and immediately cast a rebuff spell, but he was still at half-power and it had little effect. Thane hit them all with an immobilizing spell, and they were captive, unable to move.

Marissa scooped up the Nyrra and held it tightly in her arms. "I have Dantin! Let's take him and go before they can combine their powers and get out," she said to Thane.

But he had other ideas. "I'm going to get rid of them," he said. "Dantin will reward me handsomely for it."

"Fine–but make it quick."

They'd ignored Lexie, standing off to the side. She was just a dog, after all. But Lexie had a secret that Chloe had given her when she touched her; a spell they would be able to hear outside in case something went wrong. Lexie barked, but alerted the Will-O-Wisps to the danger.

Instantly both Chloe and Daphne appeared in a dazzling column of light. Swiftly they bound both Thane and Marissa, in a cocoon of magic and dragged them to where the other witches stood in Thane's binding spell.

"Drop the spell," Chloe commanded Thane. When he hesitated the Will-O-Wisps focused on him and he crumpled in their of powerful and magical grasp. When they stopped he immediately complied, releasing the others.

"Are you all right?" Daphne asked them. When they nodded she turned on Marissa, who still held the Vessel of Nyrra with Dantin's soul inside.

"Give it to them," Daphne said.

Marissa glanced at Thane, remembering what he'd just gone through and handed the Nyrra to

Schmidt. Then the two Wisps bound the Blue/Blacks together, and in a blinding flash, disappeared with them both.

Schmidt peered into the Vessel of Nyrra for several seconds, looking to make sure Dantin's soul was encapsulated safely inside.

"Well?" said Olivia apprehensively.

"He's in there." Schmidt offered it to her, and they passed it around one by one to look into it, satisfying themselves that Dantin really was trapped while Schmidt and Locke removed the protection spell from around the castle. Malila was the last one to hold it and after a thorough examination of the Nyrra she looked at the other witches.

"We need to find somewhere secure to put this. We don't want him to get into another body where he can come back and find us. Maybe Taylor can take it by ley-line to another world."

Alejo plucked the Vessel from Malila's hand.

"Fuck that–I am sick of this guy!"

He slammed the orb to the floor as hard as he could and it shattered, releasing both Dantin's essence and his soul into the room. It spread out in a grey miasma across the floor, the tendrils of vapor curling as if to grab onto something, but then flattening as it thinned and dissipated across the room. Within a minute Dantin dissolved unceremoniously into nothingness as they watched.

Suddenly Dantin's chimera burst into the workroom, a smoky entity that darted about, flashing to each one of the witches in turn as they stood there, swarming around them to try and identify where Dantin was located. Olivia's chimera Eidolon was right behind it, on guard in case it had evil intent, but it swirled through the workroom without doing harm, looking for its partner witch. When it didn't find Dantin it stilled, a hostile presence that seemed ready to strike if provoked. Schmidt pointed to the bits of broken Vessel scattered across the floor and the chimera immediately went to them.

But Dantin was gone.

Without ceremony it left, passing through the wall and disappearing. Eidolon's purple mist settled around Olivia briefly to greet her before it, too, disappeared.

"Not much on ceremony, is he?" asked Michael.

Olivia smiled. "Not usually. He went after Dantin's chimera to make sure it left here for good. They've never trusted each other." She shrugged. "I'll see him at home."

She looked around at the others. "Home. That sounds really good, doesn't it?"

"I'm going with you," said Alejo. "I'm not letting you out of my sight for a long time." He took her hand, marveling that he could do so as her lover, and that she loved him back. Finally.

Schmidt waved Olivia over to him. "I really should check you out and make sure you're all right."

Alejo shook his head, not letting go of Olivia. "You can do that later. Right now I want to be alone with her." With that, he scooped her up in his arms and they disappeared, leaving only Olivia's delighted squeal in the room behind them.

The remaining witches burst into laughter and Schmidt chuckled, too, foiled for the moment. "Well, she couldn't be in better hands. I'm going to clean up this place."

"We'll help," said Michael, but Schmidt shook his head. "No, you two go on. I need to speak with Malila alone, anyway."

Malila looked at Schmidt curiously but nodded at the other two. "You've been through a lot. You both need rest."

Taylor shrugged her shoulders. "Well, I can't go home–that's where Olivia and Alejo are. There's no way I am raining on that parade."

Michael put his arm around her. "Come stay with me for a few days. I've got a week before I have to show up in Montreal for the next race."

Taylor looked at him apprehensively, thinking of all the revelations Dantin had shown from her past and doubting Michael's intent. He whispered in her ear, reassuring her.

"Don't worry. Just like we agreed, we get to know each other slowly until you are ready. Just like before."

Taylor leaned away to look at him disbelievingly, and then affectionately. "Thank you," she whispered.

He kissed her cheek and then turned to the others. "Are you sure you don't need some help?"

"No," Schmidt said, "go on."

After they disappeared Malila was curious to know what Schmidt had to say to her. "What's going on?" she asked.

"Well, while we were in one of the realms looking for a Nyrra I ran into a demon who had some very interesting things. Curse related things."

Malila felt a jolt of electricity run through her. There was something about his expression...she hardly dared think what she was hoping he'd brought her.

"Can you help me and Locke?"

Schmidt shook his head. "I'm sorry, not quite that good of news." He felt awful for disappointing her. "Something else that might be nice, though."

Malila sighed. "What?"

Schmidt produced a strange-looking vial of powder from his pocket. "A transference spell. The demon put the spell into this talisman and then crushed it up so I could take it with me. It's only enough for one use."

Malila's eyes widened as she looked at the vial. It would release her from one of her paramours.

"Does it work both ways?"

"Yep. You can choose a different paramour, or give him a different partner. Got anyone in mind?" Schmidt was smiling at her expectantly.

Malila turned a disbelieving face to him. "Really? Of course it's Alejo. We'll have to ask them before we link him to Olivia instead of to me, but I hardly think they'll say no."

"I daresay you're right."

"Maybe before Olivia I would have picked someone else, but this is the perfect remedy for everyone involved."

Schmidt smiled. "Now you see why I wanted to know details when you first came to me? You never know what I'll run across when I'm looking for the solution to something else."

Malila gave him a nod of her head and smiled. "Right, as always."

"I'll keep looking for something to free you and Locke, but honestly, I've never heard of it. Your curse binds you both tightly, and Locke's very existence is predicated on it."

"I know." She shook her head sadly. "Schmidt, I don't know what is worse–being without him after he died or living with him like this. I should have known better than to try and cheat fate."

Schmidt put his arm around her shoulders. "You can't think that way; you'll destroy yourself with regret."

Malila nodded as Schmidt went on. "You have good to do here, you know. You're the only one who can help Olivia master the Blue/Black until she gets used to it ... and Alejo, too, I think."

"I saw that happen when we were connected by the Nyrra. Was it the charm that turned him?"

"I don't know; it happened so damned quick after he absorbed it that I have my doubts." Schmidt regarded Malila seriously. "You know he stabbed himself with that sword, too, don't you?"

Malila looked at him, surprised. "I suspected it, but how did you know?"

"I just know him, and I know how much he loves Olivia. I was with them after Paris." Schmidt held the vial of crushed talisman to the light, watching the prismatic reflections off the iridescent powder inside. "Mmm. Pretty colors."

Malila was trying to figure it out. "So it could be the sword or the charm that turned them." She gave a start. "Oh, and they've both killed Dantin, too."

"So–the sword, the charm, and killing the same witch. You can't get much more alike magically." Schmidt was realizing the confluences that now surrounded the couple. "And if they agree to being linked by your infatuation spell ... oh, this is going to be good."

When Alejo disappeared with Olivia, he had taken her directly to her bedroom and tossed her on the bed, laughing. Then he turned serious as he gazed down at her.

"What is it?" she asked him.

He sat next to her on the bed. "Olivia, this isn't a temporary whim I'm indulging myself in.

I've known for a long time that I'm in love with you."

He sounded so serious that Olivia remained quiet, looking into his face as she listened to him speak in his soft Latin accent.

"Now that we're together like this, I don't want to rush it. I don't want to miss any of this." He looked at her eyes, her hair, her lips, drinking in the sight as if trying to fix the image in his mind forever.

"I may have tossed you on the bed as if we were playing, but that's not how I feel, Olivia."

Olivia moved her hand up to touch his hair and then lowered it, brushing her fingers lightly across his chest and down his arm. She looked into his face.

"Kiss me." She tilted her chin to raise her lips to him.

Alejo leaned down and kissed her gently, barely grazing her lips with his own. Olivia matched the delicacy of his touch and they immersed themselves in the feeling of gossamer kisses, hardly breathing, barely touching, wanting to experience every nuance. They explored the newness of their lips so familiar, yet unfamiliar to each other, and the exquisite feel and taste of each other's tongue. They kissed like that for a long while before Alejo finally lifted his lips from hers, leaving them both dizzy from sensation.

He pulled off his shirt and then moved to unbutton hers, slowly revealing the silky skin and drinking in the sight of her breasts that he could caress now, after aching to for so long. They were round and fit perfectly into his palms, and he smiled thinking that they were made just for him to hold. He kissed her nipples gently, watching them tighten and point to attention for him before he moved on, slowly removing her clothing until she lay naked on the bed before him.

Alejo let his eyes travel over Olivia completely, drinking in every inch of her. He wanted to commit her to memory, to know her intimately and save the experience forever in his soul. He had dreamed of being with her like this, and had a sudden ridiculous fear that it was a dream, that it would go away. Looking at her wasn't nearly enough suddenly, and he knelt on the bed beside her, sweeping his fingertips slowly over her skin to explore. He moved lightly, hardly touching her flesh, and was rewarded by her sinuous reactions and gasps of ecstasy. He explored her for half an hour that way, learning every inch of her and discovering what pleasured her by her responses.

Olivia let go under Alejo's caresses, indulging herself in his touch. It vibrated on her skin, so light it was maddening, but any closer would have been too much. And any farther away would have been too little. It made her heady, intoxicated. It was perfect. Alejo was perfect for her, she thought dreamily.

Alejo watched her face as she sighed in pleasure, still amazed he was actually with her. The thought made him even harder than he already was and now it was uncomfortable, his erection trapped in his jeans. He pulled them off and lay naked beside her.

"I want to see you," she whispered.

Alejo complied, stretching out but lying still, not wanting to rush her before she was ready. Then he noticed the gooseflesh on her thighs. He gestured toward the fireplace in her room, creating a full draft of flames to warm the air around them.

"I'm sorry; I should have thought of that."

Olivia shook her head and smiled.

"Alejo, I'm not cold, I'm ..." She gave a tiny laugh. "I'm a little nervous." She realized she had butterflies suddenly and was trembling. "I think I'm still getting used to the idea. I purposely never let myself think of you as more than a friend because it wasn't an option, and here I am in love with you."

She turned her face up to his. "Alejo, I am really, deeply, vastly in love with you. More than anyone else I've ever known. Ever."

"*Dios*, Livy, if you knew how long I've wanted to hear that..." he broke off and wrapped his arms around her, kissing her deeply. They both grew urgent and Olivia pressed against him.

"I want you in me," she whispered. "I don't want to be separate from you anymore; I want us to be as close as we possibly can."

"How would you like me?" Alejo wanted to make sure that their first time was everything she wanted it to be.

"Face to face. I want to see you when you're inside me. I want you to see me, and I want to kiss you." She drew her knees up and Alejo knelt between them. Olivia looked down between his legs.

"Oh, that is so beautiful...look at that." She reached down and grasped his hard shaft. "And all for me," she smiled up at him.

Alejo couldn't even answer her. He threw his head back and groaned at her touch. He was acutely aware it was the first time she'd held it, a memory he'd been hoping to have for a long time.

"I don't want to wait any longer," said Olivia. "Come here." She pulled him toward her gently and when he was close enough she lifted her arms to embrace him, cradling his hips with her thighs. He entered her very slowly, both of them savoring each moment and each other's expressions. Even when he was fully inside they waited, just feeling each other; her the fullness of his girth, and him the close grip of her around him.

"Oh, my God," breathed Olivia, "you feel incredible, Alejo."

Alejo kissed her throat and nestled into her cradle of warmth, smiling.

They couldn't hold still for long, though. Olivia canted her hips to let him in deeper, wrapping her legs around his waist and starting a rhythm that was languid at first, and then more insistent. He matched her stroke for stroke, even when she grew urgent. He could tell she was climaxing and it nearly drove him to orgasm, too, but he wanted to watch her in that moment, to know her that way. He clenched his teeth and held back as he watched her get lost in the feeling, indulging in how beautiful she looked completely stripped of pretense, unaware of anything around her.

He smiled down at her when she could focus again. "Very nice," he said to her.

Olivia looked a little startled at first, and then laughed a little shyly. "Yes, it was, thank you very much." She wrapped her legs around him again. "Would you like one, too?"

Alejo smiled and nodded. "Oh, yes. Very much." Then he turned serious and wrapped his arms around her.

"I love you, Olivia."

She looked up at him. "I love you, too, Alejandro. More than anything."

A week later Alejo visited Taylor at the Sorrento Hotel. Michael had left for Montreal and she moved in there rather than go back to Olivia's. Alejo tried to talk her into returning.

"Why don't you come home instead of staying here? I don't understand." He asked her as they exited the Sorrento and crossed the street.

"No, I don't want to intrude; it's only been a week and I want you to be able to enjoy each other without anything else to think about. I also don't want to wonder whether you're secretly wishing I would leave so you can get time alone."

Alejo opened his mouth to answer, but then shut it. He had no reply to that, especially because she was right. For a nineteen-year-old she had an old soul, he thought.

"Well, then, dinner tonight at Palomino's like we did last winter?"

"Yes, absolutely." Taylor smiled up at him. "I'd like that a lot."

Alejo had offered to walk Lexie with Taylor while they visited. They took their time, heading up First Hill as they talked and passing through the medical district toward Broadway until the commercial bustle had thinned out. Now they were in a run-down, worn neighborhood on the back of the Hill, but it was pleasant enough, quiet and tree-filled.

"So I told you I would tell you how I picked Lexie's name," Taylor said to Alejo as they walked along.

"That's right, you did. So how did you?"

"I named Lexie after you." Taylor's smile was mischievous.

"What? How did you get Lexie from Alejo?" Alejo stopped dead to look at her.

"Alejandro is Spanish for Alexander and I named her Alexandra. Lexie for short."

"Oh, *magnífico*, your dog is named after me. Thank you very much, Taylor." He scowled at her affectionately. "I thought you were kidding."

"Nope."

"Ah, well. So now I have a namesake. Things could be worse." He shrugged his shoulders, and then suddenly he laughed aloud. "Things have been worse."

He turned and scooped Taylor up in his arms, lifting her off her feet in a tight hug. "But now things are the best they have ever been, aren't they, my little *sobrinita*? Everyone is so happy!"

"Speaking of which, what are you doing here with me? You waited two hundred years for Olivia to love you. Go make up for that lost time."

Alejo put her down and kissed her cheek. "You are right. I need to see her right now." He looked around them in the quiet neighborhood and seeing no one, disappeared right off the street.

Taylor looked after him in surprise; that was a risky move he had pulled, disappearing in plain sight like that. She looked down at Lexie.

"I guess he really did need to see her."

She looked up at the June sun that had recently returned to Seattle. "It's a beautiful day, isn't it, Lexie? Come on–we have somewhere to go."

They kept walking through the old neighborhood until Taylor stopped across the street from an old craftsman house with a sagging wraparound porch. She knew this house; she'd purposely made her way here after Alejo had gone.

It was the same house Dantin had shown them inside Locke's prison cell.

Vaguely, Taylor could see activity through the front window, a hint of movement but no detail. She could have spelled the house to show her anything she wanted, but inside was the last thing she wanted to see again. Memories unwanted and vile flooded back through her as she stood there. They felt like bloated, rotted, decomposing things, those memories, and Taylor realized she was capable of hate after all.

She whispered to the house across the street and the man inside of it.

"You shouldn't be allowed to do what you did to our mother and get away with it." She stared at the house with narrowed eyes, rubbing her fingers together tightly to restrain herself as she thought of all that had happened there.

"I am going to make you pay. I haven't decided how yet. I'm still a Silver-Tint and want to stay that way, but I will make you so very sorry you ever hurt anyone." She was smoldering as she looked at the hated house across the street.

She didn't notice Dantin's chimera as she stood there, so intently was she focused on the house. It was nearly invisible as it lofted over her, reading her feelings. What is it that could make a Silver-Tint this way? it wondered.

The chimera gave Taylor a wide berth, slipping away from her and taking a broad path around the block and then back to the house to slip inside. Seeping like an invisible mist into room after room, it fed on the horror that was once there, gaining in strength and feeling a disturbed and twisted human presence that still lingered. Not a witch, not by any means, but human. And every human had a little witch ability. Easy enough to slip into the person and read them.

It slipped into Taylor's stepfather.

ABOUT THE AUTHOR

Image by Barbara Roser Photography

Cathleen Dunn writes urban fantasy in her real life while holding down a full-time job to pay bills. She lives in Seattle with her husband, rescuing greyhounds, attending the Opera and Symphony, and doing random volunteering. She's been onstage with the opera several times, has been known to paint faux finishes and murals inside homes for her friends, and occasionally goes hunting and fishing with her husband.